GOOD INTENTIONS

MW00334491

Happy reading!

Good
Intentions

By

KATHRYN R. BIEL

KATHRYN R. BIEL

©Copyright 2013. This book is a work of fiction. Names, characters, places, and incidents are either products of the author's imagination or are used fictitiously, and any resemblance to actual persons, living or dead, business establishments, events, or locales is purely coincidental.

All rights reserved.

No part of this book may be reproduced, scanned, or distributed in any printed or electronic form or by any electronic or mechanical means including information storage and retrieval systems, without permission in writing from the author. The only exception is by a reviewer, who may quote short excerpts in a review. Please do not participate in or encourage piracy of copyrighted materials in violation of the author's rights. Purchase only authorized editions.

ISBN: 0615833373
ISBN-13: 978-0615833378

DEDICATION

This book would not have been written without the love and support of many people. I need to first and foremost include, my husband, Patrick, who did not laugh when I told him that I wanted to write a book and to my parents, Philip and Mary Rose Kopach, who in addition to years of love and support, watched my children on Sunday afternoons so that I could write instead of clean my house.

I need to thank my best friend, and the mayor of Kate-ville, Michele Vagianelis, who read the book, also without laughing, insisted she was included in it, offered up some really good material, and has listened to me throughout the whole process.

To my original crew, Christine, Devany, Gabriela, and Becky, who provided the original inspiration for the setting in the first place.

CHAPTER ONE
September 2000

*R*emind me again why I'm doing this.

That's what I muttered to myself as I stood on my step stool, leaning over my too-tall, hand-me-down bureau to apply my makeup. In contrast to my college days, which seemed like a lifetime ago rather than a few months in the past, I now hated going out on Friday nights. Instead, I wanted to veg. My first month at work had flown by, but the four weeks under my belt hadn't helped me get my paperwork done any faster on the one night I wanted to leave on time.

That's the way it always goes, isn't it?

So here I was, running around like a chicken with my head cut off, trying to make myself presentable for this stupid night. Everything about it irked me. The fact that I didn't get to come home from work and relax. The fact that I had to shower twice in one day. The fact that I even bothered to shave. All it did was eat up precious time. Time I needed to pull myself together. I don't know why I even bothered. It's not like anyone would be feeling my legs tonight, but I would wear a dress and feel pretty. That never happened with my khakis and polo and sneakers at work.

Yes, a dress was a must.

At least my hair was low maintenance. My pixie cut meant it basically had one style. I could not figure out why I was going this extra mile. The music blasting through my CD player did little to boost my energy.

Okay, it helped a little.

Anything to make me feel better about being set up on a sort of blind date. I searched my memory for the times I'd met Ryan, who was to be my companion for the evening. He was my best friend's best friend. So it wasn't actually a setup or a blind date. There was no reason to be nervous.

Or to shave.

Yet, both had happened.

I had insisted to Matt that I didn't need Ryan to pick me up, or whatever you call it when you're walking, and that I could just meet the three of them at the cute Italian restaurant in Allston. It didn't make sense for Ryan to walk past Ruggerio's to get to my place. But as usual, I lost out to Matt's argument. One of these days, I'd stand up for myself and mean it.

It had been a while since I had seen Ryan. He would periodically come out from Ohio to visit Matt. Was last fall the last time he was here? Time's a blur.

Matt had gone back to Ohio for our final clinical in the spring, so it had to have been at least a year. Try as I might, I couldn't quite conjure up details of Ryan's face or physique.

I guess I had never seen him as date material. Since he was Matt's friend, it was kind of a weird situation, like dating your brother's best friend, or something equally as icky. Needless to say, I hadn't wanted to do this tonight. Or any night.

Dinner tonight would be a splurge, delaying my plan for phasing out my hand-me-downs and bargain-basement finds. Like the shoes I was currently wearing. Though there was something about the red patent leather stilettos that I loved. I hoped the food would be worth the sacrifice. Matt laughed at my frugality, but I tried to stick to my guns. He simply couldn't understand where I was coming from in many matters, from finances to dating.

This evening, much to my surprise, was a result of the relentless determination of Matt's girlfriend, Irene. Generally, she barely tolerated my presence. The feeling was more or less mutual, and I usually avoided spending one-on-one time with her. Which was my code for "I think she's a complete and total bitch." But here I was, getting ready for a nice, cozy, intimate dinner. I wasn't sure if I should be thankful or suspicious. Right now the only thing I felt was tired. But as time ticked on, that feeling was slowly replaced by butterflies.

The buzzer rang, startling me from my daydream. I grabbed my purse and half-stumbled to the door as I pressed the button and yelled, "Be right down." I straightened up and smoothed my dress one last time and put my cardigan on. It had been a while since I had been out on a date, let alone a date with an audience.

A judgmental audience.

It would be fine. It was no big deal. It wasn't really a date anyway. Just a group of friends going out to celebrate life in the real world with real-world jobs.

If Ryan hadn't come to get me, it wouldn't feel like a date, and I wouldn't be running around like a fart in a mitten, all nervous.

The time to suck it up and pull myself together was here. I locked my apartment door behind me and headed downstairs, making it down the first segment without incident. As I descended the bottom set, my attention shifted to the person standing in the foyer. I bent forward to get a better look and my ankle twisted. I slid down three steps with my right ankle bent under me. My skirt rode up, and all I could think about was feeling grateful that I was wearing nice underwear.

It was probably a good thing I shaved.

I righted myself at the bottom of the stairs and looked up, horrified, all while scrambling to pull my skirt down. There Ryan stood, grinning at me. I returned his smile as I did a little curtsey. I tried to take a breath as I opened the glass door and said, "And now, for my next act ..."

Ryan laughed and said, "I thought we'd get a drink first. I didn't realize you would have a head start."

Heat flamed my cheeks. "I guess you can dress me up, but you can't take me anywhere."

Ryan's ebony eyes smiled. He was the epitome of tall, dark and handsome. He belonged on the cover of a magazine. How could I not remember him? His voice was smooth as he said, "Looking like that, I'd take you anywhere. How long has it been, Maggie?" He pulled me toward him.

"At least a year, I think. Maybe? I dunno." I said, giving him an awkward hug. Wow, he smelled good, like sandalwood and citrus.

"Yeah, I think it was some tailgate party. Good game. You okay?" he asked glancing at my feet. His arms were still around my waist.

"Fine. Let's get going," I said, breaking free and pushing through the outside door. I couldn't meet his gaze. I felt like such an ass. I blew the evening before it even started. We walked down the outside steps of the building and turned left, heading towards the main street. The restaurant was only a few blocks away, and I was glad. My red stilettos were not exactly walking shoes. But they were fabulous and completed the look. My ankle throbbed a little. I tried not to limp.

"You settled in yet?" I asked, finally breaking the silence that had stretched at least a block

"Getting there. Boston is so different from Ohio. Lots to get used to. I guess working is a lot to get used to, too. Just glad that Matt is letting me crash with him for a while. It's good to hang out with him again. Didn't see enough of that kid while we were in school."

"Yeah, I know he missed you. Not that he'd say as much. You know how emotional he can get though, crying all the time and stuff. Kissing your picture, holding his pillow."

Ryan chuckled. "That's Matt to a T."

We arrived at the restaurant, still laughing at our mutual friend's expense. Ryan opened the door for me. I turned to him as I walked by and asked him if he thought Matt and Irene were here yet. As I did, Ryan and I collided. It was like hitting a solid wall. All muscle underneath. Wow. I inhaled and sucked in my stomach, trying to appear as thin as possible as his hand reached around my waist to steady me. He kept his hand around my waist as he guided me into the restaurant. Obviously, he realized that I wasn't even capable of walking properly. Ugh.

And yes, Matt and Irene were already there, sitting close to each other. I took another breath and sat down in my chair. Ugh again.

Already on the table was a bottle of cheap champagne. It was a celebratory dinner after all. The four of us now held our advanced degrees, with piles of student loans, but had paychecks coming in to pay for them. We had entered the world of the working-class stiff.

Irene had landed a job at a public school in Brookline. How she would teach kids was beyond me. Matt and I had passed our physical therapy boards and had been employed. Matt was working at a sports medicine clinic downtown, and while I was working at a pediatric clinic. Ryan, most impressively, had finished law school and had landed a very prestigious job in the Suffolk County DA's office.

And this dinner would be perfect, with my stunningly gorgeous date, if I hadn't already blown it the moment I slid down the stairs and then plowed into him walking into the restaurant. At least I managed to eat without dropping food down the front of me, which was probably a first for me.

Irene was very pleasant and her typical digs and potshots were surprisingly absent. Instead, she went out of her way to compliment me on my shoes. "They make your legs look fabulous!" she gushed. I thought I detected an element of surprise in her voice as if she thought I had tree stumps under my jeans or khakis.

Of course, Ryan looked down at my legs. I crossed them and drew them underneath the chair. And I blushed. And again mentally phewed that I'd shaved.

Suddenly, I was very nervous. Guys like him didn't date girls like me. He was so gorgeous, and it was almost difficult to function around him. I knew I better enjoy it while it lasted, which in my estimate, was probably about fifteen more minutes.

After our dishes had been cleared, Irene and I went to the restroom. Despite the uneasy feelings between us, we stuck to the "girls go to the bathroom in pairs" creed. Irene looked stunning in a sleek little black dress. Of course, she looked stunning in a burlap sack. Her hair, as always, was shampoo-commercial sleek and shiny, while shine dared not to cross her flawless complexion.

While touching up our make-up, Irene commented, "Ryan cleans up well, doesn't he?"

I smiled, thinking that he would look great dirty too. But that smile of his bit right to my core. "I'm kind of blinded by his stunning white teeth. How long is he crashing with Matt for?"

Irene grimaced. "Too long." Her bitter tone betrayed her otherwise smooth exterior. Ryan's crashing at Matt's meant that Irene wouldn't be able to move in any time soon. She flashed a dazzling smile at me. "Unless he can find a reason to move on ..."

Everything clicked into place. The reason for the dinner—and the compliments—now made sense. Pairing Ryan and I up would kill two birds with one stone. I wouldn't be a threat to her and Matt, not that I ever was, and she'd be able to move into Matt's place. Maybe it was the wine; maybe it was the fear of flying solo. Whatever it was, I couldn't help but wish that her plan was successful. I shook my head at myself and dropped my lip gloss back into my purse.

When we got back to the table, the guys were just finishing paying the bill. I'd had no expectation Ryan would pay for me. I looked at him and cocked my head to the side. As I sat down, I leaned over to whisper into his ear. "Thanks, you shouldn't have done that."

He winked at me. "You can pay me later."

The wine upped my flirting game. I raised my eyebrow. "Oh really?"

He flashed that dazzling grin, "Yeah, I pulled a muscle in my low back moving my stuff into Matt's, and I heard you might be able to work it out for me."

I grinned back, biting my lower lip and angelically shrugging my shoulders, "Well, backs are Matt's specialty, not mine. Maybe he can give you a little rub down later. I can't help you if you're over four feet tall."

At that moment, Matt and Irene stood up. I didn't want dinner to be over. My liquid courage was just kicking in, and I was just feeling relaxed enough to enjoy Ryan's company without feeling insignificant and plain. It was only eleven p.m., early by Boston nightlife standards. Suddenly I was no longer tired. There was a chill in the air. Fall was here. I involuntarily shivered and crossed my arms, my cardigan doing little to warm me.

Irene turned to Matt and said in a saccharine voice, "Honey, that rigatoni isn't sitting so well. I want to go home ... now." She tapped her foot impatiently. I looked at Ryan and then at Matt. It appeared as if our evening was over because *she* said so.

"Well, I guess I'll see you guys later then. Ryan, good luck with the new job this week. Lemme know how it goes." I turned around to walk home, trying to hold my head up high while not letting my shoulders slump in defeat.

Ryan's hand shot out and grabbed my elbow, stopping me and pulling me back and around. Of course, I stumbled a little and fell into him again. At least this time I could blame the wine. "Where do you think you're going? They might be headed home, but our night is just beginning." He smiled again, and I felt weak in the knees.

Matt shifted and said quietly to Irene, "Are you sure you're not up for getting one drink? It's Ryan's first time out since he officially moved here."

Irene gave him a cold look. "Yes, I'm sure," she replied icily. "But if you don't care enough to see me home, that's fine." The tone implied that it was anything but fine. Typical. Also typical, Matt dropped his head, and mumbled to us, "See you guys later. Ry, take care of her, okay?" And then they turned and walked away.

Ryan shook his head and muttered, "Since when did he become a eunuch?"

I rolled my eyes, not wanting to put words to my true feelings.

Ryan continued, "How long has *that* been going on?"

"Well, let's see. They've been together for about five years now, so I'd say four years and eleven months."

"Huh. I never noticed it before."

"Really? That's all I ever see from her. She was actually very well behaved for most of the evening. I didn't know she was capable of acting so congenial." I looked down at my feet, knowing I'd said too much. So much for not saying anything.

I was trying to think of a cute, funny line to cover up what I had just said when Ryan spoke. He still had his arm around me, holding onto my elbow. I was still leaning into him. He looked down at me and asked, "Are you gonna take me out for a drink or what? Do I have to beg?"

"A little begging would be good." I looked directly into his eyes and smiled. Oh man, I could listen to him beg all night long. Focus. "Do you have any preferences?"

"Petite, cute, funny. I like brunettes, am partial to freckles and a Buckeye fan is a must."

"I meant, where did you want to go, but I can tell you that you just happen to be in luck. I like to think that I am funny, although most people do not find me as humorous as I find myself. I am genetically incapable of tanning, and my grandfather was a walk-on to the team in the 30s." I started walking down the street, strutting a little more than I would have done in jeans. Or sober.

Ryan seemed frozen for a minute and then caught up. "Are you kidding? He really played?"

"Well, he was on the team. Playing time is another story. But he used to get rides from Youngstown down to

Columbus with Paul Brown before he became the coach. My dad used to have the team picture hanging up in our family room."

"Cool. You'd be a celebrity at OSU."

"No one here in Boston even thinks it's a big deal. I'm not sure if I've even told that to anyone other than Matt. Don't have too many Buckeye fans out here. More of a baseball and hockey town."

I stopped and gestured towards a sleek-looking establishment. It was not a bar we went to often, generally more for the Euro-trash crowd. I wasn't trying to impress Ryan; I just wanted to go someplace where I wasn't going to run into a hundred people that I knew. Not that I wouldn't have wanted to show him off. But I didn't think that I would have this kind of time with him again, and I wanted him all to myself.

CHAPTER TWO

The bar was moderately crowded, but we managed to find two stools near the back. They were crowded together, and our legs were pressed up against each other. The female bartender immediately appeared in front of us, not surprisingly. Ryan looked at me to order first. I ordered a Guinness. He had a surprised look and said, "Make it two," holding up his fingers to emphasize. I smugly smiled at him. "What did you expect, a white wine spritzer?"

He laughed and said, "No, I had you pegged for the sex-on-the-beach type."

"Too much sand in uncomfortable places. But I don't mind an occasional skinny dip."

The bartender brought our beers over and placed them down. I paid her and took a slow sip of my beer. What the hell was I doing? Why was I acting like a total ass? It's not like this was a random date that I would never have to see again.

But then I felt a warm hand on my knee. Holy crap! I thanked God, yet again, that I'd taken the time to shave.

I rambled on. "Well, only skinny dipping in pools though. I get skeeved out with the thought of too much nature near my, um, nature, you know? I don't like lakes at all. Too much seaweed. It's squishy and gross. And only when it's warm out. I don't want to be chilly, you know?"

Please someone shoot me so I stop talking.

Ryan was looking at me, drinking his beer, an amused look on his face. I sighed and took another drink. Why did I have to act like an idiot just because he was hot? He looked like he had a question. "What?" I asked. It was abrupt and rude, not at all how I meant to sound.

Someone—*anyone*—put me out of my misery. *Please.*

"I was just wondering ... why we haven't hung out before? I mean, the other times when I've been up to visit."

I shrugged. This was not where I thought he was going. Frankly, I was surprised he was still sitting there and hadn't bolted yet.

Another sip.

"I think Matt was hiding you from me. I didn't know you were this funny. Gonna have to get on Matt for being so selfish." He wrinkled his brow a little as if searching his distant memory. Then a look of "a-ha" crossed his face. "You have a boyfriend," he stated, almost accusing.

I gave him a confused look. "Um, not that I'm aware of. I've been single for, oh, a while." It had been a year.

Depressing.

I had probably only even had one date since then. I tried to remember what ex he could be talking about. Ryan filled in the blanks. "Who was the jack-off you were with at the tailgate? The one doing keg stands?"

"Ohhh," I laughed. "That fine specimen. Shortly after that lovely performance, he informed me that I would no longer receive the pleasure of his company since he was already spending his free time with a mutual friend. I had to spend the next six months sitting in class with both of them every day and socializing with them together outside of class.

It was hell." I paused and took a long sip of my Guinness. "Now, imagine her shock when she found out that he was cheating on her with his married supervisor while we were on our last internship. Ellen was waiting for him in the car one day while he ran into a store. She opened the glove compartment to see what was in there to find a stash of love letters, not to mention her *underwear* in there. He tried to blame her for being a snoop, and then turned it around, saying if she had been a better girlfriend, he wouldn't have *had* to cheat on her."

"I was wondering why you tolerated him. You always seemed so cool and down to earth. Didn't seem like your type."

"Of course he was my type. He was a slacker loser who treated me badly. What's not to like? I have impeccable taste, you know," I said, raising my eyebrows at him in a wonderfully self-deprecating gesture.

"Did you learn from it?"

"Of course; I learned that I will always go after the wrong person. I swore off guys pretty much. I just don't want to deal with it anymore. I'd rather be alone than be treated like crap again."

I put my elbow on the bar and tucked some hair behind my ear. It was at moments like this that I wished I had long hair to play with to distract a guy from my personality. I leaned on my hand and slowly lifted my Guinness with the other. I don't know how I was still making eye contact with him. His hand was still on my knee, warm and sending even warmer sensations elsewhere. He looked at me, staring into my eyes. I couldn't feel my feet.

He smiled and continued, "At least I know he won't be hard to compete with. He makes me look better already."

"Like you need any help looking better."

Please tell me I did not say that out loud. Must drink more to end the embarrassment. Or maybe I should stop drinking so I can save some semblance of dignity. Option A. I drained my beer. And continued rambling, "And you? Anyone you're moving out here from Columbus?"

Please say no. *Please say no.*

He shook his head. "No, no one. I was kind of focused on school and then passing the bar. Had my eye on the prize."

And now, those beautiful eyes were on me.

No, they weren't, I told myself. He was just being nice and didn't want to go home to face icy Irene.

FOCUS.

He continued, "I don't date a lot."

Yeah, right.

He shrugged, "I don't know what kind of vibe I'm putting out there, but I seem to attract a lot of women who are very interested in the superficial and don't have a lot of substance behind it. So, I figure, why waste my time and theirs when I know that it's not going to go anywhere. I know it's kind of harsh and abrupt, but I can usually tell about midway through the first date if there will be another one. And pretty much, the answer is no. At least, it used to be ...." He stopped and looked at me. "And even when the date turns into more than one, I seem to be really, really bad at the relationship thing. It's just never really clicked for me. I can't seem to read women. I mean, when they're on the stand, I can, but I have no idea what a woman wants from me." Now he was starting to ramble.

Could *I* be making *him* nervous?

"You ready for another?" He gestured at our empty glasses, finally taking his hand off my knee.

I swear my leg was burning. I nodded, and he caught the eye of the bartender. She had been staring us down since we started talking. I tried not to notice as she flirted with him. I reached for my purse on the bar, but he put his hand on mine. "My turn."

I excused myself and walked as steadily as I could to the bathroom. I needed to pull myself together. I had a nice little buzz on and could not afford to lose any more control before turning into a bumbling idiot. Let's face it, it was a fine line to begin with. I may have been a little drunk, but I could not—would not—throw myself at Ryan. It would make him uncomfortable, and then it would be weird in the future.

Matt was so happy that Ryan was finally here. The situation with Irene was already tenuous at best, so I couldn't make it any more awkward if I hoped to continue my friendship with Matt. Pull it together!

I returned to my seat, trying not to melt as Ryan gave me a beautiful grin. He took a breath and then started with the questions. "Midgets?"

"I think they prefer being called Little People, but I'm not following you."

"Why can't you help me if I'm over four feet tall? Do you specialize in midgets?"

I laughed. "No, kids. I work at a pediatric clinic. I'm not into the whole orthopedic thing like Matt is. I don't want to treat forty-year-olds with low back pain my whole life."

Our conversation flowed easily, and I finally relaxed. I switched from Guinness to ice water in the interest of self-preservation. Talk of our career hopes and childhood has us talking for hours. Naturally, I glazed over my childhood, not wanting to get into it, keeping it light and vague. It was easy to divert by asking Ryan questions about his childhood.

I'd had a lot of practice with that maneuver.

The conversation was easy and fun. I laughed more than I have in a while, and by his expression, Ryan seemed to enjoy himself as well. Before I knew it, the bartender was announcing last call. In disbelief, I looked at my watch. 1:45 a.m. I wasn't even tired.

Wow.

Ryan stood up to leave. He was stunning looking in his dark slacks and a cream shirt that showed off his olive complexion. I sighed and stood up. "You okay?" he asked, concerned.

I forced a smile and lied, "Just tired." I didn't want this evening to end. Even though he was hot, it was more than that. I liked him, his personality. He intrigued me, which is more than I can say for most of the guys I met. I wanted to talk to him for days on end, but I doubted that would happen. It was time for me to turn back into a pumpkin.

Maybe I'd see him in a few weeks at Matt's. It was football season. Maybe we could watch a game together. It was a hope.

He put his arm around my waist again and guided me out of the bar. It was a sweet gesture, more protective than romantic. He had already seen my impressive balance. He probably didn't want to be embarrassed by having to watch me fall again. I took advantage of the situation by leaning in slightly.

Got to make lemonade where you can.

I've made enough lemonade throughout my life to open up a stand.

We walked in silence back to my apartment. When we got to my stoop, I fished my keys out of my purse. Suddenly, his grip around my waist tightened, and he pulled me into him. I looked up at him in surprise.

"I promised Matt I'd take care of you, didn't I? Let's get you home and into bed," he murmured, as his free hand tipped my chin up. I closed my eyes and met his kiss.

Wow.

That was all I could think. How was this happening? His lips were firm against mine, and his breath was hot. I couldn't feel my feet again. I was afraid I was going to faint.

I pulled my head back and looked up at him. He was probably about six-foot-two, so that gave him almost a foot on me. A little less tonight with the killer heels. I smiled tentatively, which he returned.

"I've been waiting to do that all night. Are you going to invite me up?" he asked hopefully.

"Um, okay. Sure." I stammered, as I fumbled with my keys and opened the outside door. I wanted to take his hand as I led him up the stairs, but I wasn't sure. What kind of message would that send? What kind of message did I want to send? I was pretty sure I could have him spend the night. Did I want that? HELL YES. No, wait, that would be bad. No, it would probably be really good. No, I could not let this happen. Oh crap.

I led him up to my second-floor apartment and unlocked the door. As I was pushing it open, he grabbed me again and started kissing me. We staggered through the door, kicking it closed behind us. I steered him toward the living room. I pushed him down to sit on the couch and straddled his legs, sitting on his lap. We continued the make-out session with our arms around each other, bodies pressed close together. Eventually, and I'm still not sure how, I stopped and pulled away slightly. "I'm not being a very good host. Can I get you something?" I managed to croak out.

He had his head buried in my neck and was kissing along my collar bone. One of his hands was caressing my thigh, underneath my dress. "Um, I'm good. Really good." He stopped and smiled up at me.

I couldn't help it, I burst out laughing.

Ryan smiled but didn't get the joke. "Not the reaction I was hoping for. Is this *not* good?"

"Oh no, it's very good. Too good. I almost don't want you to leave." Damn straight I did not want him to leave. It had been a long time since I had had even this much action. Let alone with a guy as attractive as Ryan.

I wasn't sure if I was ready for this, but I didn't want him to go either. Would it be wrong if I imprisoned him here in my apartment forever?

Get a grip.

I used the pause in the action to remove myself from his lap and sit down next to him. I snuggled into his side, keeping his arm around me. "Music," I finally said.

"What about it?"

"I should put some on. It's too quiet." I was afraid that he could hear my heart racing.

"Yeah, it is quiet. Do you live here by yourself?"

"No, I have a roommate, but Deborah's away this weekend."

"So, what's your plan for tomorrow?" he asked, straightening himself up. His cheeks were flushed. I saw him glancing around my apartment, taking it all in.

"Sleeping in a little, if I can. Walking down to Haymarket to get some stuff. Grocery shopping. Maybe a nap. This whole work thing is taking it out of me. And I should go to the gym, but I won't."

"What's Haymarket?"

"It's a farmers' market in the North End, I guess you could say. Sometimes I get my veggies and fish there. Usually, the quantities are too big for just me to eat though. The joys of cooking for one."

Oh good lord, how much more desperate could I sound?

"Do you want some company? I mean, I need to stock up too. Can't expect Matt to feed me forever. What time do you want me to pick you up?"

So he was going to leave. Good. Unless it's because he didn't want to stay. Okay, re-group.

"Well, I was going to walk. It takes about an hour or so, but I like to get out when the weather is nice. Are you up for that?" I said softly, looking down.

"Walking, interesting concept."

"You live in Boston now. You'd better get used to walking. I mean, I guess we can take the T if you want, but it takes almost as long to get there." I looked up hopefully.

"Sounds good. Why don't you call me when you wake up, and we can go from there?" He paused. "You know, I'd rather you just woke me up in the morning, but I, um," he broke off.

I dropped my head down again. Pull it together. "No, it's fine. I've been trying to kick you out for a while now." Trying to be glib. "Now get out." I smiled at him and stood up, pulling him up off the couch.

He stood up, still holding my hands. He leaned in and kissed me again. "I'd better go, or you will have to physically remove me."

Anything physical was fine by me!

I led him to the door and said, "So I guess I'll call you in the morning?"

"Definitely. How do you take your coffee? I'll bring some over."

"Oh, thanks. Skim milk and sugar, please. How did you know that I cannot function without my caffeine?" I laughed.

He laughed. "You not only have a Mr. Coffee, but an espresso maker too. Anyone with the capability to procure that amount of caffeine is serious about their coffee.

Remember, I'm a prosecutor now." He tapped his temple. "I'm all about the details." He gave me one last quick kiss and turned out the door. In a daze, I closed it behind him. I sighed and kicked off my shoes.

I walked into my bedroom and stood there. I wanted to collapse onto my bed, but I knew I'd never get up. My feet and legs were killing me, and my ankle was swelling. Tonight my bedtime routine included ibuprofen and a bag of ice for my tender ankle. Once in bed, I wanted to think about the evening. I wanted to relive every glorious moment. I wanted to dissect my appalling comments and try to judge his reactions. I wanted to think about every touch, every kiss.

But all I did was fall asleep.

CHAPTER THREE

I knew I was awake even without opening my eyes. I was afraid to open them; afraid that last night was a dream.

A really good one.

I laid there, trying to process my thoughts. The dull headache and stomach ache that confirmed the presence of too much alcohol. My right ankle hurt and there was something cold pressing down on it. The bottoms of both feet ached, screaming to be rubbed.

My body indicated that last night could have happened. With my eyes still closed, I touched my hand to my lips. They felt the same. But the memories brought a rush of heat to my body, and my eyes flew open.

Holy crap, I'd had a serious make-out session with Ryan Milan.

I inventoried the situation. Lots of kissing, good. Hands stayed relatively tame, not so good. Plans for today, good. He left last night, not so good. No sex. Unable to determine at this time whether that falls in the good or not so good category. Probably good in the fact that it'd be too complicated for a one-night stand.

However, he was *hot*. And in the light of day, and without the benefit of alcohol, he'd probably change his mind

25

about me. I sighed and rolled over, stretching diagonally across my whole bed. I squinted and lifted my head so I could see my clock. 9:38 a.m.

Should I go back to sleep or should I get up and call Ryan? Was it too early? It would seem desperate. But I didn't want to keep him waiting. Frankly, I didn't want to give him time to change his mind either. I forced myself to stay prone until at least 10 a.m. That I could manage.

At 9:57, my phone rang. Who the hell could be calling me so early? Had to be Rachel. None of my other friends would be up and social at this time on a Saturday morning. I grabbed the phone and croaked out a hello. I was not expecting the velvet voice that purred, "Good morning, Sunshine. Are you ready for that coffee yet?"

I paused and stared at the phone itself as if it could provide an answer. "Ryan?"

"I knew you had guys lined up waiting to wait on you. Do I need to get a number, like at the deli?"

"Ding. Now serving number twenty-four. What number do you have young man?"

"Well, as luck would have it, number twenty-four. So do you want your coffee now?"

"Um, yes?"

"Why does your answer sound like a question?"

"Because I do need some coffee, as you can probably tell. But I need to become vertical and try to become a little human too. Trying to see which need is more pressing."

"And?"

"Must attain vertical and become human first. Can you give me a few minutes?"

"No problem," he said cheerfully. "See you in twenty." And he hung up.

Holy crap! There was no way I could pull myself together in twenty minutes. As I launched myself out of bed, the Ziploc bag, now full of melted ice, otherwise known as water, hit the floor and burst open.

Great.

It was only after I grabbed the towel off my doorknob and mopped the floor did I realize I'd just used my last clean towel. No shower for me but there wasn't time for one anyway. At least that spot on my floor was now clean.

A visit to the bathroom revealed a fuzzy reflection in the mirror. My ankle was still smarting from last night and didn't appreciate the extra trip back down the hall to retrieve my glasses. I popped two more ibuprofen and stuck my mouth under the faucet to wash them down.

While brushing my teeth, I looked at my reflection in the mirror trying to survey the damage. Despite efforts to wash my face last night, I still had mascara tracks under my eyes that made me look reminiscent of a rabid raccoon. The dark-colored bags under my eyes were puffy. Part of my hair stood up in the back, while the opposing side was flat. I washed my face again, this time using cold water to reduce the puffiness. I used my shirt to pat my face dry and went back to my room. That took me seven minutes. There was no way I was going to be ready on time.

I put my contacts in and blinked a few times. Hurriedly, I dug through my drawer looking for clothes. I managed to find, in addition to my favorite jeans, a coordinating bra, and underwear. Not sure why I even bothered. I had to be delusional if I thought Ryan and I would pick up where we left off.

A girl could dream, couldn't she?

I rummaged through my sock drawer and pulled out an old ankle brace. I jerked it on my right foot and pulled my gym socks on over. The pressure hurt, but I knew I'd need the support. Whipping open my closet door, I grabbed a violet-colored tee that made my eyes look more green and was flattering to my chest, along with a zip-up hoodie, and sneakers.

My stomach churned when I gulped down the glass of water on my bedside table, grimacing at how the lukewarm water tasted. I needed something in my stomach ASAP. I dashed into the kitchen and opened up the breadbox. I grabbed a piece, stuffing the carbohydrate goodness into my mouth.

I still had to fix my hair and makeup. I wet my hands in the kitchen sink and ran them through my hair, running back to my bedroom as I furiously combed down one side of my hair while simultaneously trying to encourage the other side to life. God, I missed being able to put my hair in a ponytail.

I completed my three-minute makeup routine and popped my silver hoops in. Sunglasses on the top of my head, and I was done. Seventeen minutes. I was gonna make it.

Wait—did I put deodorant on? That was close. I danced through my floral body spray just in case I wasn't as fresh as I thought I was.

I was ready to—crap. Where was my wallet? In my purse. Where was that? I looked at the table by the door where I usually put it. Nope. Think, what did I do when I walked in last night? I didn't walk in, I stumbled in, half wrapped around Ryan.

I pause for a moment to think about that. Got it! Purse tossed on the love seat next to the table. I grabbed my license, ATM card, and cash and tucked them into my back pocket. I ran back to the kitchen and grabbed my canvas knapsack out from under the sink. It had been my mother's during the '70s and was perfect for something like this. I grabbed my keys off the hook, surprised that I'd managed to hang them up the night before.

Nineteen minutes. Damn, I'm good.

I ran down the stairs and managed not to fall this time. Of course not, there was no audience. I tried to slow my pace as I went through the first door. I opened the outside door and walked down the four steps. I glanced up the street to see Ryan just ten feet away, grinning broadly. He held out a coffee as he closed the gap between us. "Morning, Sunshine. Skim milk and sugar, as requested."

I frowned as I took the cup and opened the lid. "Isn't that how you wanted it?" he asked.

"Yes, thanks," I replied. "But now you have an unfair advantage. How do you take yours?"

"I already told you what I like. Light and sweet."

Swoon.

"Uh." I tried to recover. Must keep it together, must keep it together. "Did you want to sit and drink the coffee or just get going?" I was doubtful that I could walk and drink my coffee without spilling it down the front of me. "We could sit here," I pointed to the stoop, "or we could walk a little way and find a bench somewhere more scenic."

"Why don't we find a bench? I don't want to be accused of loitering on your front steps."

We started walking down Commonwealth Ave. I kept stealing glances at Ryan. Good thing I had the sense to grab my sunglasses so that my staring wouldn't be blatant. He had a shadow of stubble. He was wearing jeans and sneakers, a gray Henley, and a black baseball cap. He looked casual but still gorgeous.

Ryan was one of the beautiful people. He didn't even have to try to look good. He probably would have to try to look bad. But I wondered how many people really ever bothered to listen to Ryan and get to know the person he was. I was so lost in thought, I kept walking, even after Ryan had stopped in front of a small, green space with a bench.

"Hey!" he called after me. "You wanna sit?"

"Sure," I said, snapping out of my thoughts. "Just in my own little world. Trying to compose a list of what I need today." Just trying to compose myself.

We sat down and began sipping our coffee. The sun was out, and it was going to be a perfect day. Sunny and warm, but fall. We were in a great spot for people-watching. Foot traffic was light on a Saturday morning.

"Are you really Maggie?" He asked.

"No, I'm a secret Russian spy that was crafted to look exactly like Maggie."

"No, I meant, is your real name Maggie, or is it a nickname?"

I laughed. "Nickname. My full name is Magdalene. Only the nuns ever called me that. Or my dad when I was *really* in trouble. I think it killed the nuns to have to call me that. They didn't like that I was named after a prostitute."

"A prostitute?"

"Yeah, Mary Magdalene in the Bible was in the world's oldest profession. I never wanted to disappoint their scandalous excitement by telling them that I was named after a cat."

"A cat? How do you go from a prostitute to a cat? Okay, that's a sentence I never thought I'd say." He laughed. "It sounds like a riddle."

"My mom's younger brother, Dan, got two cats when my mom moved out. He's thirteen years younger than her, so he was about twelve when she was getting married. She helped him name them, Jake and Maggie. Fast forward about five years when my parents started having kids. Those were the only names my mom really liked. My brother was Jake, and I'm Maggie."

"Was?"

Dammit. I already knew he was observant. I should have known he'd pick up on that. Better to get it over with quickly. I took a deep breath and said in one exhale, "My brother and mom were killed in a car accident when I was seven. I was in the car too. I missed the better part of the school year recuperating from my injuries. I broke my legs, pelvis, and back. I guess I'm pretty lucky to be walking." My voice lowered and my head dropped.

"Is that why you work with kids?"

"Yeah. My PTs were so awesome. Miss Cheryl became kind of a surrogate mother for me. She was tough but warm. I knew I wanted to be just like her when I grew up."

"I'm sorry. Matt never told me."

"Not really light conversation to make in passing. I don't talk about it much, and I don't usually share details. But it's okay. I've had almost twenty years to adjust to it. I think that's why I gravitated to Matt. I think he reminds me of Jake. Kind of like the brother figure that I've been missing."

"So you guys like never dated?"

I shook my head, a little confused. Why didn't he ask Matt this? "He's been with Irene the whole time. I don't think it ever occurred to him that I'm a girl."

"Oh, I'm sure it did. He's not blind."

Wow, what did he mean by that? I stared at him for a minute. Eventually, it occurred to me that I needed to say something. "But you don't need to look into the shadows when you have a sun goddess orbiting around you."

That's how I felt compared to Irene. She was bright and beautiful, and I was ... me.

He stared at me for a moment. "What's the deal with Irene anyway? She's a little, um, frosty?"

"The sugar-coated version or the hard truth?"

"The truth, the whole truth, and nothing but the truth."

"Yes, sir. She's pissed that you moved in with Matt. He was finally done with school, so that means he won't be seeing as much of me, which makes her happy. She was hoping he would ask her to move in with him and set up house, but you preempted that." I paused, unsure if I should share my suspicions about the dinner last night. I took a sip of my coffee and looked at him.

"Makes sense. If Matt didn't want me to move in, why didn't he say something?"

"Because that's Irene's plan, not Matt's plan. He's happy with the status quo right now. I don't think he's ready to settle down yet. And that pisses her off to no end. As does his friendship with me."

"Well, I guess I'll stay put until he says something to me. Maybe I'll try to feel him out a little, see if he wants me to move out sooner rather than later."

"I'd guess not, but what do I know? I'm pretty sure it's you he wants to spoon with instead of her."

"Nice, how did you know?"

I laughed and stood up. "You ready to go?"

Even though we walked for almost an hour, time flew by due to the easy conversation. I never even tripped. He had to keep asking me to slow down. "For a little person with short legs, you walk fast!"

"I've spent the last five years perfecting it. If it meant I could sleep a few minutes later, then it's worth it!"

We got to Haymarket and wound our way through the crowded streets and vendors. We each stocked up on fresh produce. The fishmonger had some beautiful swordfish steaks that I couldn't resist. I bought four, planning to freeze some.

Ryan just stood with a confused look on his face. "We don't get a lot of fresh fish in Ohio. It's not usually even worth ordering in a restaurant unless you're at the Red Lobster."

The fishmonger laughed with a thick local accent, "That's not even real fish. Welcome to Boston, Kid!"

My canvas bag was a little heavy, even slung on my back, so I suggested that we take the T back. We headed underground to the Haymarket station and bought our tokens. I gave Ryan a little background of how the T runs and picked up a map for him. We waited for a B-line train, the station hot and noisy. We were able to find seats, and I plopped down. I was acutely aware that our shoulders and arms were only centimeters apart. I wondered if he realized it too. As if answering my question, Ryan turned to me, pulling away, and asked, "Do you ever get used to traveling like this?"

"Definitely. When I go home, it's weird having to drive everywhere. I pretty much only use my car to get out of the city, like to visit my dad or head away. Mostly, I just pay for it to sit, and I try to avoid parking tickets. I guess I'm a city girl at heart. It's all in the mindset. You just have to plan your travel time well and dress appropriately for the weather. Yeah, in the pouring rain, I do drive a little more, but that's about it. I'd rather live like this than in suburbia and have to drive everywhere."

As the T came up to street level, I told him that he could continue on one more stop past me, and that would put him a little closer to his place. He didn't say anything. I didn't know how to take that. Maybe I said something to irritate him, or maybe he had just had his fill of me. As I approached my stop, I stood up, thanked him for the coffee and company, and said goodbye. He smiled and gave me a nice, friendly peck on the cheek.

I didn't expect him to chase after me or anything, but I kind of wished he would. Or call out to me asking me to go out with him tonight.

Oh well, I knew that the magic of the previous night would not last in the daylight hours. I'd had a great night last night and a really great morning. It was perfect, so what did I have to complain about? I trudged the two blocks home and tried to put him out of my mind. After all, I had an exciting afternoon of laundry to keep me occupied.

I spent the rest of the afternoon running up and down from the basement doing my laundry. I watched Ohio State pummel Northwestern and wondered if Ryan and Matt were watching the game too. Most likely.

Around seven, I forced myself to go to the gym. I did not want to, but I felt like I needed to get out for a little distraction. The gym was virtually empty, predictable for a Saturday night. I tried to tell myself that this workout was worth it if someone was going to be seeing me naked, especially someone with a perfect body ... STOP!

No, I would not permit *that* train to leave the station. The empty gym meant the only person to watch was me. I tried to look objectively, to see what someone observing me would see. I was moderately attractive. Cuter than anything else. Not the kind of girl that guys would cross a room for, but the kind that a guy would feel comfortable talking to if we bumped into each other. My legs were toned and muscular from years of therapy. If only they weren't so pale. My midsection could definitely use some toning but didn't look bad. I did ten more crunches at the end of my set for good measure and headed to the locker room. I pulled on my baggy sweats and sweatshirt and got another drink. When I exercised, my face turned bright pink, and my hair was glued to my head with sweat. I headed out into the now chilly autumn night.

I was about a block from home, walking while watching my feet, as usual, so I didn't trip when I heard voices. I looked up to see four figures walking towards me. They were talking and laughing.

Oh shit.

It was Matt, Irene, Ryan, and Irene's friend Samantha. I was tempted to vomit. They were all dressed casually but were obviously headed out. Together. "Mags!" Matt yelled, obviously happy to see me. "Whatchya doing?"

"Returning home from my photoshoot for Cosmo before heading to dinner at the United Nations." I rolled my eyes. I looked like a frumpy drowned rat with a sunburn. There was no doubt that I smelled.

Please, sidewalk open up and swallow me whole.

I could not believe that Ryan saw me like this, while he was out with another girl, no less. There went any chance I had with him. So much for having him see me naked anytime soon. I guess I could have skipped those extra crunches.

Irene, being Irene, gave me the up and down look and smirked at me. "Well, we're headed out. Samantha had to work last night, so we re-scheduled for tonight."

That certainly clarified how our "double date" had come about. I was a stand-in from the beginning. Nice. I stood up as tall as I could and tried to spare a tiny shred of dignity, "Have fun. Gotta get inside, see ya!" I started jogging away.

Silently I said a prayer that Matt wouldn't comment on my running or the fact that I never run. That my motto was that I only run when my life is in danger. To me, this falls into that category. Fight or flight, I pick flight.

Every time.

CHAPTER FOUR

In the following weeks, my roommate Deborah and I dissected every comment, gesture, silence, and action about my encounters with Ryan until there was nothing left to be discussed. Ryan had piqued my interest, which hadn't happened in a long time.

I couldn't stop thinking about him. It was almost to the point of obsession. Even Jared, my last disaster of a relationship, had merely been based upon drunken make-out sessions with little in the way of a real relationship to back it up. If we hadn't been in classes together, we would've had nothing to talk about.

So different from how I felt with Ryan.

We could talk to each other for hours. But it didn't seem to matter what a great time I thought Ryan and I had had. It didn't seem to matter that we were able to talk for hours and that it was easy being together. It didn't seem to matter that I thought it was one of the best make-out sessions I had ever had. He ranked as one of my top ten kisses. Maybe top five.

What mattered was that I didn't hear from him. I talked to Matt sporadically over that time, checking in about the job. We usually ended up discussing patient problems or cool things that we had learned. We updated each other about classmates that we ran into. I tried to casually ask how Ryan liked his new job. Matt's response was vague and only indicated that Ryan was busy. I couldn't tell if it was Matt running interference so I wouldn't dwell on why Ryan never called—which I was doing—or if Matt was in oblivious-guy mode— which he probably was.

Deborah had her own drama to help occupy the time. After spending the night arguing with her long-distance boyfriend on the phone on Saturday, she emerged from her bedroom with a triumphant look on her face. "I am officially single, and I want to go dancing!"

"You're on sister!" I'd never been a fan of James's. Moreover, I could use a fun night, which I night out with Deborah was guaranteed to be. She was a social butterfly, and guys flocked to her, usually paying for most of our drinks. We could be goofy together.

Our night started as usual; a dance music CD in the stereo and a glass—or four—of wine while we got ready. Sometimes, the getting-ready rituals were the most fun part of the night.

Once dressed and made up, we made the round of a few bars down on Boylston, before deciding to head back to our favorite neighborhood bar around midnight. We knew the staff, so it was like hanging out with friends. The DJ was playing great music and, with beers in our hands, we headed out to the crowded dance floor in the center of the small bar. For what seemed like the best setlist ever, we danced, stomped, and gyrated until I was lost in the music.

I was hot and thirsty, so I motioned to Deb that I was going to get another beer, unable to verbally communicate over the loud, thumping beat. She pointed in another direction. I turned and saw Matt, Irene, Ryan, and Samantha standing not too far from the door. They were watching the dance floor. Correct that: they were watching Deb and me on the dance floor.

Crap.

Deb followed me off the dance floor, and we curved around to the opposite end of the bar from where the happy foursome was.

Well, I guess I know why he hadn't called.

Deb and I flagged down the bartender and ordered two more bottles of beer. We grabbed our bottles, and I began to down mine. Deb leaned over, "Holy shit, he is *hot*. What is he doing with Sam?" Sam was as pretty as Irene but even more of a bitch. At least she always had been to us. She was the type of girl that Ryan said he usually attracted, but that didn't make it to Date Two. Well, this had to be at least Date Two, if not Date Ten. I shrugged and tried not to cry.

Just then, we heard the familiar guitar opening chords to one of our favorite songs. I looked at Deb, and she grinned, "They're playing *our* song."

It was enough for me to snap out of my funk, at least for the moment. I winked at her and grabbed her hand, and we skirted out to the dance floor to let it all hang out and sing at the top of our lungs. As the song ended, I saw the warning look in her eyes. I steeled myself and turned. Ryan was standing behind me, smiling.

Now, I wish I could say that I barely glanced in his direction, except to give him a cool hello and then continued on with my night. I wish I could say that I was put together and nonchalant. I wish I could, but I can't.

Thanks to copious amounts of wine and beer inhibiting my every wise thought and action, I shrieked, "Ryan!" and launched myself at him. I threw my arms around his neck and pressed my body into his.

Despite my sloppiness, he looked amused, "Having fun?" he shouted over the music. His eyes were warm, and his hands were around my waist. It was hard to tell if he was holding me or holding me up.

"Come on and dance with us," I yelled back and pulled him out to the dance floor. Ryan was a good sport. He kept looking at me and smiling. I was touching him. A lot. I didn't care. He was out here with me.

Matt, Irene, and Samantha soon joined us up on the dance floor, and it looked like we were one big, happy group of friends. At that moment, I was so happy. This was turning out to be a great evening.

Until I turned around to see Samantha was winding herself up and down Ryan, and Irene was rubbing herself on his back. The message was clear—there was no place for me here. Pissed off, I abruptly turned around and stormed off the dance floor. I sidled up to the bar and asked for water. I wasn't sure if I was going to cry or punch something.

"Hey."

I turned and looked at Matt with a dirty look on my face. "Hey, what?" I snapped.

He was taken aback by my aggressive tone. "What's your problem?"

"Nothing. I'm peachy keen right now." I was biting back tears. "Don't let me spoil your evening. Better yet, why don't you leave so that you don't spoil mine?"

Deborah appeared next to Matt. "Don't you think you should claim your girlfriend?" She gestured to the dance floor where Irene and Samantha were performing what could have been described as a fully clothed threesome with Ryan.

Matt laughed, "Better him than me. Samantha is vicious. I have never seen her on the hunt like this. She's been all over Ryan for weeks now. Practically glued herself to him. Can barely get her to leave our apartment."

My mouth fell open. I felt like I had been punched in the gut. Matt was still rambling on, oblivious to how he had just shattered my world. I looked over at the spectacle on the dance floor, in time to see Samantha and Ryan kissing. Irene had stepped back, a smug look on her face.

I looked at Deborah and said, "I gotta get out of here. I'm gonna be sick." I bolted, pushing my way out the door. The only thing that could possibly make this night any worse would be to throw up all over the place. I made it to the door, and the fresh air hit me. Okay, I was going to be okay. I thought about what Matt had just said and what I had just seen.

Oops, no I was not going to be okay. I ran into the alley next to the bar and threw up.

Awesome.

I heard someone come up behind me. Probably Deborah. "I cannot even believe it; can you?" I muttered without looking.

Instead, I heard Matt's voice. "Dude, what's wrong with you? How drunk are you?"

I turned around and wiped my mouth. I looked at him and said, "Nothing. Just too much to drink. I'm gonna grab Deb and head home."

Matt knew I was lying, but I didn't want to get into it with him. He pulled me into a tight hug. "I don't know why you are upset, but tell me what I can do to help."

I sighed, leaning into his chest. "I had my hopes up for an unrealistic expectation and it all just hit me at once."

"What unrealistic expectation?"

I looked at his face, so sweet and innocent. So utterly clueless.

"Don't worry, I'll get over this too. Just like I always do." I laughed bitterly. "You really think I'd be used to getting dumped on by now. Happens often enough. This is why I don't date. I'd rather stay home and be lonely than get crushed all the time."

"Who did you go out with? Did you have a date tonight? Where was he? I thought you were with Deborah."

"Matt, are you blind? You are such a shithead!" And with that, I turned and stormed home.

The next morning was painful. I was hungover with a splitting headache that threatened to last most of the day. I'm not sure how much of it was from alcohol and how much was from crying. Deborah had caught up with me outside and we went home. I apologized profusely for being such an ass and cried. And she cried over James. He was an ass, but she still was going to miss him. We agreed that we were pitiful and we were asses and men were asses and cried some more.

At some point, I would need to call Matt and apologize, but I couldn't bring myself to. Not yet.

No, this Sunday would be spent with Deborah and me laying at opposite ends of the couch, watching TV through puffy and tired eyes. We again dissected the events of the previous evening.

My stomach rolled with queasiness. I needed to eat something, but nothing I had in the house appealed to me. I said, "What do you think the odds of a bacon, egg, and cheese sandwich materializing out of nowhere are?

Deb laughed. "About as likely as Samantha getting leprosy and having her nose fall off."

"Well, one can dream ..." I retorted.

About ten seconds later, the buzzer rang. Deb and I looked at each other with confused looks. I was closest, so I got up and shuffled over to the door. "Hello?"

"Lemme in." It was Matt.

"Be right down." About now, I was cursing the fact that the buzzer was still broken, and I had to walk down the stairs to allow him access. I opened the door and just looked at him. He held up a bag and a cup and said, "Peace offering?"

A smile stretched across my face. There were two breakfast sandwiches and a large Coke, no ice. He knew me so well.

"Deal."

"By the way, you look like shit." He was not wrong. I was dressed in old flannel pajama bottoms that were starting to fray and a wife-beater, no bra. I kept my arms folded over my chest to cover the girls. I wore my glasses, last night's makeup, and I couldn't even imagine what my hair was doing. The smell of old cigarettes and stale booze wafted from every pore.

"Thanks. I feel like it too. Does that make you feel better?"

We went back up to my apartment. I held up the bag as I walked through the door and said to Deb, "Uh-oh, I hear there may be an outbreak of leprosy in the near future."

Deborah grabbed her sandwich and thanked Matt. She went into her room to give us a little privacy. I flopped back down on the couch and wrapped a blanket around my upper half, mostly to cover my boobs. "Um, sorry about calling you a shithead last night."

"I wasn't even sure you'd remember that. You were pretty out of it. I've seen you pretty drunk, but I've never seen quite that mood before. I haven't seen your temper flare like that since probably sophomore year. What brought it on?"

He still didn't get it. I guess no one had even for one second considered that Ryan would go for me. I mean, why would he? No one expected me to be crushed because it was such an unlikely scenario. Matt had never seen me as dating material; why would Ryan?

I was a fine friend. A great friend. But that was it. That would always be it. Tears threatened again. I shrugged my shoulders and said, "Dunno. Too much to drink I guess."

He looked at me skeptically. "You need anything?"

I drew myself into a little ball on the couch. I shook my head. "No, the sandwich and soda hit the spot. Thanks again, you know me so well."

He stood up to leave. "Gotta take care of my best friend. I'll call you later to see if you are okay." He ruffled my hair. Like I was the dog or his kid brother. "'K thanks." I mumbled. I closed my eyes and heard him walk across the living room and out the door.

If I couldn't have Ryan, at least Matt was still my friend. I hadn't totally ruined things.

Not yet.

CHAPTER FIVE

I wish I could say that things got better. They didn't. Nothing changed, and I think that was worse. I barely talked to Matt, and when I did, it was strained and generic conversation.

I was sad, lonely, and pissed.

My pining over Ryan was present but starting to fade. I mean, we kissed a little one night. No big deal. It didn't mean anything. Obviously.

But I was sad that I felt like I had lost Matt too. The irony was not lost on me. One of the reasons that I held back and did not sleep with Ryan was so that it didn't affect my friendship with Matt. But it still did, and I didn't even get a night of possibly mind-blowing sex—or bragging rights—out of it.

I felt cheated.

But then, the Friday before Thanksgiving, I was grocery shopping, wearing my heavy winter coat made me look like the Stay-Puff Marshmallow Man when I ran into Ryan.

Figures.

The big Ohio State vs. Michigan game was on the next day. Matt and I usually watched it together, but I had not heard from him, so I planned to watch it by myself. Even if I was pitiful, there was no reason why I shouldn't have my traditional chili to keep me warm, since it's not like anyone else was.

My hand was sliding over the hot peppers when I heard a voice over my shoulder. "You don't want to make it too spicy. Some people can't handle the heat."

Without missing a beat, I replied, "You need a little heat to make things interesting." And then I immediately hated myself for sounding so corny. I pasted on a smile and turned around.

Ryan was genuinely grinning back at me. "Maggie Miller, where the hell have you been?" He looked like he was really happy to see me, even going so far as to hug me.

I was shocked. Why was he asking me where I've been? Where did he think I'd be? The fifth wheel at Matt's? Did he really think that I wanted to hang around and watch him make out with Samantha while I got death glares from Irene?

Oh my God, I was so in the friend zone that he did not even consider me a girl. I might as well have a penis.

But I loved how it sounded when he said my name. And that when he hugged me, an electric current went running through my body. And that was through the puffy jacket. I finally pulled my racing thoughts together enough to come up with a very witty retort. "Around."

"I thought you'd be over a lot more now. Matt is a mess. He says he's not, but he just mopes around all the time."

I stepped back. "What are you talking about?"

"You don't know?"

I shook my head, confused.

"Irene dumped him. She gave him an ultimatum about her moving in. He hesitated like, two seconds in replying, and she stormed out. That's it, finish-done. Oh, and apparently she's sleeping with a co-worker. She called and demanded he bring her stuff to her, and when he got there, he found her with some dude. He's pretty messed up about it."

This doesn't make sense. Why wouldn't he call me? "He never even called ..."

"I told him to. I was wondering why you hadn't been over. I said you were going to be pissed when you found out. Then I said Irene had better watch out because you were going to kick her ass."

I shrugged my shoulders, trying to smile. I was hurt and confused, but mostly I was sad for my friend who was apparently devastated and wouldn't even let me help him. Were we even friends anymore?

"But you're coming over tomorrow, right?" Ryan's voice broke me out of my train of thoughts.

"Umm, not sure I was invited" I mumbled looking at my feet.

"Consider yourself invited. And if you feel the need to cook for us, feel free. I've heard stories about your cooking."

I smiled at Ryan, temporarily forgetting I was angry with him. It was so hard. He was so warm and friendly. His smile made me want to melt. I was still trying to pull myself together after the hug, then the news about Matt.

"I was going to make chili, as long as you think you can handle my heat."

"Oh, just let me try." He winked at me, "But maybe I should pick up some Tums, just in case ..."

"Are you sure it will be okay with Matt ... and um, everyone else?" Meaning Samantha.

"No problem. If Matt wants to pout, then consider yourself my special guest. Which means you, I mean, all the food is just for me." He leaned in and said this last part into my ear, with his hand wrapped around my waist, pulling me a little closer. I think my feet went numb again.

He pulled back and smiled. "See you tomorrow. Come on over any time after ten." And with that, he turned and was gone.

I was still there, holding a jalapeno, my mouth hanging open. My brain was having difficulty processing what had just happened.

Matt … and Irene. Done. He never called me. Even after she was out of the picture.

Ryan didn't mention Samantha at all. Would she be there tomorrow? Damn, I should have found a way to ask. Maybe Deborah would come as reinforcement.

My evening was spent in a flurry in the kitchen, going all out with game day treats. In addition to my chili prep, I made cornbread and Buckeyes, naturally. I was cleaning up by the time Deborah finally came in, so I gave her the rundown. She had to work tomorrow, so I would be flying solo.

"You have to call me if *anything* happens! I should be home by five."

Despite my fatigue from the week and the cooking, my mind was a swirl of activity. My brain refused to still long enough to sleep until close to midnight. I slept in and awoke with plenty of time to shower and cook the chili before it went in the crockpot. Once everything was lined up on the counter it occurred to me that I'd never be able to carry it all over to Matt and Ryan's. Deborah didn't have to work until noon, so she gladly drove me over.

"Remember, call me if anything big happens!" she called as I got out of her car.

Loaded up like a pack mule, I steeled myself to walk in. Time to face the music.

CHAPTER SIX

I artfully juggled the crockpot and the heavy bag slung over my shoulder as I walked up the three flights of stairs to Matt and Ryan's apartment. When I got to the door, I banged it with my foot, precariously balancing on the other. It was a miracle that I didn't drop everything.

Ryan answered the door with a smile. *Oh, that smile.* "I see you come bearing gifts," he greeted.

"Yep," I said, as I handed him the crockpot, "as promised." I breezed by him to get to Matt, who was walking across the living room at that moment. I threw my arms around him and clung to him. His arms reached around me and held on tight. He put his head down and buried it in my shoulder. I held onto him for a minute and then I stepped back and playfully punched him in the gut. "You suck."

"Oww," he recoiled, rubbing his stomach. "What was that for?"

"Why didn't you call me?"

Ryan laughed at us. "I told you I thought she would kick the shit out of Irene. I didn't think she could take you too!"

I turned to look at Ryan, sharing his laughter. Matt took advantage of the situation and put me in a headlock. "What was that?" he said, joining in the fun. Matt released me, and I retrieved the crockpot from the coffee table, where Ryan had put it down to watch us wrestle. I brought it out to the kitchen and plugged it in. I put the various contents of my bag in the fridge and grabbed a beer. I opened it and returned to the living room, plopping myself on one end of the couch, opposite Matt. "No, seriously, why didn't you call me?"

He dropped his head and looked sheepishly down at his hands. "Firstly, I did think that you would kill Irene. And then I didn't want to hear you gloat."

"Gloat, about what? Kicking her ass?" I could totally take her. I'm small but scrappy.

"No, about how you were right about her. You've never been a huge fan of hers, and I wasn't in the mood to hear it."

I stiffened, offended. "Matt, I thought you knew me better than that. I am first and foremost your friend. You have always been there for me. Jeez, how many times have I called you up in the middle of the night because some loser or another crapped all over me again? Do I need to remind you of the Jared and Ellen fiasco?"

I shudder, thinking of that disaster. "How many boxes of tissues did I go through? I don't know how I would have ever gone to class again if you had not been there sitting beside me. I owe you big time, and this is the one time I could have started to repay you."

Matt shrugged, a little embarrassed. Ryan was in the kitchen, making himself busy. I didn't care if he heard this not. This was about my friend who was in pain. It didn't matter what opinion some guy formed of me.

I continued. "Secondly, I don't think you are ready to hear my true feelings. Knowing you, which I think I do, I think there's a pretty good chance that you and Irene will get back together. And if," I paused, meeting his eyes, "that happens, all you will remember is all the smack I talked about her. If you are truly finished, which I doubt, I will give you my opinion much, much later."

He smiled at me, and I returned it. "Now tell me what happened."

My stomach churned as he told me of the ultimatum and subsequent fight. As he recounted how she called, a few days later demanding her stuff back, only to greet him at the door, wearing a robe and with men's clothing—not his—strewn about the place. A toilet flush from the bathroom was all Matt needed to hear.

I really did want to kick Irene's ass now. How dare she hurt my friend? How could she go from wanting to move in to screwing someone else in the span of days? I knew she was cold, but this ...

A thought dawned the pieces snapping together in my brain.

Matt looked up and saw me smiling. "Could you please not take so much pleasure in my pain?" he said coldly. "Jesus!"

My face fell apologetically. "No Matt, that's not what it is at all. Ten bucks says she didn't sleep with anyone else." He looked at me with confusion. I continued. "She demanded you come over right?"

"Yeah."

"It was a setup. Totally. Sure, there probably was a guy there, but I would guess she made it look as bad as she could. He was probably the super, fixing a leak or something. She wants you to see that she can get anyone no problem, and that would drive you crazy. Then you'd want to fight for her and beg for her to come back. She knows she'll never do any better than you; she'd be crazy to throw it away. I'd bet this was her plan to speed things along."

"Diabolical," Ryan said, walking into the room. So he had been listening.

"I wouldn't put it past her," I affirmed.

Matt just shook his head, not knowing what to think.

"I can't tell you how to proceed. I'm just here to provide my two cents. Is there any other service I can provide today?" I bowed a little. I thought I heard Ryan choke on his beer a little. It took every amount of self-control in my body not to turn around and look at him. I sat frozen until I heard him walk back into the kitchen.

"Well," Matt said sheepishly "my neck has been killing me all week."

I sighed, being overly dramatic. "I provided you with valuable knowledge today and have not mocked you in any way. This will cost you."

"Deal."

I got up. "Where's your bag?"

"Bedroom."

I went into Matt's room and saw his black duffle by the closet. I retrieved the small container of massage lotion and returned to the living room. Ryan watched me suspiciously.

I pointed at Matt. "Sit on the floor, I'll get behind you." Ryan continued to watch us as Matt slid to a sitting position on the floor in front of the couch. I climbed over Matt and sat down behind him, my legs straddling his shoulders. I opened the container and applied a little lotion to my fingertips. I began working and kneading at his shoulders and neck muscles. I worked my way up and down his shoulder blades, stopping and concentrating when I would feel knots and spasms. The game was on, and I continued working, letting my hands guide me while my eyes were focused on the TV. I ended with some mobilizations of the neck vertebrae and patted Matt on the shoulders. I stood up and went into the kitchen to wash my hands and check on the chili. I needed another beer too. I poked my head out. "Beer?"

53

Matt, now fully reclined against the couch, looking super relaxed, raised his hand. Ryan stood up and came into the kitchen. "So what was that? You lied to me," he said accusingly.

I just looked at him.

"Matt is definitely over four feet tall. Why does he get a rubdown?"

"Matt was my lab partner, so he knows exactly what my skill level is. I have to use that line or every Tom, Dick, and Harry I meet will want a free massage. I can't lie to Matt. He knows that I am more than capable. Plus," I winked, "now he owes me one. I like to think of us as friends with benefits, just not the 'traditional' kind of benefits."

"So, what? I'm just like every other Tom, Dick, and Harry that tries to hit on you that you have to give the brush off?" He seemed angry.

"Uhh, no. I was just making a joke," I stammered. "If you want to provide me with legal service, I'd be more than happy to rub you down."

And now I sounded cheesy, lame, and like I was a prostitute. Why can't I flirt like a normal human being?

He gave me a sly smile. "Well, I guess I have to hope you find yourself in trouble soon." He walked back out into the living room to watch the game.

How the hell was I supposed to take him? Was he mad? Flirting? Jealous?

What reason would Ryan have to be jealous?

CHAPTER SEVEN

B y the end of the game, the apartment started filling with people. Friends dropping by to drink and eat. And drink some more. By the time Deborah showed up with some of her friends, the day's drinking was starting to catch up with me.

Okay, I was drunk.

It took me a minute to realize the squealing I heard was coming from me. Someone produced a camera and the flashing didn't help the room stay still or clear.

Soon, all the food and drink had been consumed, so the large group of us went out to a local sports bar to watch the evening games. By about ten, I was more tired than buzzed, having been drinking for far too long. I'd hit my wall and needed to go home. I motioned to Matt that I was leaving. He seemed like he was having a fun time, which was a relief after how upset he'd seemed earlier today.

I found Ryan sitting in the corner of a booth, flanked by a few girls whom I vaguely knew. "Hey, I'm taking off."

He tried to stand up, "Wait! Lemme walk you home." He climbed over his booth mates and grabbed my arm.

I shrugged. "Okay, you don't have to."

"I know I don't have to, I want to."

Wedd walked for about a block or so when I realized that I didn't have my keys. All my stuff was still at his apartment."Crap."

"What?"

"My keys are at your place."

"No problem, we'll just detour there."

We turned up the next block and continued to walk in silence. I was tired, but I was becoming more alert thanks to the cold November night air. Ryan didn't say much. I thought about the last time he had walked me home, how he had his arm around me, and the ...

No. I could not let myself go there again. That wasn't going to happen again, as he had made abundantly clear. Or had he? He seemed almost jealous of Matt earlier today.

"Where are you? Hello?"

"Oh sorry, just lost in my head again. Did you ask me something?"

"No, you just looked far away, and you were speed walking again."

"Sorry. Just tired, I guess."

"Usually being tired makes people move slower, not faster."

We had reached his place, and I stood behind him as he unlocked the door. Without really paying attention, I followed him into the dark apartment. He walked forward about six steps, and then whirled around, crashing into me.

"Oh sorry," I mumbled. I steadied myself by grabbing onto him. His arms went around me for a millisecond to steady me, and then they were gone. I tried to find the lights but ended up reaching aimlessly around on the wall. Ryan reached over my shoulder and flicked on the lights. I blinked my eyes a few times, trying to adjust. We stood there looking at each other for a minute. Finally, he broke the silence, "Do you mind if I check a few scores before I take you home?" Ryan asked.

"You don't have to take me home, I'll be fine."

"Don't be stupid. I'm not letting you walk home alone."

"It's no big deal. I walk everywhere by myself all the time."

"I am not discussing this any further. You are not walking home alone."

"Okay, okay, okay." I relented. While Ryan waited for the score updates, I made myself comfortable, getting a drink of water. I was so tired. I kicked my sneakers off and reclined on the couch. Ryan was on the couch too, so there was nowhere for my feet to go, except in his lap. He rested his hands on my feet. I let out a content little sigh and promptly fell asleep.

I heard voices a little later on, but they were not strong enough to fully wake me. I felt my body being jostled around slightly, and I struggled to open my eyes. Ryan's face was right there. He was carrying me. Had I been more alert, I probably would have taken advantage of our proximity. "Hey," he said softly. "You fell asleep. Just stay here."

I tried to say yes, but I'm pretty sure it came out like, "Mmmhmm." He put me down gently on his bed and said, "I'll be out on the couch if you need anything." I think he kissed me on the forehead, but I could have imagined it. And he was gone.

It didn't matter though because as soon as I shimmied out of my jeans, I was dead to the world again.

Hours later, I woke to what sounded like a door opening and closing. Sunlight filled the unfamiliar room, and I looked around, searching my memory as to my location.

Ryan. I was in his bed. Alone.

I was sprawled out, with my bare leg hanging out from beneath the sheet, and firmly planted on the floor, to stop the bed spins.

Wait—why didn't I have pants on? Oh, that's right, I took them off myself. I lifted my head slightly and saw them at the end of the bed. I shifted my gaze to the door. Was that the sound I'd heard?

Ryan was peaking in. "Sorry, didn't mean to wake you." He came in and let the door close behind him. "Just wanted to make sure you were okay." His dark hair was tousled, and he had a face full of stubble. He looked so sexy in his T-shirt and shorts.

And here I was, without pants on.

I tried to sit up, but with my one exposed leg hanging down, all I could do was myself up on my elbows. "I'm fine. Um, thanks for the bed? You didn't have to do that you know."

"No problem, the couch is super comfortable," he said in a voice that indicated the contrary. He crossed the room and sat on the edge of the bed next to me. I drew my leg back under the covers. "I called Deborah and left her a message that you were staying here, just so she didn't worry."

"That's the sweetest thing any guy has ever done for me." Whoops, didn't mean to say that out loud.

"That's so sad."

"Why is that sad? I think it's so nice that you did that," I said defensively.

"No, it's sad that that simple thing would be the nicest thing a guy has done for you. What kind of guys are you dating, anyway?"

"Well, you may not have noticed, but they aren't exactly lined up right now. And, as I told you before, I have excellent skills in picking loser bad boys who treat me like shit. The more of an ass they are, the more I seem to like them.

I have impeccable taste." I flopped back down and put my arm over my face.

He shook his head. "So I need to be more of an ass?"

"What?" I said, staring up at the ceiling, my eyes wide.

At that minute, Ryan's door flew open and it was Matt, jubilant, "You'll never guess ..."

He stopped in his tracks. It took him a minute to process that Ryan was not alone. "Oh, sorry, didn't mean to interrupt ..." I sat up to look at Matt and his eyes widened as we locked stares. He backed out and closed the door.

"Crap," I said as I flopped backward, keeping my face covered in my hands.

Ryan pulled me close to him and wrapped his arms around me. "Is it Matt? Are you, I mean do you want to be, ummm ..."

"NO!" I said pulling my hands down from my face. "God no. I just don't want him to be mad at me."

"Why would he be mad at you?"

"Well, this probably looks like we, well, um, you know. I don't want him to be pissed at me for corrupting you or throwing myself at you. I told you, I have an awesome track record with guys, and Matt will be pissed if I hurt you. Plus, I don't want to put Matt in the middle of, well, whatever this is. Or isn't."

"Oh." He seemed upset.

"Does that bother you, that I care about what Matt thinks about us?" Oh God, I wish there was an *us*. "I mean, Matt is my best friend and I well, I don't know." I had no idea what Ryan wanted. What his intentions were? If they were the same as mine, wouldn't he have slept in here with me?

He didn't answer the question. "We should go talk to Matt. He seemed like he had good news."

"Okay." I started to get up, and then I realized that I did not have pants on. "Could you hand me my jeans?" I mumbled, looking down at my bare legs and gesturing to my jeans, on the other side of him.

Ryan turned quickly away and grabbed them. He tossed them back to me and walked out of the room without looking back.

Well, I guess that about says it all. He couldn't even stand the sight of me half-naked in his bed. I looked forlornly at the door before sliding back into my jeans. My socks, on the other hand, were among the missing. I had a habit of kicking them off while I slept. One was tangled up in the sheets while the other was under the bed.

I hiked up my jeans one last time as I walked out into the living room. Matt was buzzing around, picking up beer bottles and other various remnants of yesterday. He stopped when I came into the room and ran to me. He picked me up, spinning me around. "You are a goddess."

"That's common knowledge," I glanced at Ryan, scared to meet his eyes, as Matt put me back down, "but what has brought this to your attention now?"

Matt rambled excitedly. "After you guys left last night, Irene came into the bar. I confronted her and told her that I didn't think she had slept with anyone else. She was stunned. She couldn't believe that I figured it out. That *you* figured it out." We were spinning again. Not great the morning after drinking. "I told her that I loved her and didn't want to lose her, but I just wasn't ready for the next step. That I wanted to be with her, but she needed to be a little more mature about the whole situation."

Matt released me and I stepped back stumbling a bit as the room continued to rotate. "So, what did you do then?"

"I told her that *if* I decided to take her back, she would have to stop trying to manipulate me and let the relationship proceed at its natural pace. And now, I'm letting her swing for a few days." He grinned. "Now let's go to the diner and get some breakfast. You're looking a little queasy. You need a little grease."

"Thanks. I go from being a goddess to queasy. Awesome," I grumbled.

I sat down wearily on the couch. My hungover mind was trying to process what was going on around me.

Matt and Irene were going to get back together. Not the best news, but Matt seemed really happy. I wanted my friend to be happy.

And Ryan ... I had no idea what the hell was going on. One minute, he seemed interested, and next, he was giving me the cold shoulder. I was starting to get whiplash.

Maybe we needed to sit down and talk. Yeah, I'm sure that wouldn't be awkward. He obviously was not into me. Maybe he was still with Samantha. I bet she wasn't around because of the whole Irene and Matt thing.

He came out of his room and tossed his hat and sweatshirt to me since my hair was hopeless. They were huge on me and made me look like a small child. He smiled at me and tapped the bill of the hat down over my eyes. He turned around and headed towards the door. I could have sworn that I heard him mutter, "Cute."

As we headed out to the diner, Matt was happy, rambling on about his confrontation with Irene. He was so proud of himself for standing up to her. I wish I could have felt the same way.

Next week was Thanksgiving week. With being new hires, neither Matt nor Ryan was able to secure the time off to go back to Ohio. Their mothers were traveling out here together to cook for their boys. I was headed home on Wednesday morning to celebrate my favorite holiday. I had already emailed my dad the shopping list and was prepared to start cooking as soon as I walked through his door.

Both guys walked me home. I hugged Ryan then Matt and wished them a Happy Thanksgiving, promising to call later on in the week. I didn't specify who I was going to call.

I didn't know myself.

CHAPTER EIGHT

It was always good going home to see my dad. We were close, and I missed him. I worried about him being alone. We had a lot of family around, including my mother's parents and her younger brother, my Uncle Dan, and his wife and kids. There were aunts and uncles and cousins too. We would be having twelve for Thanksgiving, and I threw myself into cooking. I loved all of the prep work and the comfort foods. Wednesday night, when I was home and elbow deep in pie dough, my dad sat down at the counter and looked uncomfortable.

Through many stops and starts, he finally said, "Marcy and I are doing it. We're getting married."

I don't know what reaction he was expecting, but I bet it wasn't to be showered in flour as I threw my arms around him in a joyous hug. I wanted my dad to be happy, and Marcy made him happy.

He'd been single since Mom died. Though my dad's joy at settling down again caused a pang deep within my heart. It's what I wanted for myself as well. I wasn't even looking for a ring and kids. I just wanted someone to want me. Could that be Ryan, or was I making another bad decision? When Marcy came over later, I was thrilled to congratulate the happy couple. I really was.

I called Matt and Ryan late Thanksgiving night and got the machine. I gave them a generic holiday greeting and hung up. I had an early Black Friday shopping date with Marcy. She was perfect for both me and my dad. The rest of the weekend of family and fun flew by, and before I knew it, I was on I-90 heading back into Massachusetts.

The completion of Thanksgiving meant that the holiday season was here. I was determined not to go through it lonely and miserable. I needed to be happy with myself, whether or not Ryan was in the picture. But I did need to talk to him.

Life conspired against us, work eating away at our limited free time. Finally, on Friday night, I was hanging out with Matt—too tired to go out anywhere—when Ryan finally trudged through the door at nine p.m. He was virtually dragging his briefcase. He walked in and took off his long winter coat. I caught my breath at the sight of him in his suit. My heart soared. Even with his tired eyes and his feet shuffling, he looked mouth-watering. His tie was loosened, and he took it off as soon as he could.

The caretaker in me jumped up, suddenly full of energy. "You look exhausted. Have you eaten yet?"

He shook his head and shrugged out of his suit coat. He carefully folded it and draped it over a chair. "No, and I'm too tired to even think about trying to make something. If there was cardboard on the table, I'd probably eat that."

"Sit down, lemme get you something." I hopped up and went to the kitchen to heat up a plate of the lemon chicken and pasta with broccoli that I'd made earlier. It'd been a nice treat to catch up with Matt, even if he talked about Irene the whole time, and I totally chickened out from asking him about Ryan.

Matt followed me into the kitchen. "I'm gonna go see if I can find Irene. I think it's time to let her off the hook. Thanks for dinner and the talk. Behave yourself." He kissed me on the cheek and left. What could he mean by that? Did he know something that I didn't? Damn, I should have asked him about Ryan before he got home! Now I was flying blind.

I poured Ryan a glass of Pinot Grigio and brought it out to him, along with the plate of food. "Thanks," he said, diving right in.

I refilled my wine glass as well and sat down next to him. I was on my third—or fourth—glass. I rambled on while he was eating. Slowly, a little light came back into his eyes, and he didn't look so worn out. He finished eating and put his plate on the coffee table. He drained his wine glass and filled it up again. "That hit the spot. You're a great cook."

I smiled at him, "Thanks. You need anything else?" Please say me.

He gave me a sly look. "Do you need legal help yet?"

I laughed, "Not that I know of, why?"

"That's too bad because I could really use a massage." He looked like a little boy and was batting his gorgeous dark eyes at me.

"Well, it is the Christmas season. I guess I could get in the spirit of the season and be generous. What hurts?"

"Everything. No, it's not that I hurt, I'm just tired. I think I logged in close to sixty hours this week. Tonight is an early night."

"Back or feet?"

"Umm, back." He drained his glass for the second time. "Would it be best if we used my bed?"

Um, OKAY! Thank you, Jesus!

"Yeah, that would probably be good." I tried to pull myself together.

Holy crap, he wants me to give him a massage in bed! Calm down.

I tried to breathe deeply and not skip with joy and anticipation. I went into Matt's room to find his massage lotion. Oh boy. I reminded myself that Ryan just saw me as a friend and would probably ask Matt for the same treatment. Well, probably not, but he still didn't see me that way.

But maybe, just maybe, he did?

I went to the bathroom and then washed my hands, letting them run under the hot water to warm them up. Matt used to yell at me in lab when my hands were too cold. I took a few deep breaths and tried to make myself seem clinical. I told myself this was not about sex.

Oh please let it be about sex.

I grabbed the bottle of wine from the coffee table and brought it, as well as our glasses into Ryan's bedroom. He had put on a Dave Matthews CD and only the bedside lamp was on. Ryan had changed into gym shorts, and he still had his white t-shirt on. He had taken the time to hang up his suit. He looked at me almost sheepishly. "I suppose you need me to take this off?"

"It would be easier that way," I said, trying to keep my voice professional. Clinical. Not sexy. "Are you able to lie on your stomach?" I asked, gesturing to the bed. I put the wine down on Ryan's desk, careful not to put it near the stacks of books and papers that seemed to be towering on every flat surface. I took a large swig and put my glass on the nightstand.

This was either a very good or a very bad idea. Ryan took off his shirt and laid down. Holy crap. His body was near perfect, with firm muscles and definition everywhere, just as I had suspected. Even in the middle of winter, in Boston, he still had a good color to his skin. Or maybe, it just looked that way since I was so pale and pasty. And I was about to explore every inch of his torso.

This was a very good idea.

I climbed onto the bed, kneeling next to Ryan's gorgeous and half-naked body. Deep breath, Maggie, you can do this. Wait for him to make a move.

I applied a little of the massage cream to my hands and got to work. As I worked my hands up and down Ryan's back, kneading and rubbing, I tried to keep my mind occupied so that I did not do anything inappropriate. I tried to concentrate on the music but decided it was too sexy. I tried not to read anything into the music selection. It was probably what was in the CD player, not a soundtrack to seduction. But seriously, "Crash Into Me?" What am I supposed to read into that? I gazed around the room, trying to absorb the details as I let my hands work themselves over Ryan's back. I was about to start chanting "baseball, baseball" to myself to keep my brain occupied and in a clean place. I looked at his collection of books. They were mostly textbooks and law books. I suppose that did not leave much time for other reading. He had some pictures out of him with his parents and other family members, including what had to be his two older sisters. The pictures of him with the small children were probably his niece and nephew that he talked about the first time we went out. His room was cluttered but in a neat way. I could see into his closet where suits, shirts, and ties were hung up precisely.

I was so busy trying not to think about Ryan, that it took me a few minutes to realize how relaxed and still he had become. He was asleep.

Seriously? I stopped the massage, although I did let my hands stay on his flanks for an extra moment or two. Okay, three.

He was lying across the middle of the bed. I climbed over him and sat up by the nightstand and took a sip of wine. I contemplated my next move.

I should leave. Ryan was peacefully sleeping, and Matt most likely was not coming home. There was no need for me to stay. Except that I wanted to. I finished my wine, and laid down next to Ryan, as close to him as I dared. My face was turned to his. I wanted to shake him awake and yell at him. *Notice me! Like me! Want me!*

What the hell was I doing? I think I officially had just crossed over into psycho-stalker mode. No, I had to pull it together and go home. To my empty apartment. Deborah was skiing, so I would be alone all weekend. The thought of leaving Ryan, however comatose, to go home alone made me want to cry.

I let out a little sigh and started to get up. Ryan stirred a little and reached his arm around my middle and down to my hip. Oh no. What was I going to do now? Ryan rolled onto his side, his arm contracting around me and pulling me into him. I could have sworn that I heard him mumble, "Don't go."

That was all I needed. I laid there for a while, my body pressed into his. This was what I was hoping for, wasn't it? Well, ideally, he would have been conscious when he spooned me, but beggars can't be choosers. I laid there, listening to Dave Matthews, being held by the most gorgeous man I had ever laid eyes on. Sleep claimed me quickly as well.

I woke up in the morning, still curled up on my side. However, my pants were off. Again. I knew I did this myself, as I could never sleep with something on my legs unless I was super cold. And since I had a human blanket, the cold was something that was very far from my mind. Ryan had his arm wrapped around me and nestled in close to my body. He was pressed tightly to mine, with my rear end cradled by his pelvis. He had a leg in between mine and my top leg was extended back over his. I couldn't be sure, but I thought his face was buried into the back of my neck.

It was the most intimate position I had been in in a very long time. He began stirring, and reached his arm down and placed it on my hip. I shifted my body away slightly, although we were still touching at our pelvises. He was gently caressing my upper thigh, his fingers lightly moving over my long faded scars. "Not that I'm complaining or in any way judging, but why don't you have pants on?"

My answer would not make sense to anyone but me. "I can't sleep with stuff on my legs unless I'm really cold. I don't like the feeling of it. If I fall asleep fully dressed, I will take the stuff off without waking up. I'm not even aware I'm doing it."

"Oh," was all he said.

"I think it's from when I was in the hospital and stuff. I had casts and braces and traction and all this stuff on my legs and didn't wear pants for a few months. I can't relax and be comfortable now because of it, especially with jeans. And since that's what I was wearing ..." My voice was low, barely above a whisper. It always seemed to make people uncomfortable when I talked about the accident, which was why I seldom did.

He said, still letting his fingers trail up and down my hip and thigh, "And this? It's part of that?"

"One of the surgeries. I really don't have too many scars, not on the outside at least."

I pulled away and rolled over to look at him, placing a few inches in between us.

He looked into my eyes. "I guess I fell asleep. Sorry, I was just exhausted."

"I tried to get up, but you said, 'don't go' so I stayed. I hope that was okay." I tried to rationalize myself. Please don't think that I am psychotic ...

He smiled at me. "Perfectly fine. I'm glad you stayed. I like having you here. That was one hell of a massage. I thought I melted. I have not been so relaxed since I started this job. No wonder you hold out on people. I'm going to have to put you on retainer so that you'll be at my beck and call."

I couldn't help but smile. I would love to be at his beck and call.

He continued, "And speaking of retainers, I have to go into work today to check some emails."

"That sucks, especially with how much you've already worked this week."

"I guess since the criminals of the city don't take a break, I don't get to either. But where I was going was that I have to go into work for a few minutes. If you don't mind, would you want to come with me? I can show you where I work, and then maybe you could help me out with something?" He looked at me hopefully.

I narrowed my eyes, "I'm suspicious by nature. What could you possibly need my help with?"

"Christmas gifts for my niece and nephew. I know you work with kids, so I thought you might have some ideas. I need to preserve my role as the Funcle."

"Funcle?"

"Yeah," he smiled. "I'm the fun-uncle."

"Makes sense. When were you thinking about going?" I wanted to go home and shower.

"I was thinking about a shower first."

My mind started racing with numerous innuendos and flirty lines I could say. Instead, I stammered, "Sure. I, um, I need to go home for a while anyway. How about we meet at the T stop by my house in an hour or so?"

"Okay, I'll call you when I'm leaving here."

I rolled over and sat up on the edge of the bed, pulling the sheet around my waist. I reached for my jeans and pulled them on. I fished around until I found my socks and donned them as well. Ryan was not saying anything. He was still lying on his side, propped up on his elbow. I glanced back over my shoulder, and he was smiling at me. He looked irresistible in nothing but shorts, and he was in danger of being tackled.

By me.

I virtually raced out of his room and tried to casually say over my shoulder, "See you in a little while." And I was out the door.

And I'm sure I sounded anything *but* casual.

*****

It was always easy between us, making for a pleasant afternoon. It felt like we could talk forever and still not know everything there was to know about each other. I told him about my father's upcoming marriage. He talked about his family, mostly his niece and nephew. Family was a recurring theme and the strain of being away from them was apparent.

Ryan took me to his office, where he introduced me to his co-worker, also in checking emails on a Saturday. She was a well-put-together brunette named Liza, and I couldn't help but admire her. She was the embodiment of casual elegance, with confidence and power exuding through her invisible pores. Even in her Saturday, dress-down garb of dark jeans with high-heeled boots and a navy cashmere sweater, you could tell she was no one to mess with. Maybe it was the pearls.

Or maybe it was the way she smiled warmly at Ryan and a little less warmly at me. Okay, message received. She was interested in Ryan too.

What warm-blooded female with a pulse wouldn't be?

Ryan opened his email and wearily sat down. "Crap, this is bad. Maggie, this may take a lot longer than I anticipated."

I got the hint. "No problem, I'll just head over to Downtown Crossing to do a little Christmas shopping. Thanks for the company and showing me around." I turned to head out. I felt like I was always running out on Ryan. I wondered if he noticed that too?

"Maggie, wait!" he said, getting up from his desk and crossing the room to me. Maybe he did notice …

He hugged me.

Just a hug. Dammit. When was he going to kiss me again?

With his arms still wrapped around my waist, he said, "Sorry, this is not how I hoped today would go. I'll make it up to you, promise."

I didn't know whether to smile or cry. I went for the smile and nodded. "Talk to you soon."

I turned to walk out the door. I saw Liza watching out of the corner of her eye. Ryan called out, "I still owe you for last night. Don't forget."

I turned around and said, in the most seductive way I could manage, "Oh, I won't." And I left.

As I shopped, I tried to quash my disappointment. His comments were certainly something to be hopeful about. On the other hand, I had spent the night in his bed twice, ended up pantless both times, and only managed to get a little cuddling.

I was so confused. At least with the normal losers that I ended up with, you knew their intentions right from the beginning. Sex and nothing more. With guys like that, there was never any mystery, but there was never any of the intrigue that I was finding with Ryan either.

I didn't want to get my hopes up too much that more would occur between us, though I desperately wanted more. If I got my hopes up any further, I would be completely crushed if, and when, things didn't work out between us. This was different than anything I'd ever felt.

I was indescribably drawn to Ryan.

These were the thoughts running around in my head as I tried to focus on Christmas shopping. It was hard to be blue this time of year. I loved the lights and the decorations, and it probably didn't hurt that my birthday was right before. When I was a kid—before the accident—I used to think that the whole season was a celebration for me.

I found gifts for my Uncle Dan. His son, my cousin, was fourteen and also a Red Sox fan, so his was the easiest gift I found. I bought a necklace for my cousin, Lindsay, who was ten. It was a "grown-up" piece, but I knew she would love it. I found myself looking at gifts for kids, even though Ryan was not with me. His nephew was three and his niece was two. Looking, I thought a set of large trucks would be perfect for his nephew and found the most adorable tea set for his niece. I would give him the suggestions later. If I talked to him again.

With him, you never knew.

CHAPTER NINE

Disappointment swelled throughout the week with each passing moment that the phone *didn't* ring. Why wouldn't he call me even to say hi?

I simply didn't get it.

I forced myself not to call. Mostly by sitting on my hands every night. I had never shown such restraint, but it didn't seem to be getting me anywhere. I practically tackled the phone when it rang on Thursday, but it was only Matt with an invitation to hang out at their place on Saturday. He told me to bring Deborah too or whomever I wanted. I agreed like I always did. It wasn't like I had many other offers, plus I hadn't talked to Matt a whole lot since his reunion with Irene. I missed him, but he seemed happy when I was able to briefly talk to him, which was what was important.

By the time Saturday afternoon rolled around, it was snowing, and I wondered what type of turn-out there would be tonight. While I wanted to dress to impress, the need to stay warm prevailed, resulting in my typical jeans and my favorite black turtleneck sweater. Deborah and I bundled up like Sherpa about to ascend Everest, stopping at the packie on our way over.

Irene answered the door when we knocked. She looked almost friendly and even smiled at us. "Hey, guys! Welcome, welcome, welcome!" Interesting how at home she seemed, playing the hostess here.

We deposited our goods on the table and removed our coats. Matt swooped in and grabbed them from us. Our boots went by the door, in a long line of other winter footwear covered in snow. I recognized Liza, but the couple was unfamiliar. Ryan shouted from the kitchen, "Bob and Suzanne, from the office. Introduce yourselves."

A few minutes later, Matt's friends, Aaron and Christian showed up. The snow was really coming down by now. A few people called to say they didn't want to venture out. It looked like the evening was going to be more an intimate and cozy party than anyone originally thought.

Eventually, we all ended up lounging around on the couches and chairs in a large circle. The lights were turned out, except for Christmas lights on the tree and around the window. The decor had Irene written all over it.

All of this had Irene written all over it.

The night outside looked purple from the snow, and it was wonderfully romantic. It occurred to me that there were equal matches of men and women, that everyone could pair off. I fleetingly wondered, if forced to, who Ryan would pick— Liza or me? It was nice and cozy, not shouting over the din of a bar.

Christian worked in HR for a large, well-known public relations corporation. He was telling stories about weird talents that people listed on their resumes, such as pole dancing. He laughed and asked Liza what "unique" talent she could list on her resume, quite flirtatiously. Suzanne, quite brazenly, interrupted and suggested that we play a game.

"Let me explain the rules. First, everyone writes down a question. We'll mix them together and draw them randomly. Everyone has to answer. If you don't want to answer, you do a shot."

Christian piped up, "I've got my question."

I was going to be in trouble. I couldn't do shots without throwing up. Looks like I would be spilling my guts tonight.

We all filled up our drinks and then settled in. Irene was sitting on Matt's lap in the oversized armchair. Deborah and I sat on the love seat, and Aaron and Christian were on the floor in front of us. Liza, Suzanne, and Bob were opposite us on the couch. Ryan was on the floor, in front of Liza, and was directly across from me.

Irene, showing off, took the first question. She read out loud, "What is your theme song?" She laughed. "Oh, that's easy. 'Dancing Queen,' Abba."

Matt went next, "'Born to Run,' Springsteen." Fitting. He'd run the Boston Marathon five consecutive years.

Everyone laughed at Christian's "I'm Too Sexy." Not what we'd expect from the uptight HR type.

Bob, very buttoned up and conservative made everyone laugh by naming "The Thong Song." Suzanne laughed, saying, "Well, I guess you could say it's my song too!"

I was trying to think about what to say. Do I go for the funny or sexy answer or the truth? I heard Deborah say, "Better Man." I smiled at her. She'd been honest, and I decided to do the same.

It was my turn. "'Tracks of my Tears' by Smokey Robinson." It had certainly described my recovery from Jared, forced to publicly smile while I watched him and Ellen flaunt their relationship. It summed up my whole life, always forcing a smile, no matter how sad I felt. I felt all the eyes in the place swivel to me. Aaron broke the silence. "Man, that's the most pitiful thing I've ever heard. I reject that answer, you are way too happy. Come up with another."

I had to laugh. That smile wasn't forced.

"Umm, 'Changes in Latitudes, Changes in Attitudes?'" I replied.

"Better," Aaron retorted, "but still melancholy."

Questions about favorite quotes and favorite movies had us all laughing and smiling, and we ended up saying our favorite lines for over an hour. And for the record, I will say my favorite movie is *Gone with the Wind*, but in reality, it's *Tommy Boy*.

The next question was "Where do you see yourself in ten to twenty years?"

Suzanne immediately answered, showing no fear. "Partner and with a summer house on Nantucket." Bob grinned back at her, stupid in love. "Partner, a summer house on the *Vineyard*," he looked pointedly at Suzanne, "and a semi-pro golf career."

Irene chimed in next, "Married to Matt, of course."

Matt stammered, and said, "Hopefully running my own sports med clinic. Or better yet, PT for the Sox."

Interesting, Matt didn't mention Irene. She caught that too and was *not* happy about it.

Finally, it was my turn. I was about to start when Irene interrupted me with a snarky comment. "Let me guess. Married with children, the house in the suburbs with a white picket fence, a minivan, and the whole nine yards."

I glared back at her and said calmly, "Actually, Irene, you would be wrong. I want to travel the world. I want to see the sights, tour Europe, go on an African safari. I always see myself living in the city. I don't necessarily want to be married, but I would like to have someone to share my life with. I hope to still be working with kids but don't plan on having any. So Irene, no, I don't see the whole white picket fence scenario. That's you, not me."

You could cut the tension in the room with a knife. Ryan, God bless his soul, broke the tension by taking his turn. He said, "I hope to still be in public office, possibly the DA or Solicitor General, if I'm back in Ohio. Working my way towards a judgeship. I like Maggie's thought about sharing my life with someone, but no kids." He stared right at me while he said this. Then he smiled, the softest and warmest of smiles.

My stomach turned into molten goo.

Deborah, Aaron, Christian, and Liza all took their turns, but I couldn't focus on what they were saying. I couldn't help but look across at Ryan. It seemed like our lives were compatible. Was this a sign that things might work out between us?

Dammit, I should have paid attention to Liza's answer. I bet she was a better match. And more importantly, I should have paid attention to Ryan's reaction to Liza's answer, to see if it made him light up, the way his answer did to me.

Deborah reached for a folded piece of paper and read her question. It was the one about unusual talents. She laughed, "I can do a thousand sit-ups in one session."

I didn't doubt it. The girl was jacked.

Irene's was being able to read and write upside down. No, duh, she's a teacher. Skills that any good teacher should possess, not a special talent. The guys tried to one-up each other with masculine traits.

Liza, brazenly out of the blue declared, "I'm double-jointed" with a knowing smirk. All the guys turned to look at her. I swear I saw at least one of them drooling.

I tried to come up with a good answer. But I couldn't think of anything special. I was sure that Ryan must be as impressed with Liza as I thought he should be. Why should he think I was anything special when Liza was so perfectly put together and so perfect for him? When it was my turn, all I could answer was, "I don't have any special talents. I'm a jack of all trades, master of none."

There was grumbling about whether I should have to do a shot. Deborah piped up, "Oh! I know your talent! We can tell always tell what type of alcohol you are drinking by how you act."

Christian demanded, "Explain before we render a verdict."

I said, "Well, I don't consider it a talent, but when I drink vodka, my face turns bright red. When I drink beer, I like to dance and get a little frisky. When I drink red wine, I cry a lot. When I drink rum, I want to fight. I broke my hand one night punching a wall over a guy. I also decked my ex-boyfriend's brother in the face one night because I didn't like how he referred to me. Again, not a talent, merely a reaction."

Ryan said, "For God's sake, take that Rum and Coke away and get the girl a beer, dammit!" Everyone laughed as Matt almost dumped Irene out of his lap when he jumped up and said, "I know—you're psychic!"

I laughed. I'd forgotten about that.

Christian said, "Really, psychic? What am I going to say next?"

I laughed again. "Okay. Not really psychic, but I have had a few episodes of, um, I don't know, like precognition. Usually centered around a guy. I don't think it's a true talent, but that I maybe pick up on clues subliminally and process them. Like I knew that my high school boyfriend was back with his ex-girlfriend and was going to break up with me. And there was the night sophomore year that I dreamed that Brian and I broke up, and then the next day we did. And of course, there was the Jared fiasco." I paused to take a drink.

Liza leaned forward. "Do tell," she goaded.

I rolled my eyes and continued, "Matt called one day and asked if Jared was coming with me on a trip to Maine that the group was taking that weekend. I told him no, I didn't think we would be together by then, that we would be breaking up. He told me I was crazy, that he had just seen us together, and we looked fine, but I just had a feeling. I called Jared and asked him to come over. He thought it was a good idea, that he wanted to talk to me."

"Uh-oh" I heard Suzanne say. I nodded and continued, "And when he got to my place, he said that we were too serious, and I wasn't what he was looking for. He apparently was looking for something else, because he was banging a fellow classmate."

Christian grimaced, "Has it ever happened not around being dumped?"

I laughed. "I know, I pick some real winners, right? Sometimes, a song or a person that I haven't heard or seen in a long time will randomly pop into my head. Then I will hear the song or run into the person. But, it did happen one time, when I was little, but it's depressing." I stopped.

Deborah took my hand and squeezed it. She gave me a go-ahead nod. I took a breath and continued.

"I was seven and my mom was taking me and my brother to visit her parents, across town. It was summertime, the Fourth of July, and we were going for a cook-out. Jake was laughing at me because I wasn't big enough to ride in the front seat. I stuck my tongue out and told him that I wouldn't be caught dead in the front seat. Then something popped into my head. I asked my mom if it hurt to die. She was startled and tried to shush me, to not talk about death. Like mentioning it would somehow bring it about. I told her that I thought if death came quickly, then it wouldn't hurt and that it would be more painful to be the one left behind. Exactly twelve minutes later, a drunk teenager in a large truck ran a red light and took out the front of the car. My mom and brother were killed instantly and the lower half of my body was shattered. The only reason that I survived was because Jake was in the front seat. Where I wouldn't be caught dead." I broke off, got up, and ran into the nearest room, which happened to be Ryan's, unable to hold the tears back any longer.

I stood by the door and looked out the window at the snow, unseeing for a little while, letting the tears flow. It had been a while since the pain had touched me like that, and I was unprepared for it. I normally kept those doors locked tightly. I heard the door open, and I tried to wipe my eyes on my sleeve.

"Matt, I'm fine. Sorry to ruin the mood." I felt arms around me and I turned around.

"Oh, Ryan. Sorry. Matt's the one who usually cleans up my drunken messes." I tried to smile at him. He shushed me by putting a finger to my lips, and then leaned in and kissed me. Gently.

"I'm sorry. I had no idea."

"It's okay. I've had years and years of therapy to conclude that I did not cause the accident. That some drunk asshole kid did. And he has paid for it. But I was right; it is more painful to be the one left behind."

He kept his arms around me and stared into my eyes. I continued, "You see how I am just a mess. This is why I'm always alone." I laughed. "Run, run now, run fast."

Before he could respond, Deborah poked her head in. "We're all braving the snow and heading to the bar. You in?"

"No, I'm gonna take my drunk ass home and stop bringing everyone else down."

"Be careful. Oh, and don't wait up. I like Christian—he's pretty cute!" She winked at me and was gone.

I turned back to Ryan. "You'd better get going. Liza will be disappointed."

We heard voices get loud, then the doors closed, and then the apartment was quiet. "I don't think she'll miss me."

He leaned in, kissing me. I kissed him back, wrapping my arms around him and grabbing his hair. His hands were around my waist and were lifting me up. I wrapped my legs around his waist and let him carry me to his bed. Before I knew it or could stop to think, our clothes were off, and we were finally together.

Afterward, I was lying on my back next to Ryan. I ran my hand through my hair and covered my eyes. "Holy shit" I whispered, more to myself than to him.

He rolled on his side and propped his head up on his elbow. He leaned in and kissed me. "You okay?"

"Just trying to regain some composure," I said, blushing in the darkness. "What was that?"

"That was phenomenal."

Yes, yes it was.

"No, I mean what just happened?"

"Well, you see, when a man and a woman ..."

I cut him off by smacking him lightly on his chest. His beautiful, sculpted perfect chest. "Stop. You don't like me like that. I'm a mess. And just a friend."

He laughed. "No. That's not what I usually do with friends. Do you think that would have happened if that's what I thought? I have been trying to get you alone since the first time we went out."

"Huh?"

"How drunk are you right now? You seem a little out of it."

"I must be pretty drunk because I think I just had mind-blowing sex with a god. I'm probably passed out, and this is the best dream I have ever had."

"You're not dreaming, and there's more where that came from." Suddenly, his mouth was moving on my body and his hands were everywhere.

Thank you, Jesus.

In the early morning, I sat up woozily on the side of the bed. I wasn't too hungover, but I was incredulous about the previous evening's events. *Had that really happened?* I grabbed a t-shirt from the end of the bed and pulled it on. My eyes were burning from sleeping with my contacts in, and I desperately needed something to drink.

Ryan was still sleeping, his back to me. I wanted to run my fingers up and down his back and touch everywhere. This was not good. I just had a drunken hook-up with my best friend's roommate, so this meant the walk of shame from hell. Matt and I were finally back in a good place, and now I wouldn't be able to hang out here anymore. Plus, well, I tried not to think about what a blubbering mess I had been last night.

A total disaster.

"Good morning, Sunshine." Hands were around my waist.

I looked over my shoulder at Ryan. I can only imagine how awesome I looked and smelled. I groaned at the memory of my drunken sob story, and what an embarrassment I had made of myself.

"What's wrong? Are you sorry about last night?" He sat up and looked at me.

"Yes, I mean no, I mean I don't know" I rambled. "I mean, it was really, *really* good, but it's hard to feel good about a drive-by. I kind of thought I was over that part of my life."

Why the hell was I being so honest? Someone, please duct tape my mouth.

"A drive-by?"

"That's what my girlfriends and I refer to as a one-night stand. Somehow sounds less pitiful."

"Who said this was a one-night stand? Unless that's all you want it to be ..." he trailed off.

I shook my head, burying my face in my hands.

"No, it's not all I want."

"Well, good, that's settled, because I want to be with you. And not just for one night. For a very long time. What do you think about that?"

"I don't understand."

"What's not to understand?"

"What are you saying? Like, a relationship? Is that what you are talking about?"

"I hadn't thought about what it would be called, but I guess. I just want to talk to you and see you, and do a little more of what we did last night."

"Just a little more?"

"Okay, a whole lot more. But I also just want to be with you. Well, that and eat your cooking. I don't know exactly what you call that."

"Good. 'Cause you know I can't do 'relationships.' I'm incredibly bad at them. I swore off them. But I like you. A lot. Too much."

"Well, it's settled then. Are you okay about this?"

"I *think* so. I think as shocking as this sounds, especially given my mood last night, I might be happy."

"Happy?"

I smiled up at him. "Yes, happy. Last night was wonderful. It just came out of left field. I've been so confused about you and me. I mean, sometimes, I thought you were flirting with me, and then other times, I knew you looked at me like a friend. I was so pissed at you for kissing me and then never calling. I mean, we seemed to connect so well, but then, nothing. And then you were with Sam, and I knew I had no shot, and I was so sad. And then Liza was here, and she was flirting with you. You are always surrounded by beautiful women who are much better for you than I am."

I needed to stop rambling and shut up.

"Sunshine," he murmured, smoothing my hair back. "You've got it all wrong. I thought I totally scared you the first time we went out. You kept pulling away, and I could barely keep myself off of you. I thought you must have seen me as a creep. Even the next day, I tried to flirt, and you weren't buying it. I've never been good at the flirting thing, and I told you how bad I was at the relationship thing. I can't gauge how women take me. I always think I come on too strong, and I didn't want to blow it with you, so I dialed back. But anyway, I kept hoping you'd call or come over."

I cut him off. "You know, for a prosecutor, that's a pretty passive way to go about things ..."

He put a finger to my lips to silence me. "*Anyway*," he continued, "I was so happy to see you out that one night at the bar, and I thought I had a shot with you then. It was obvious you'd been drinking, but so was I and I thought maybe we'd get together then. Then all of a sudden you were mad and storming out. Matt said you'd had a date that went badly. I guessed since you were out on dates with other guys, that you weren't interested in me, and I decided not to pursue you."

"You were there with Samantha, and I saw you kissing! You were the date I was talking about. Matt is such a clueless shithead!"

"She kissed me, and I guess you missed the part where I told her to leave me alone and walked away. She'd been bugging the crap out of me for weeks, and I couldn't shake her. I told you, I don't waste time with people who don't interest me. And I was interested in you. So, it was you or no one."

"Oh, I thought you and she ..."

"And I thought you hated me."

"Well, I did a little, for picking her over me."

"Silly girl, I didn't. I picked you. From the moment you fell down the stairs in front of me."

"Sorry about not responding to the flirting thing. I kept trying to flirt back, but I thought I sounded like a psycho moron, so I kept silencing myself."

"Well, don't do that again." He kissed me.

"So you don't just want to be friends? I'm not just one of the guys to you?"

"Trust me, I don't do this with my guy friends." He leaned in and kissed me again. It took me a minute to catch my breath.

"What about Liza?"

"What about her?"

"Well, she likes you."

"And I like you, so that's that."

Oh my.

"So really a drive-by?" he asked with a smile. "Is there any other terminology you use out here that I should know about?"

I laughed. "Someday, I'll explain to you the difference between a hook-up and a Jersey hook-up, according to me and my friends."

"See this is what I like about you. I told you, petite with a good sense of humor. But even last night, when you were very serious, I still really liked you."

I kissed him again. "You know I never talk about the accident. It makes people uncomfortable, and I don't want to get into details anyway. I'm not as together about it as I like to pretend I am. When I look deeply, which isn't often, I still have a lot of holes, and I don't know if I will ever fill them. Kind of like a broken vase that you Crazy Glue back together. All the little tiny shards are missing, and when you look close, you can still see all the cracks." I paused, "Okay, now you need to tell me something deep and dark about you, so I don't feel like as much of a freak." I smiled weakly.

"My dad has pancreatic cancer, and it's really hard right now, being here away from him and the rest of the family. I put a lot of pressure on myself to live up to his standards and expectations. He never got to go to college; he went to Vietnam. So he wanted me to have a big career for as long as I can remember. I don't know that it was what I was meant to do, but I have been focused on it since I was in first grade. I want to make him proud through my own type of service since I didn't serve in the military. I can't imagine letting him down or disappointing him. I'm gonna devote myself to my career and public service. I don't know how to do things only halfway. And right now, I only really want to focus on my career and nothing else, so I don't let him down. And I can't see that changing."

"Oh, I'm so sorry. How is he doing?"

"About as well as to be expected. That's why I can't wait to go home and see him at Christmas. Most likely it will be his last one. This move has been hard on me. I shouldn't have left him now. I didn't want to come out here, but he wouldn't hear of me staying for him. He said that a job opportunity like this was rare, and I needed to take it. If I stayed, it would have let him down, and I couldn't do that to him, not now. Again, I feel like I'm always letting people down, and that I can't make everyone happy. Like I can't live up to everyone else's ideals for me. And in the end, I try so hard to please everyone else that I make myself unhappy. I end up paralyzed because I don't want to do anything to disappoint. I'm afraid that no matter what I do, someone will be let down. So I do nothing. And that's why I'm here but wish that I was with my dad. Your turn again."

"Ryan, I am so so sorry." I hugged him tightly. "I had all of the best therapy, both physical and psychological, that money could buy. The kid who hit us was the son of the richest guy in town. Owned car dealerships. Anyway, I was fourteen when I told my shrink that, although I chose not to let the accident define me and my life, it was not my choice to make and will forever be the most defining event of my life. And that it would be the story of my life. The choices that I made were irrelevant, and the choices that others made would be the ones that defined me. And then I decided I was done with therapy. I mean, in an instant, I lost my mother and brother. I had survivor's guilt, which never really goes away." I stopped for a moment and swallowed.

This was the hardest thing to say.

"I lost my best friend and the person who shared all my most personal memories. I will forever be living for my brother, having the life that he was denied. I carry the weight of my mother's expectations. I make decisions based upon what she would have wanted for me, or what my brother would have been doing. But part of me will always be the little girl who had to grow up without a mother. The one who was left behind."

I haven't said that out loud to anyone since I was in therapy. I continue, "I get what you're saying about expectations. I played soccer for years, just so my dad would be able to coach a ball team, even though I hated it. I never disobeyed him. I studied hard and went to school. I didn't stay home and marry a local boy because my mother wanted more for me than that. I am put together because she would have wanted me to move on. I don't dwell on the accident or talk about it, because I'm not supposed to make others uncomfortable, especially my dad. I am happy that my dad is remarrying because he won't be alone, and I know my mom would have wanted him to be happy. But really, I'm not at all together."

I have abandonment issues that will never go away.

"It's probably why I pick people who are destined to leave me. It's messed up, huh? I'm afraid of being left, so I seek out people who are incapable of staying. Because of that, I now have trust issues too, because the guys who can't commit are usually out screwing someone else. I cannot let myself open up to someone, to trust that they will not leave me. If it were someone that I really cared about, and they left me, I don't think I could survive it."

My voice breaks and the tears I've been holding back finally escape. "It would crush me down in such a way that I don't think I could ever recover." I swallow hard. "I don't think I could bring myself to have a child because I could not bear to leave my child, as my mother left me. I feel like I can't be a mother since I didn't have one. I don't think I will ever be whole again, and I cannot willingly inflict that on another."

I stopped to look at him, to see if I had totally scared him. I had never been this candid with anyone, outside of my shrink. It was that type of opening up that could lead to me being hurt again. Not even Matt or Deborah knew the depth of my damage.

Yet I continued, "I think I like to work with kids because I try to put them and families back together. I minored in psychology so that I could add a counseling component to my therapy. And I feel like if I get my fill of kids through work, I won't need them for myself. I've come to the conclusion that it's better to be alone by choice than to be left again."

"Wow."

I expected more. He must be truly horrified.

"Did I scare you?" I expected him to jump up and leave, even though it was his apartment.

"No, not at all. I am touched that you told me that. That had to be hard to say."

"I don't believe that I did not just freak you out."

"No, what you said makes sense to me."

"Then it would seem that we are both a mess and require lots and lots of therapy."

He leaned in and kissed me again. "Maybe, but at least I guess we're on the same page about not having a family. And don't worry, I'm not planning on going anywhere."

Somewhere, in the back of my head, those precognition bells started going off. Yes, he was going somewhere.

And soon.

CHAPTER TEN

I t was a perfect day.

After our morning heart to heart, Ryan took a quick shower, and then we went back to my place so I could get cleaned up. I took my contacts out and put my glasses on, another sure sign that my defense walls were coming down. I had never felt so close and connected to someone in my life.

We got take out, then crawled into my bed to watch movies. He sat up against the headboard, while I laid between his legs up against his sculpted chest. Through laughter and cuddling, he told me about how he had almost an obsessive drive for perfection in school and now in his career.

For the first time, I opened up more about my recovery experiences and the losses I still felt. When the evening time finally rolled around and 60 Minutes was over, Ryan sighed. "I have another atrocious week at work coming up. A lot of long days. I don't think I'm going to be able to see you until the weekend."

What the hell? What about the being together crap? Was it just a line, and since we didn't have sex again, he was bailing?

He continued, "This is not a brush-off or dumping in any way, shape, or form. You've seen me at the end of my day. I'm useless. I'm hoping that if I can cram all my work into the week, then my weekend will be totally free to devote to you. I want to take you out on Saturday, and I don't plan on leaving until Monday morning. Is that okay?"

"Sure," I said, as breezily as I could. Jesus, I was a paranoid mess. My birthday was Saturday, almost a week before Christmas. He didn't know that it, and I didn't want to put any pressure on him. He was upfront about his job and its demands, and I had to appreciate the honesty.

My previous partners wouldn't know honesty if it jumped up and bit them.

He'd been candid about the priority of his work, not to mention his near-obsessive drive. It's not like he was going to change all that because of me. I didn't want him to. At least this is what I told myself to try and keep rational and sane.

Not an easy task.

I kept busy during the week. Ryan called a few times, late at night and exhausted. The conversations were nice, but brief, mostly recounting our daily activities. I appreciated that he made the effort, even though he was so busy.

No matter how I dissected every conversation and nuance, the only logical conclusion was that he must actually like me. I certainly felt the same.

But it was more than that.

Even though we were in the beginning stages, I felt like our relationship had been building for months, whether or not we called it a relationship. I had a deeper level of openness and trust than I'd ever had with any of my previous relationships.

I was falling, if not already, in love with Ryan. An uneasy feeling settled upon me that I tried to shake but couldn't.

Saturday was approaching. I decided to live a little dangerously and to go shopping for a new outfit on Thursday after work. Although I did not like to think about it, as of Saturday, I would not ever have to justify spending money again. I could stop being a spendthrift. My life would dramatically change, just by turning twenty-five.

I squashed those thoughts, continuing to look for sale items. I ended up buying a little black mini-skirt and a fabulous low-cut emerald green silk blouse. But my real splurge was a fantastic pair of knee-high black boots. They were gorgeous and made my legs look great.

And they made me feel sexy and powerful. Every girl should have a pair.

I was on the T, returning home from my shopping expedition when I ran into Matt. I smiled and lifted my bags. "Had to treat myself to a new outfit for Saturday. Ryan and I are going out."

"He does know that it's your birthday, doesn't he?"

I shook my head. "And don't tell him either." I did not want to discuss my twenty-fifth birthday with anyone. But Matt wouldn't let it go. I wish I'd never told him.

"So I guess you haven't told him about your birthday present this year then, then?"

"It's not a birthday present. It's blood money. It's the cost of my brother and my mother's lives. Just because I can officially access the trust doesn't mean I will. It's going to stay in that account. The only difference is I'm the one who keeps it in the account, rather than my dad."

"I don't understand why you don't want the money. You would never have to work again."

"It's not that much. And again, it's hard to justify spending the money on trivial things when it's payment for the lives of my family. I don't see inheriting the trust as a meal ticket. I've told you over and over, my plan is and has always been, to keep the money in trust for a 'rainy day.' And since I don't plan on having any children rain down on me, I will probably eventually leave it to my little cousins and some charities. End of discussion."

I gave him a warning look.

I wish he'd forget about it. There was a reason why I didn't talk about it. Money does weird things to people.

"Okay, okay," he said, lifting his hands in peace. "I don't understand. Just like I can't understand about your 'rainy day' or not having kids or whatever. You'd be a great mother, and you could make sure they were well provided for. But I just want to make sure that you are taken care of."

"And that's exactly why I don't tell anyone about the trust. I don't want anyone seeing me as a meal ticket. So don't make me sorry that I told you!"

It was already too late for that.

"Okay, simmer down. It's forgotten. Now, since I can't tell Ryan that Saturday is your birthday and that you officially become a millionaire that day, can I at least drop some hints to him as you might like to go out to eat?"

I smiled at my best friend. "That, you can do."

The T was approaching my stop. Matt would make sure Ryan took me to my favorite places, so I was sure it would be a great evening. Of course, I could go to McDonald's with Ryan, and it would probably be fabulous.

For the first time in a very long time, I didn't dread turning twenty-five. The weight of inheriting the trust did not seem nearly as heavy anymore. Not to mention I had the potential to be spending the night, the first of many, with the man of my dreams. Things were good.

By the time Saturday rolled around, I could barely contain my excitement. Deborah and I went for massages and pedicures, her treat to me. It was relaxing, but I couldn't help but wish the time away so it would be that much closer to my date with Ryan. After when we were home lounging, the buzzer rang. I was looking quizzically at Deborah when I pressed the intercom. "Delivery for Magdalene Miller."

As I bounded down the stairs, a huge smile erupted. There was a large flower arrangement, containing mostly pink roses, which were my favorite. I took the flowers and beamed an elated 'thank you' to the delivery guy. I floated back up the stairs and triumphantly carried the flowers in.

Matt had to have told Ryan about how much I loved roses. After all, my middle name was Rose, just like my mother. I set the mammoth vase down and pulled the card out of the plastic holder. I'd never received flowers from a guy before. My hands seemed barely able to work well enough to open the envelope.

Happy Birthday to my best girl, my little Rose. See you next week, Love Dad.

My stomach dropped, and I felt like I was being crushed by a heavy boulder. Deborah watched the color drain from my face. "My dad," I croaked out and my eyes filled over with tears.

"I know it's stupid. I just thought ..." I broke off.

Deborah was hugging me. "It's okay sweetie. I would have thought the same thing too. But that was sweet of your dad."

I nodded and pulled myself together. "Yeah, it really was sweet. I bet Marcy helped him. God, why do I have to be so stupid, getting my hopes all up?"

Dejected, I went to the bathroom and took a long, hot shower. I took my sweet time enjoying every pampering thing I could do before getting ready. I was going all out for Ryan tonight, even adding sexy black lingerie underneath. I was just starting to put my boots on when I heard the buzzer. I heard Deborah call that she would get it, and I hurried to get ready. I wanted to stun Ryan coming out of my room.

I heard the voices come closer to the door and then into the apartment. I realized that there was something not right about them, but couldn't place what was wrong. I stepped through my door and attempted to give a sexy little pose, with my boots and mini-skirt, with my legs apart and my hips shifted to the side. I froze, midway there. It was Matt standing there, not Ryan. He was frozen, looking at me.

"Where's Ryan?" I asked, still hoping that this was not as bad as it looked, even though I knew it was going to be.

"Honey, he's not coming."

I think Matt kept talking, but I spun around on my heel and turned back into my room. But Matt was right there behind me. "Maggie, wait! It's not what you think!" He added gravely, "It's his dad."

I turned back to look at him. He continued, "His mom called a little while ago. He took a turn for the worse and is in the hospital. They're not sure how long," his voice broke off. It took me a minute to realize that Matt would be grieving this loss as well. He had known Mr. Milan his whole life. Matt swallowed and continued, "Ryan was on the phone calling the airlines. They got him on a flight, but he had to race to make it to Logan. He felt awful about you, but you know how torn he's been about leaving his father. Now he's wondering if he even made the right decision, coming here. I honestly think, if he hadn't met you, he wouldn't have stayed this long."

I knew what it was like to lose a parent, and Ryan was facing losing his, most likely soon. I had kept him from being with his father—where he wanted to be. I felt awful about what Ryan would be facing, for his loss. Awful that he had chosen me these last few months.

And most of all, even though I knew it was irrational, I felt cheated that I didn't get my one special night.

Matt and Deborah took me out to eat for my birthday. I couldn't be mad, yet I was still crushed. I tried to attend to the conversation, but couldn't. I painted a semi-smile on my face, passing through the night in a daze.

Ryan called me the next morning, apologizing profusely. He sounded terrible, and I would bet that he hadn't slept. I dismissed his concern, instead asking about his father. He was in the hospital awaiting hospice, and the prognosis was grim. It was a matter of when not if.

The only definite in Ryan's life was he was not coming back to Boston. He had already called his boss and taken an indefinite leave of absence. "I know that this might kill my career, but I can't leave home right now. I hope you understand."

My head did. My heart didn't.

On the other hand, my brain kept trying to plot out scenarios in which we could continue our relationship. If he wasn't working, surely we would be able to talk on the phone more. And I could fly out in a few weeks to see him. Mid-January, after the holidays.

Focus. I had to focus on what he was saying. I knew how career-driven he was, and what this sacrifice meant. He would have a hard time reconciling his decision to put his career on hold to be there for his family. It was agony for him in more ways than one. There was no way I could make this any harder on him. He was torn apart already and was about to go through one of the worst experiences of his life.

He paused and swore under his breath, "Maggie, you are the most remarkable woman I have ever met. I wish things could be, um, different. I hope you can understand why I have to do this. I wish we could have been together." His words sliced through me.

Knowing why you were being dumped, however rational and valid, didn't make it hurt any less.

CHAPTER ELEVEN
January 2001

I hate January. I always have. I always will.

Back in Boston, trudging through the snow and iced-lined streets, those words became my mantra. It was below zero, with a wind chill even lower. Everything seemed bare, stripped of the festive decorations. I had a post-holiday season hangover.

I was tired.

I was depressed.

January had never been a good month because both my mom and brother were born in January. So in addition to that, I was dealing with the post-holiday let-down period, as well as my father's marriage. That was the only good thing right now. This year, my grief was so close to the surface it felt palpable.

It wasn't my dad's marriage or the holiday hangover. It wasn't even because of my mom or Jake.

It was because Ryan was gone. He was in Ohio and was not coming back. His father still clung to life, and Ryan had managed to find a job there. He could make his father proud, while not being far away. His life had come together.

And he had made no mention of me being a part of his life.

Here I was alone again.

Even Matt was leaving. He and Irene had planned an eight-week trip to Australia, New Zealand, and other Southern Hemisphere destinations. They were leaving at the end of the month. Deborah and Christian were hot and heavy and spending all of their time together. Not only had I been dumped, but all my friends were too busy for me.

I moved through January like a zombie, going through the motions. I was tired and never felt like socializing.

Ryan stopped taking my calls.

I called about once a week, and he never once called back. A granite block dropped on me could not have produced a more crushing feeling.

The bleakness only got bleaker when my dad called to tell me he and Marcy were moving to Florida. Her family lived there, and they were ready to retire.

My dad wanted to split the proceeds of the house evenly with me. I didn't need the money and he knew it, but wouldn't hear my argument. The only relief was that we'd moved into this house after the accident. It didn't tie me to my mother and brother.

I'm not sure I could have survived that loss too.

On the last day of January, this cursed month, I stopped over at Matt's to say goodbye before his trip. I hadn't been over there since, well, since Ryan. I tried to push the thoughts and feelings deep down as I trudged over. The sight of the apartment was shocking.

Ryan's stuff was gone. His room was empty. The books and desk were gone. The pictures were gone. The bed where we ... gone. It made the hollow feeling in my chest overwhelm me and the room began spinning. I thought I was going to throw up.

Matt quickly ushered me to the sofa and sat me down. "Maggie, what's wrong?"

"I don't feel very well. I didn't eat today. Maybe I have low blood sugar. Do you have any soda?"

Matt disappeared before returning with a cup. I drank the soda and then sat back and closed my eyes. I pressed the cold cup to my forehead. "It's just so final," I finally whispered.

Matt looked at me with concern in his eyes. "Are you going to be okay? I've never seen you like this, this shaken up. Even after Jared. What's going on?"

I shook my head. "I know it's stupid. I mean, it's not like we were even really together. I just felt, I mean I thought, oh crap." My eyes filled with tears. I whispered, barely loud enough for him to hear, "I think he could have been the one. And now he's gone. And he won't even call me back."

Matt's arms were around me, enveloping me. "Maggie, I know this won't make it easier or better, but I think he feels the same way. I've never seen him like this about a girl. He is torn up about leaving you. He has been beating himself up for leaving you, especially how he did. But I don't think he realized that you felt as strongly about him as he did about you."

Now it was my turn for the blank stare.

Matt continued, "He said that he was afraid to let you down by leaving, but that he didn't think that you were as deep into your relationship, or whatever, as he was. I heard him telling his sister that he had a girlfriend, but that she lived in Boston, so it wasn't going to work out." His use of the past tense made me even sadder. He got up and got something out of his room. "I got these pictures developed from the Ohio

State-Michigan game. I didn't know if you would want to see them." He handed me a picture envelope.

I numbly took it and flipped through the pictures. My heart stopped when I saw the one of Ryan, Matt, and me. I acutely remember it being taken. I was sitting on the kitchen counter, and Ryan was standing next to me. He had slid in close to me with his arm behind me so that it looked like it was around me. My head was tipped in toward him. We both had a light in our eyes. Matt stood on my other side, slightly away from me.

I knew what picture would be next in the pile. After that picture, Ryan had then turned to Matt and said, "Take one of me and Mags." He had thrown his arms around me, and I had reciprocated. We were both smiling with our whole faces for the camera, with my head leaning into his chest.

We looked like a very happy couple.

I looked at Matt. "Can I have these?"

"Sure, take them. That was a good day, wasn't it?"

I nodded and stood up to leave. The tears were flowing. "I'm going to miss you while you're gone." I hugged Matt and held onto him for a minute.

He said, "I'll email you when I can. Be okay, okay?"

I left quickly. I had to get out of there. I needed to get home. Waves of nausea rolled through me, having the decency to wait until I got home to produce vomit.

I spent the rest of the day in bed. I would feel better for a little while and then crappy again. My dad called with the news that he and Marcy had found a small house on the east coast of Florida, located along a canal that connected to the intercoastal waterway. More importantly, there were already a few offers on our house, and it looked as if we might get a little more than the asking price for it.

It was good news, and it was impossible not to be happy for my dad. He told me that he was going to pack up all my things and move them down to the new house, so "you don't feel like there's not a place for you to call home." A touching gesture that I appreciated.

"When are you coming to visit?" he asked hopefully.

"I'm not sure, Dad. Things are busy here."

"Don't put it off for too long. Relax in the sun. Maybe look at a house or two. You could live here. Nothing is keeping you there anymore."

He hit the nail on the head.

I didn't even have to tell him, and he knew.

Over the next two weeks, things got worse as Valentine's Day assaulted me from every angle, despite my best attempts to ignore it. On a good year, I hated Valentine's Day. This year, it was interminable. Irrational depression plus the most romantic holiday of the year does not make a happy Maggie.

Eventually, I would get over this I told myself. Matt would come back and cheer me up. I would go out again, and I would meet people. Maybe someone special.

I doubted though, that I'd ever feel about someone else the way I felt about Ryan. As the dreaded day approached, I started thinking about the romance of Valentine's Day and what couples were planning for the night. My mind wandered, thinking about the last time I had planned anything. Valentine's Day was one of those big holidays geared towards couples that I naturally and instinctually hated since I was usually alone.

I was solo for New Year's this year, not to mention my birthday. I stopped and stared at the calendar.

No no no no no!

I ran to the corner pharmacy, getting in right before closing. I was trying not to freak out, and the practical part of my mind took over. Might as well grab the deodorant and lotion I was running low on before I made my way to the family planning aisle. I paid for my purchases, not able to look the cashier in the eye. I ran home and was breathless.

For once, I was relieved that Deborah was spending the night at Christian's again so I could have this moment to myself.

And three minutes later, I sat down on my bathroom floor and cried until I could no longer see those two little pink lines.

Eventually, I pulled myself together. I went to my computer and emailed Matt:

02/13/01: Hey! I need to talk to you. I wouldn't bother you if it wasn't important. Please write back, or call me if you can. Please.

I tried to collect myself. It was late, so I decided to go to bed. There was no way I'd be able to sleep. I got out of bed before realizing that I couldn't even have a glass—or bottle—of wine or even take a sleeping pill! I laid down and put the TV on. It was a terrible movie, but it was mindless and allowed me to fall asleep.

By mid-morning the next day, I'd already scheduled an appointment for later that afternoon. I met with the nurse-midwife who explained how things work. She must have sensed my hesitancy, or maybe it was because I was alone.

"Are you planning on keeping this pregnancy?"

I wanted to say no. I wanted to schedule and have an abortion right then and there. But I couldn't, for three reasons. One, because it was against my family's beliefs, and my mother would have disapproved; two, because this was a child I created with Ryan and it would forever tie me to him; and three, because I was already in love with my child.

02/21/01: Matt, please call me. I need to talk to you. It's IMPORTANT. I need your help. PLEASE CALL ASAP!!!

No one knew my secret. Not even Deborah. She'd mentioned moving in with Christian, but I knew she didn't want to leave me all mopey and depressed. They had fallen fast and furiously in love, and she was sure that he was it.

I tried hard to be happy for them. Her new relationship left me alone most of the time. When she was around, so was Christian, and their obvious infatuation cut through me. And made me a little nauseous, as if I needed any more of that. The writing was on the wall. We were going our separate ways.

I wanted to tell Deborah but continued to hold my secret. It was hard, though, keeping it from my dad. I had prepared him for so long that I didn't want kids, so I knew he'd be ecstatic, despite the non-ideal circumstances. I called and left one last message for Ryan, asking him to please call me back.

When Matt finally answered, it wasn't what I expected.

02/24/01: Auckland, NZ
Mags! The trip is awesome. We're having such a great time. Sad news, Ryan's father died yesterday. He emailed me. I won't make it back for the services. Just thought you'd want to know. See you in few weeks!

I needed to know how to pursue. Why was Matt sending me such a blasé email? Didn't he understand just how desperate I was? What did I do now? Should I tell Ryan? I knew what his feelings on the issue were. He hadn't called me since Christmas, despite my repeated attempts, so that pretty much told me how he felt about me. He was dealing with a lot of stuff, and I didn't think he would want to deal with an unwanted child from an unwanted woman either. How could I dump this on him now? He would probably be pissed when he found out, but how could he? I would never ask him for anything. I had the means to support myself and this child. I would send a condolence note. If Ryan responded, then I would tell him. I would put the ball in his court. This was probably not the best idea, but I was in survival mode, and it was the best I could come up with.

Ryan,

I am so sorry to hear about the passing of your father. I know this must be an incredibly difficult time for you and your family. Please know that my thoughts and prayers are with you. I wish that I could offer some true words of comfort to ease your pain at this time. All I can tell you is that you will carry an emptiness around with you that can never quite be filled. For some, the rest of their lives are fulfilling and the emptiness becomes very small. For others, it remains a gaping, wide-open hole. I guess you can tell which category I fall into. I would have liked to be there for you and to hold your hand through this ordeal. Please know that I would be there for you if you asked. Please contact me, I would really like to speak with you now.

Love, Maggie

I knew the love part was wrong, but I didn't know what else to say. Sincerely didn't quite seem to fit the bill, and in my heart of hearts, I did love him.

What was it going to do, scare him away? I mailed the letter on the twenty-fourth of February.

And then I continued on with my life. I took my prenatal vitamins and hid my morning sickness. But I needed a plan. What I needed was to tell someone. I called Matt and left a voicemail, knowing that he'd eventually check-in.

"Matt, it's me. I really, really need to talk to you. I, um, shit, well, it's that rainy day that I was never planning on having. Call me on my cell. Can you believe I finally got a cell? Now I'm as bad as all the people we make fun of on Newbury Street. The apartment phone is being disconnected. My cell number is 617-555-2589. Call me soon. Love you."

I sent Matt one more email, complete with shouty caps.

03/05/01: Matt! CHECK YOUR MESSAGES. IT IS IMPORTANT. THIS CANNOT WAIT UNTIL YOU GET HOME!

Still no response.

With nothing else to do, I flew down to Florida for a long weekend to see my dad and Marcy the first weekend in March. It was beautiful and peaceful. For the first time since my birthday, a peace settled over me, right there in their backyard, looking at their dock.

You couldn't help but have tranquility here. I kept to myself the first day there, trying to figure out my next move. There was a small house for sale at the end of the street, three houses down and also on the water. I was never one for rash decisions, but I no longer had the luxury of time.

"Hey, Dad," I said, settling in next to him at the edge of his dock. "I made some calls today. I'm thinking of investing in some real estate."

"Real estate? Where?"

"Right at the end of the street, neighbor!"

He looked at me and grinned from ear to ear. He boomed "Neighbor, well I sure do like the sound of that!"

The time to share my other surprise was here. "Maybe I shouldn't call you neighbor," I dropped my head, swallowed, and then looked right at him, "maybe I should call you Grandpa."

"Grandpa?" His smile faded into a look of disbelief. When I nodded through tears, his smile returned and he jumped up, pulling me to my feet, and hugged me. "This is the best day I've had in a long time!"

He turned and almost started running to the house. "Marcy, come and meet our new neighbor. Grandma Marcy, get out here now!"

That was done. They were happy. For the first time in a long time, I felt content with the direction of my life. I returned to Boston, gave only one week's notice, and told Deborah that I needed to get out of Dodge for a while. I remained aloof, saying that I would probably travel. I sold most of my things and packed my stuff in record time. With a U-Haul attached to the back of my little Ford Escort wagon, I left Boston without looking back. I waited for Matt to call. He never did.

Neither did Ryan.

CHAPTER TWELVE
April 2008
Seven Years Later

Remind me again, why do I do this to myself?" I needed someone to calm my frazzled nerves. I'm not sure what possessed me to think I could create a dream princess castle birthday cake for my little princess's third birthday, complete with hand-dipped ice cream cone turrets. Insane. I'd been working the entire time Sophia had been napping, and I wasn't done yet. I moved faster. Even the air conditioning did nothing to cool me down. With the back of my hand, I swiped hair back toward my ponytail. "Why can't I just order one from Publix?"

Michele chuckled as she dipped a finger in a bowl of frosting by the sink. "The boys played great. Jake and Owen are so cute together."

She glanced around my kitchen that now looked like the site of *Cake Wars* if they used actual bombs. "You do this because that's not who you are. You are Über-mother, and you insist on making birthday cakes and Halloween costumes, and give the rest of us mothers a complex about our shortcomings. Career, kids and you do it all alone. Amazing!"

I shrugged sheepishly. "I'm not alone, I have my dad and Marcy three houses away. Plus my uncle is one town over. Not to mention, I have my *wonderful* mommy friends, without whom, I would go crazy. How else would I have figured out the inner-workings and politics of the PTA?"

She laughed as she stood up to leave, "What time tomorrow for the party?"

"About five-ish. Pizza and wings, then cake and ice cream. Not anything big. But my dad wants to take the kids out on the boat. We can drink wine while they do that." I winked at her.

Michele headed out the kitchen door and out through the garage. Everyone used that door. Despite Michele's high praises, my house was casual. The only people who ever came to the front door were selling something. Usually, something I didn't want.

I was a little startled to hear the doorbell ring about a minute after Michele left. Why didn't she just come back in? "Coming!" I yelled, wiping purple frosting off my hands on my filthy apron as I answered the door. I saw a tall figure through the glass and realized that it wasn't Michele. Great. I was sweaty and in old cut-offs. I'm sure I had frosting on my face or body. Whoever was here, trying to get me to accept Jesus Christ as my personal savior, was in for a treat.

As I opened the door, I froze. It was not some evangelical or even the cable company. This was the moment I had dreaded for seven years. In this instant, life as I knew it was over. I pushed down the swell of emotions that rushed up at me from deep down places. I steeled my face and prepared for the greeting. Our eyes were locked, staring each other down. Then suddenly, his eyes shifted to something behind me.

"Mom, who is it?" Jake said as he barreled up to me and stopped by my side.

I cleared my throat. "This is someone I used to know. Mr. Slavin."

Jake stuck out his hand to shake, as I'd taught him.

"And this is my son, Jake," I said back to a stunned Matt.

I turned to Jake and asked him to run over to his grandfather's and play for a minute while I visited with my company. He looked at me, not understanding. I gave him my sternest of looks, and he went out. About one minute later, the phone rang once and then was silent. "He's at my dad's safe. Come in. What can I get you to drink?" I took off my apron and turned to walk to the kitchen.

"Seriously, Maggie. What the hell is going on?"

I stopped in my tracks and spun around, still clutching the apron. "What do you mean, what the hell? How dare you? You have no business showing up here like this. To do what, pass judgment? No, thanks, I think I'll pass."

"Does he even know?"

"Know what? I don't know what you are talking about."

"Does Ryan know that he has a kid? 'Cause he's never said a thing to me about it."

"What makes you think he's Ryan's?" I countered, trying to stall.

"Because I have eyes. He's the spitting image of him. That's exactly as I remember Ryan growing up, except he has your smile."

I wanted to crumble. I willed tears not to come. Then I remembered that Matt deserted me, that he never called me, and the ice of anger replaced the heat of tears. "Why are you so interested now? You didn't seem to care when I needed you."

"What are you talking about?"

"The emails, the phone message. I didn't come right out and say that I was pregnant, but, Jesus, Matt, I thought you'd understand. And you never called. Ever. All I asked you to do was call me. I have not heard from you since. It's been over seven years. Seven! So you don't get to stand there and pass judgment on me or the decisions I have made. I was left by myself. Noble Mr. Milan never bothered to contact me either, so don't go all gung-ho protecting his honor. You both left me when I needed you the most. Everyone had someone else more important than me. So you know what, I made Jake more important than you both, so stay out of it!"

"What the hell are you talking about? Emails, messages? I never got anything from you. I came back from my trip, and you were gone. No forwarding address. Your number was disconnected. You ran away, and never even let me know you were alive."

"Bull shit. I emailed you, multiple times, begging you to call me. And I left you a voicemail with my cell number so you could get in touch with me after I moved. I said on the voicemail that I needed you, that it was the rainy day I never wanted and to call me."

Matt froze, not even breathing.

"What?" I asked angrily.

"When we got back, Irene listened to the voicemail. She said that it was nothing important, that you were just whining about the weather."

"Didn't you get the emails?"

"Um," he looked down, his face clouding over, "Irene used my email while we were away since she couldn't access her work one."

A red rage washed over me." Lemme guess, that bitch deleted all the ones from me?"

Matt looked like he was going to yell at me again. I started in before he could get a word in edgewise. My voice was level and cold as steel. "Are you going to tell me not to call your wife a bitch? Well, too late, because she is and always has been. She has been manipulating you your whole relationship, and now you finally have proof. I hope you are happy with her because you picked her over me. And I know that you married her because you are wearing a ring, and you have always been too pussy whipped to walk away from her. I was supposed to be your best friend, so go ahead, and defend her. Just don't come here and pass judgment for the self-preservation decisions that I have had to make, *alone*, while I was trying to support myself and my child. Now I think it's time you left."

"Maggie, wait, I'm so sorry. I didn't know."

"No you didn't, and you didn't care enough to try and find out either. So much for being my friend. And don't go playing the Ryan card on me either. I called him. Repeatedly. I wrote to him and asked him to contact me. He never did. Neither one of you thought enough of me to find me or to reach out to me."

Just then the phone rang. I looked at the caller ID. It was my dad. "Honey, Jake said that a guy showed up at the house. Are you okay?"

"Fine, Dad." I couldn't help but roll my eyes.

"Is it ..."

"No, Dad, it's an old, um, someone I used to know in college. Sophia's going to be getting up soon. Would you mind coming over and getting her so that Matt and I can have a little privacy to go over some, um, unfinished business?"

As I hung up, I looked at Matt. He had matured and filled out a little. His sandy brown hair was shorter than it was in college. He was wearing rumpled khaki shorts and a t-shirt.

I excused myself and went down the hall to wake up Sophia. I told her she was going over to Papa's house, as I changed her and brushed her hair, still sweaty from sleeping. I carried her out into the living room, where Matt had perched uneasily on the edge of the couch. He stood up and stared at me, mouth hanging open.

"And this is my daughter, Sophia. Sophia, can you say hello to Mr. Slavin?"

She buried her head in my shoulder, still a little groggy and sleepy, and said 'hello.' I took her out through the kitchen door and into the garage where my father and Jake were waiting. I assured them both that I was okay, that we just had some catching up to do, and that I would call later on when I wanted the kids home. It was such a relief having my dad to help. I thought for the millionth time that I didn't know how I would have made it without him.

I returned to the house, stopping in the kitchen to grab two beers and open the bottles. I returned to the living room and handed Matt one. "Probably need this right about now, huh?"

He took the bottle without making eye contact and took a long drink. I was calm. I felt like I had all the power, that I no longer had to justify my decisions. I sat down on the couch across from where Matt was standing. I waited for a moment and then said, "I'm guessing you have some questions for me. Let me start."

He listened, his face growing ashen as I told him about all the tough decisions I'd to make in the beginning. How I decided to make a fresh start with my dad and Marcy. I left out no gory details, including my seventy-five-hour labor that ended with my baby in distress and the cord wrapped around his neck, but by some miracle he was okay. And that I was alone for all of it.

"But, then I realized that I was no longer alone and that I would never seek someone else out again to make me feel whole. That this was as complete as I could ever hope to be. And I decided it would be enough. That my child now came first above all other needs, including any of my own. It was hard. So hard. I've had more issues with my back, so I went to work for an equipment vendor who specialized in supplying wheelchairs and equipment for children. It was a lot less physically demanding. Now I'm a co-owner of the company. It's perfect. I can work from home, especially at night after the kids were in bed. A benefit of not having a social life."

Matt said, "But Sophia? Where ..."

Even though it was none of his business, I found myself telling him anyway. "She's adopted. Do you remember my Uncle Dan? Well, his daughter, Lindsay, found herself pregnant at fifteen. So I stepped in. That way Jake could have a sibling, something I would not be able to give him otherwise. I've had her since the day she was born. I was in the delivery room, helping Lindsay. I didn't want her to be alone like I was."

Matt looked at me. "Jake and Sophia?"

"Yep, my brother and my mother. And Jake is really Jacob Philip."

"Philip?"

I nodded.

"That was Ryan's father's name."

"I know. It was the least I could do."

"Mr. Milan would have loved it."

My eyes filled up. I shrugged. "Well, just another benefit of being alone. I got to pick the names, both times."

"So you're not married then?"

"No, never have been and never will be. My life is my children now. I cannot survive being deserted again, so I decided that I won't have to if I never put myself out there." I looked pointedly at him. He knew that I was not only talking about Ryan but about him as well.

"Maggie, I'm so sorry." He couldn't bear to look me in the eyes.

"For what, for barging in here and passing judgment or for never calling me in the first place?"

"Both. I missed you so much, but I was mad at you for leaving me. I guess I figured that you would eventually call me. But you never did."

"How did you find me now?"

"Um, Facebook."

"But how? I'm not even on there." For just this reason.

"Caroline, from college."

"Oh, I just ran into her at Disney World, in February." Of course.

"Well, she posted pics, and there was one of her, you and Jake. As soon as I saw it, I knew that he was Ryan's. So I emailed her and asked if she knew where you were. She said Florida, so I began searching for you."

I didn't say anything.

Matt continued, "So are you going to tell Ryan?"

I looked at him like he was crazy.

"Don't you think he has a right to know?"

"No! Nothing has changed. He doesn't want kids and didn't want me. We are doing just fine as is." I continued, "And it is not your place to tell him. Consider him an anonymous sperm donor. He's not even listed on the birth certificate."

"He's not?"

"No, that way no one could ever trace it. You know, if he was running for office or something, and then the opposition dropped that he had this love child. I didn't want that to happen to him."

"Maggie, I don't get you. You deny him his child but do so to protect his career. It's just not normal."

"Well, I'm not normal, in case you haven't noticed. Anyway, I was in self-preservation mode. Besides, he could have called me. He didn't. Hasn't. I haven't spoken to him since the Christmas he left. What don't you understand about that? He wanted nothing to do with me. He made it very obvious that he was focused on his career, so I did what little I could to help him."

"That's where you're wrong."

"Wrong?"

"Yes, even you, Maggie, can be wrong. He was so torn up about leaving Boston. He wanted to ask you to move to Columbus but was afraid you would say no. He thought he would scare you away, wanting too much of a relationship, too fast."

Oh.

"I would have said yes, even before the baby thing."

"Really? I wouldn't have thought so. You were so, 'I have bad taste' and 'I'm done with relationships.' I think Ryan thought that you weren't shopping for a serious relationship."

"But that makes no sense. He was afraid to scare me away, so he left me?"

He shrugged. "He didn't see you as being ready to commit. After his dad died, I think he convinced himself that it was never really a big deal, to begin with."

"Well, it was to me," I said, barely above a whisper.

"I don't know what else to tell you. Star-crossed lovers, I guess."

117

Shit. So the last seven years of my life had been a colossal screw-up of miscommunications with everyone thinking they knew what was best for everyone else. And I had been all alone throughout it. I guessed that Ryan was not.

"Is he ... I mean, did he ever settle down?"

Matt looked embarrassed. "Um, he's getting married next month. He and Elise have been together for, like, five years. She works in the Solicitor General's Office too. They're both very career-oriented."

I dropped my head and willed myself not to cry. "So you go to the wedding and pretend that this little visit never happened, and we can all get on with our lives."

"Maggie, you know I can't do that."

"Well, you can't tell him either. It's not your place, and now, telling him will hurt him even more. I mean, what do you think that will do to his upcoming nuptials?"

"I don't know what I'm going to do about that, but I can't not have you in my life anymore. I don't know that I can go back to Irene, either, after finding out what she did. How can I stay married to someone who would so deliberately hurt someone so important to me? She's kind of, well, mean, and I don't know why I put up with it."

"You're just coming to that conclusion now? I could have told you that twelve years ago!"

"Seriously, if I had known what you were going through, I would have made you tell Ryan. And you would have moved to Ohio for him, and everyone would have lived happily ever after. But because Irene was so full of spite and jealousy, you have been alone and thought that I deserted you. I would have raised that child as my own before I let you do all this!" He was yelling now.

118

"Calm down, Matt. It's not so bad. I have a very full and fulfilling life. It just does not happen to include a significant other. My kids and I are very happy."

He looked at me, seeing through my lie. I crumbled.

"Okay, so it's tough sometimes. I was never going to end up having children, and now I have two. I mean, I have been sleep-deprived for the past six and a half years. I try to make ends meet so I can leave my trust as intact as I can for my children. For Pete's sake, I drive a minivan! I am constantly running everywhere. I never get to sit down to eat a meal. My clothes constantly have food or some kind of schmutz on them. I had to grow my hair out because I don't have time for regular haircuts. My life is dominated by princesses and action figures and Legos. I never get to read books that don't contain pictures anymore. I can't remember the last time I had a purely adult conversation that did not involve my children. And I'm lonely. I am so so lonely. I have not had a date in, oh, I can't tell you how long. And the last time I had sex was when Jake was conceived. I don't even remember what an orgasm is."

Oh my God, did I just say that out loud? I could barely look at Matt. I put my face in my hands.

Silence.

Finally, he says quietly, "Can I meet them? I mean, can I stay for a day or so and hang out with them?"

Good 'ole Matt, glossing over my verbal diarrhea. Some things never change.

"That depends. Are you going to tell Ryan or Irene?"

He looked me in the eye. "I honestly don't know, but I won't say anything while I'm here. Can I give you a hug now or what?"

He crossed the room and grabbed me. All of the tears that I had been holding back came flooding out, and I cried for a while, just holding onto him. I had missed my friend. His coming back would be the undoing of all that I had created, but it just felt so good to have his arms around me again.

CHAPTER THIRTEEN

Though I was exhausted, sleep eluded me in place of worry.

What if Matt was calling Ryan right now? Ryan would hate me if he found out, and the thought of that was unbearable. What if he tried to take Jake away from me? He was a lawyer and knew a lot of powerful people. He could probably win. *What would that do to Jake and Sophia?* They couldn't lose each other. I knew what it was like to lose my big brother, and I wouldn't let that happen to Sophia.

But it was even more than that. Seeing Matt again, I wanted my friend back. I realized how much I had missed him. I had been so lonely and isolated since I left Boston. I had friendships, but they were few and not very deep. I didn't socialize anymore outside of the play-date circle. I had shut myself off from everyone but my kids. I was even closed off to my dad and Marcy. I had stuffed all of my sorrow and loneliness down so deep and never allowed it to surface. Other than my love for my children and family, I emotionally cruised through life on autopilot. Now autopilot was disengaged, and I was flying the plane again.

And I was flying right into a large mountain.

There was something else too. I usually glazed over my lack of love life with my mommy friends, saying that I didn't want to expose the kids to some random guy. This was usually a defense mechanism to prevent the "set-up." My line was that I was sure the right guy was out there for me, but I wasn't ready yet.

And, ironically, I was sure. I had already met him, and he had fathered my son.

And then he had left me and never looked back.

Now, he was marrying someone else.

My loneliness consumed me. I longed to feel arms around me, to comfort me. Seeing Matt, talking about the past and present, and hugging him had drudged all of this up. I literally had not been physically touched—not counting the doctor—by a guy in at least three years. I hadn't even had a date since I adopted Sophia.

Who would want to date a single woman with two kids? I didn't even want to find out. And the few dates I had before Sophia ... well, they barely got beyond the handshake stage.

Laying in bed, wallowing in my own misery, I wasn't sure I could put myself together enough to face my children and my day. But I had to. That was one of the drawbacks of single mom-dom. If I didn't provide for my kids, then no one else would. And right now, I needed to give my little girl her third birthday party.

Despite my fatigue and worry, Sophia had a great party. The princess castle cake, in all of its pink and purple glory, held up. She was thrilled with her dress-up clothes and little princess dolls. Matt fit right in, catching up with my dad and Marcy, and helping out with the kids. I could see exhaustion written across his face though. I hoped he had kept his promise to not tell anyone where he was or what he had discovered.

He was great with my kids and Owen. When my dad took the kids out for a cruise on the boat, Michele and Marcy decided to go with them to give Matt and me a chance to talk.

"They're great, you know. It's so weird talking to Jake. I mean, it's just like talking to Ryan."

"I know, and I didn't even know Ryan as a child."

I looked at Matt and took a sip of my wine.

"So, have you decided what you are going to do?"

Matt shook his head. His phone rang and he pulled it out of his back pocket. He frowned at the ID. "Hey, what's up?"

He stood up and walked inside the house. He went into Sophia's room, where there was a baby monitor. I had the other end on the table next to me. I was sure he didn't realize this because he put the phone on speaker.

"Oh, man, I'm sorry she called you in the middle of the night. Not cool."

I could only guess he was talking about Irene. I froze when I heard the voice on the other end. Even through the speaker and monitor, I recognized it.

"No problem. I was worried more about you. Everything okay?" Ryan asked.

"Um, yeah, fine. We just had a major blow-up, that's all."

"She sounded panicked. Almost like she didn't know where you were. She kept insisting that you were with me."

"Yeah, I didn't really tell her where I was going."

"Oh, man, did I blow anything for you? I mean, should I have told her you were out here? I wasn't thinking. It was, like, two a.m. and she was screaming. I was trying not to wake Elise up ..."

I should stop listening. But I couldn't.

Matt continued, "No, man, don't sweat. I had an, um, I mean, kind of an emergency. And when I went to check it out, everything was okay, but then I found out about all this shit that Irene had pulled and how she's been lying to me for, like, seven years. And about really serious shit too. I blew a gasket. And she kept calling and calling last night. I finally told her that I was done with her, and I wasn't coming back."

Ryan seemed dumbfounded. "I, um, oh, wow. I don't know what to say to that. Was she cheating on you?"

"No, but she hurt ..." Matt paused. I held my breath and waited for him to continue. "She hurt people that were like family to me, just to be mean and spiteful, because she didn't trust me. And because of her actions, maybe a lot of people's lives have been fucked up, least of all mine. I can't be with a woman who would do that."

Ryan had no idea that Matt was talking about him.

Ryan asked, "You gonna be okay? When will you get back to Mass? And where are you now anyway?"

"I think I'll make it. I'll figure something out. And I'm in sunny Florida, hanging with an old buddy. Somehow, with the sun and the water and an ice-cold beer, it all doesn't seem so bad."

"Don't worry, be happy."

"That's right. Don't worry, be happy. Hey, lemme ask you something. I always wanted kids and Irene didn't, so we didn't have them. I guess, now, it's a good thing, but it always bummed me out. What if Elise wanted kids? Would you have them with her?"

Son of a bitch.

Ryan paused a minute before he answered. "You know I've never wanted kids. Not in the career plan. But I guess I always figured if the right person came along, and she wanted them, and she was truly right for me, then it would all be okay."

"So will you have them with Elise?"

Just turn the knife while you have it plunged into my back, why don't you.

"Probably not. I guess I don't feel that strongly about it."

"Well, then why the hell get married? Look at me! Save yourself some heartache, man."

"I dunno. I mean, everyone expects us to get married. Let's face it, we're more married to our careers. Elise is great, and I get along well with her and her family. I care about her. What else is there to do, spend my life alone?"

Tears were streaming down my cheeks. Here Ryan was, getting married because he was supposed to. Because he didn't want to live the pitiful existence that I had chosen for myself. My heart was breaking all over again. Not only had I not gotten over him, but he would rather marry someone he didn't really love than to have me be part of his life.

Somehow, Matt must have sensed my agony. "But marriage? Do you care about her? If you're gonna marry someone, don't you want to really be in *love* with her? Do you even know what real love feels like?"

Ryan got defensive. "Don't go lecturing me, Matt."

Matt backed down. "Sorry. Guess I'm a little more upset about the destruction of my marriage than I thought. I just don't want to see you making a mistake like I did. Apparently, everyone knew that Irene was a bitch on wheels. And I never listened."

"She was always nice to me if that makes you feel any better."

"Yeah, but she treated Ma, I mean, the rest of my friends like shit."

"Maggie."

"Yeah."

Oh God, what was he going to say?

"You know, I never got that. I mean, you and Maggie were just friends. That's what she always said. I wouldn't have gone after her if I thought there was anything more."

"But you didn't keep her once you had her."

Oh Matt, *shut up*. I pushed my sunglasses up on top of my head and hid my face in my hands as if to spare myself the embarrassment.

"Dude, you're crossing the line. But it's not every day that your marriage falls apart, so I'll let it slide. But, you're right. I didn't keep her. And I'm sorry for that. You have no idea."

I nearly gave myself whiplash as I bolted upright and stared at the monitor like it would provide answers.

"Mommy, mommy, did you see us? Papa drove the boat super-fast. Wheeeee!"

I turned my attention to my children who were climbing out of the boat. I pulled my sunglasses down and stood up. I reached over and turned the monitor off. I'd heard enough.

"Was it fun? Did you see any dolphins? I hope Papa was careful when he was driving super-fast." I put on the brightest smile that I could muster and tried to stand up straight.

In truth, I could barely breathe. The earth was spinning, and I staggered a little. Michele took one look at me and said, "Hey, you look tired. How would Jake like to come over and spend the night with Owen tonight?"

"Can I, Mom? Owen and I want to play his new DS game." Jake asked eagerly. I looked at his familiar chocolate-brown eyes and swallowed hard. His dark hair was windblown and his smile showed multiple missing teeth.

"Sure Buddy." I looked at Michele and mouthed a thank you to her. I smiled weakly at her. My smile faded when Matt came back outside. Michele reached out and touched my arm. "Call me, anytime, if you need anything. Anytime." I nodded numbly and watched her walk into the house.

"Oh, I see the crew is back. Was the boat ride fun?"

"We went super-fast. Wheeee!" Sophia excitedly explained, throwing her arms in the air and twirling around. She exuded the energy that only a child could. She was precious and beautiful, and I scooped her up and squeezed her tightly. I buried my face in her fine blond hair and wished her a happy birthday. She smelled like saltwater and fresh air and birthday cake.

It was the smell of happiness.

I had to pull myself together and remember what a happy and beautiful life I had created here for myself and my children.

My dad looked at me. A look of concern crossed his weathered face, and he frowned. God, why did my face have to read like an open book? He asked if the birthday girl wanted to spend the night at Papa and Grandma Marcy's house. She was excited and ran into the house to get her pink blankie and lamb that were her constant companions. I followed her into the house to pack up stuff for both the kids.

I was so lucky to have friends and family who supported me and came to my rescue. I needed time and space to fall apart. I brought the kids' stuff out and said goodbye to both of them, complete with hugs and kisses.

Suddenly, the crowd was gone. I sank down on the couch. I sat there, staring into space for a few minutes before I realized that Matt was still here somewhere. I stood up and looked for my wine glass. I found it and started to down the contents. I stopped myself. Drinking this into oblivion was not going to make it any better. I needed to face the music and find out exactly what Matt told Ryan.

Matt sat out in one of the deck chairs, staring out at the water, watching the sun dip below the horizon. I walked out and eased into the chair beside him. We both sat in silence for a long time. Finally, I couldn't stand it any longer. "Did you tell him?"

"How did you know I was talking to Ryan?"

"You were in Sophia's room, and there is a baby monitor out here. I heard the whole thing, right up until you were grilling him about letting me go. Then the kids came back. So, did you tell him?"

Matt looked at his feet. "No, I didn't—not yet. But I feel horrible about it, and I don't know how long I'm going to be able to keep it from him. I think you need to tell him."

"Duly noted, and ignored. Are you leaving Irene?"

"Yep, I even got a recommendation for a divorce lawyer from Ryan. I can't go back to her. Think about it. If I had found out about the baby, I would have, well, I would have done something."

"I wonder if that's what Irene was afraid of, that you would want to help me out and would leave her."

"Kind of ironic. I mean, it's seven years later, but I found out so now I'm leaving her. So, she was kind of on the money." He stopped and stared out at the water for a minute. Then he turned and looked at me. "Twelve fucking years, down the toilet."

"I wish I could say that I'm sorry, but considering how she screwed me over so royally, I only feel bad for you."

"I don't think she ever accepted that you and I were just friends. I think she couldn't believe that I was not going to cheat on her with you. I told her when we became friends that we flirted a little, but she never trusted me with you."

"I know. I'm not going to lie. When we first met, I did like you. I don't think I would have minded if you had cheated on her with me. Remember that night over at Ted and Ben's? The keg party in their basement. We flirted all night and then almost kissed. I really, really wanted to. But I figured, if you would cheat on her, then you would cheat on me. And she deserved better than that, so I stopped throwing myself at you. But then, of course, I finally met Irene. She was nasty from the getgo, but I put up with it because I didn't want to put you in the middle. It was more important to be your friend and to be in your life than to," I broke off. "Well, I guess I played that hand wrong. In the end, I was neither vindicated nor your friend."

"Why can't we still be friends now? I'm starting a new chapter in my life. I think it's time you made a re-appearance."

I started crying. Again. "Oh Matt, if it were just that easy. I mean, firstly, I have hated you for seven years. Okay, so I get that it was *probably* not your fault, other than having crappy taste in women, but I can't get over that in the drop of a hat. Secondly, I have kids and a life to think about. It's not that easy to introduce new people or lifestyles into it. And thirdly, there is the whole Ryan thing. I mean, how can you be friends with both of us, without betraying one of us?"

The air hung heavy with silence.

Finally, Matt spoke, his voice hoarse and barely above a whisper, "Why does it have to be a betrayal?"

"Because I can't see Ryan ever forgiving you for keeping this from him, and I won't be able to forgive you when you tell him and ruin my life, again." I stood up and turned to leave. Matt jumped up and grabbed my arms. "Either way, you're betraying one of us."

"Maggie, I can't lose you again." He pulled me in close, holding me to his chest. I stayed there and sobbed. His polo shirt was soaked with my tears, and I felt like they would never end. I looked up at Matt's face. He was crying too.

He wiped my cheek with his thumb. "Honey, I'll figure something out. I owe it to you. Let me be in your life. Let me be here for you now."

I stood there, in Matt's arms, staring into his blue eyes. My body was starved for human touch. He was smoothing my hair back out of my face. The wind had picked up, but I barely felt it. I was so overcome with raw emotion.

The pain at losing Ryan and being alone exploded up to the surface. Feelings of misplaced anger at Matt spun around in my head. The fear of losing my son was so real that I couldn't bear to think about it.

My world as I knew it, all compartmentalized and tucked away, had come all unraveled and pieces that were never meant to see the light of day collided with each other. I had no control over my life, which made me anxious and panicky.

I did the unthinkable.

I kissed Matt.

It was as if I had unleashed a beast. I kissed Matt hard and furiously, catching him off-guard. He stumbled back a step or two before he regained his balance and steadied himself. His arms were around me, pressing me into him, and he was kissing me back. It was not soft and romantic. It was hard and angry. He eventually backed me up against the sliding glass door. His hands were planted onto the glass on either side of my head, caging me in. He began kissing my jaw and then down to my neck. I tilted my head back and squeezed my eyes shut, trying to turn off my spinning brain.

All I wanted to do was not to think.

The phone in my back pocket vibrated. Instinctually, I reached down and grabbed it. The caller ID flashed 'Michele' and my heart skipped a beat. Matt's arms were still positioned on either side of me, and he leaned his head into his arm. Our breaths came in heavy pants. "Hey, Michele, what's up?" I tried to sound as normal as possible.

"Did I get you at a bad time?"

"Um, no, it's fine. Is Jake okay?"

"Yeah, but he is a little worried and wanted to talk to you before he went to bed."

"Okay, thanks. Put him on." I turned out of Matt's arms and went into the house. I wedged the phone between my ear and shoulder and began cleaning up the kitchen while I waited for Jake to come on the line. It was as if I was somehow able to stuff all of my overflowing baggage, emotions, and problems right back into their separate compartments and go back to Mommy mode.

It was a good skill. It meant I could function without having to face what was to come or what I had just done.

"Hi Mommy," I heard his little voice say. On the phone, he sounded so young and vulnerable, and I couldn't help but remember the promise I made on the day he was born to always protect him.

"Hey, Sport. What's going on? Are you and Owen having fun?"

"Yeah, I beat him at Mario Kart."

"Oh, that's good, but are you playing nice?" Matt had entered the house and had walked through the kitchen into the living room.

"Yes, Mommy. But I was thinking about something. Will tell me the truth if I ask you?"

"Sure, Bud. What is it?" I had no idea where he was going. All I knew was that I didn't have the energy to discuss the whole Santa Claus or Easter Bunny or Jesus thing right now. Thank God he was too young to ask about sex.

"Is Mr. Slavin still there?"

"Yes."

Could that be his question?

"Um ... I was wondering, well, is he my dad?"

I dropped the ceramic platter I was holding, and it shattered in the sink. Shit.

"Mommy, Mommy, are you okay?" Jake was yelling, and I could tell he was upset.

"Oh, I'm fine, Honey. I was cleaning up, and I dropped the big platter. My hands were wet and it slipped. Sorry it scared you."

"So is he my dad? Cause that would be cool. Then we could go fishing, just like Owen and Mr. Suarez do."

"Oh, Honey. I'm sorry to disappoint you, but Mr. Slavin is not your dad. He's just an old friend of mine from college."

"Do you know who my dad is?" Coming from anyone over the age of six and a half, I would have taken offense. But since he didn't know the mechanics of how it all worked, I cut him some slack. Still, this was the last thing I wanted to be discussing.

"Yes, Honey, I do. But it's no big deal, and we'll talk about it sometime when you're ready. Have a good time tonight and be good for Mr. and Mrs. Suarez."

"Ok, Mom. Are you really okay?"

"Yes, Sport. I'm just tired and trying to get cleaned up. I think your sister had a really good birthday. I'll see you in the morning. Love you, Sweet Boy."

"I love you too, Mommy."

Michele cut in. "Wow, I had no idea that that was what he wanted. Sorry."

"No biggie. I'm beat, so I'll see you tomorrow."

I hung up the phone and stared at it. God, I always knew that Jake was smart, but I hadn't given him that much credit for being observant.

Matt walked out into the kitchen. He started picking up the pieces of the platter. I stood there and watched him, numb. I have never gone into shock, but I imagined that this was what it felt like. Matt worked methodically and carefully. He pulled the trash bag out of the can and took it outside. I stood there, still unable to move. Matt came back in, and I was frozen. Immobile. He looked at me and said something. I couldn't process what he was saying, so I didn't reply. My eyes wouldn't focus on anything.

The only thing that I was aware of was that the whole room seemed to be shaking.

CHAPTER FOURTEEN

When I woke up the next morning, I was in my bed. I had no recollection of how I got there. I felt dizzy, and the room had a dreamlike quality to it.

I also was not alone. Matt was next to me, in my bed.

Oh, crap. What the hell had I done, and why couldn't I remember anything?

I squeezed my eyes shut and tried to remember what had happened. I remembered kissing Matt and then getting the phone call. Dropping the platter and ... nothing. There was a vague sense of watching myself like I was in a movie. I could see Matt in the kitchen. I could see him leading me down the hall. I could see myself sitting on the toilet and drinking something. Then, nothing. So, how did I get here? How did Matt get here? And what happened?

I tried to roll over but felt pinned down by the sheet. I lifted my head up off the pillow to look and tried to fight off the spinning room.

A moment later, the pain came. My back felt like I had a vice grip on either side of my spine from my ribs to my pelvis. It then spread out through my pelvis to my hips, where it felt like something was gnawing on them. The pain continued to spiral down my legs to my knees, calves, and feet.

The pain wasn't unusual. It was what I had, in some form, daily, as a result of the accident and surgeries. Yesterday, I'd been on my feet a lot in preparation for the party.

That was usually enough to cause a flare. The added stress and strain only added to it, I was sure. I needed to roll over to make myself more comfortable. I tried again, but couldn't move with Matt's body weight on top of the sheet.

Okay, so I guess that boded well for having a little less to be embarrassed about.

I reached over and touched his hand. His hand curled around mine. He was warm and it flooded my body with warmth. It had been so long since I had shared my bed with anyone, other than my children. My body ached for adult human contact, and for a moment, that ache surpassed the physical pain that I was in. I longed to be held and comforted.

My thoughts were a mess.

What exactly happened last night after the kissing? Jake's questioning his paternity. Matt was back, and I'd kissed him. Would he tell Ryan about Jake? I can't believe Ryan's getting married. What would it be like to have sex again?

Yup, a mess.

I finally worked up the energy and courage to speak. Everything was fuzzy, and my mouth felt like it was full of cotton balls.

"What happened?" I croaked.

Matt opened his eyes and looked at me. "I think you went into shock. How are you feeling?"

"Everything's fuzzy and spinning." I didn't mention the pain. I never told anyone about it. It was another thing that I stuffed way down into a little tiny box, never to see the light of day.

"I gave you a Xanax. It was in the medicine cabinet. I hope you don't mind. You needed something."

"Thanks, I guess. I've never taken it before. I can't, because of the kids."

"Oh. Then why do you have it?"

"I mentioned to my doctor one time that I have trouble sleeping because I worry so much. I mean, who wouldn't? Single mom, business owner, history of post-traumatic stress, etc, etc, etc. But you know, I can't even medicate myself. I have a hard time taking Nyquil when I'm sick because it's hard for me to wake up. But that's not the point here, is it?"

"No, it's exactly the point. You could have another parent to help you out."

"Yeah, how's that going to work? Ryan, his new wife, and I share custody of the kid he never knew he had? And what about Sophia? How am I supposed to explain to her that Jake suddenly has this other family, and she doesn't? Yeah, I don't think so."

"What about me?"

"What about you?" I sat up and glared at Matt. My back screamed, and I winced.

"I could help you raise the kids."

My mouth fell open. I knew he was being serious. I could formulate no response.

He continued. "I could move down here. I'd take the spare bedroom, of course. And you would have the help that I could have provided all along if only I had been a better friend."

"I ... don't ... know," I said slowly and hesitantly. "I mean, if you do that, how do you explain it to Ryan?"

Silence.

"I hadn't thought about that."

"So, there's that. Plus, that's not how it works. I can't just introduce you into our household, our family, as a new member. It's not like getting a new pet."

I shook my head and swung my legs over the edge of the bed. It took me a moment or three to stand up and have my legs accept the weight without collapsing. My steps were even more hesitant. I hoped Matt wouldn't notice, but seeing as how it was his profession, I knew that was yet another unreasonable hope.

"What's wrong? Why can't you walk?"

"Oh, I'm always a little slow in the morning. I think I overdid it getting ready for the party. Just give me a few minutes to work the kinks out."

"Are you always like this?" Concern edged his voice.

"Some days are better than others. This is not a good day. I'm fine. I'll be fine." And I continued into the bathroom, shutting the door for a moment of privacy.

I found my bottle of ibuprofen and downed three of them. I sat down on the toilet and put my head between my knees. How had all of this happened?

In the last forty-eight hours, my life had been blown apart. The events of the last two days spiraled me downward into grief again. I had to shake it off and keep moving.

That was the story of my life.

Shake it off and keep moving.

I walked out of the bathroom and sat down in the lounge chair that faced the bed. I had bought it, thinking it would be a great place to sit and read.

Ha! I never had time for that.

Suddenly I was overwhelmed by bitterness and resentment. Everyone else had their lives and was free to do whatever they wanted. I was living a life that I had not chosen for myself. It was thrust upon me, and I was left alone as everyone walked away.

And now, this life that I'd made the best of was being ripped away from me because everyone else wanted something different.

Where was my choice?

When did I get to be in control?

Why was everyone else so concerned about themselves that not one of them could see what havoc they were wrecking on my life?

Matt cleared his throat. "Um, so I take it, that it's a no? That you don't want me to move in and help you?"

"Oh Matt, it's not fair. You need to go home and figure out your life. What you're going to do about your marriage, about her."

I couldn't even say her name without the bile rising up in my throat. If she were here, I would probably kill her.

Matt looked down. "Okay, I just thought ... oh, I don't know. How did our lives get so messed up?"

I shook my head, shrugging my shoulders. For some things, there were no answers.

"Thanks for taking care of me last night."

"No problem. It's probably my fault that you were, um, upset."

"You think?" I retorted acerbically. "I was doing just fine until you showed up. But, it's a moot point now. Time to drop back twenty and punt. Again." Then I muttered, very softly, "Not sure how many more times I can do that."

Matt's phone rang. It was on the bedside table. He reached over and grabbed it. "Ryan." I moved over to the bed to sit next to him so I could hear the conversation.

"What's up, man?"

"Are you okay?" Ryan's voice sounded worried and almost panicked.

"Fine, why?"

"Um, where are you?"

"Still in Florida, why?"

"No, *where* are you? In Florida? Irene flew down there. She called the credit card company to find out where you were staying. She's at your hotel, waiting in your room. She called, freaking out that you didn't come back. She's seriously going psycho."

"Shit."

"I know, but I can't figure out why she keeps calling me. I mean, why does she think that I have something to do with this? Are you there with another woman or something?"

"No ..."

I hung my head in shame.

"I mean, yes." Matt stammered, "but it's not like that. I mean, oh shit."

Ryan interrupted, "Just spit it out. Something's up. What the hell is going on?"

"I found Maggie."

I looked at Matt. It was like being in the accident all over again. The truck was barreling toward us, on a direct collision course. And I knew it was going to hurt.

"Oh." Ryan exhaled. "How is, I mean, is she okay? What happened to her? Where'd she go? Is she okay?"

"She's doing well. Her dad moved down here, and she moved to stay close to him. She's happy. But I found out ..."

I braced myself for impact. This time, I would certainly die of pain.

"That she tried to contact me and leave me her information when she left Boston. Irene got rid of it. Erased her emails and messages. Maggie needed me then, and I

139

wasn't there for her because of Irene. And Maggie has spent all this time thinking that I'm a shit for deserting her."

"That's what I did to her."

"I know." It wasn't accusatory, just a fact.

"And I always feel bad about it. I was young and immature about the whole thing. Do you know what's the crazy thing? When you were asking yesterday about why Elise and I were getting married, Maggie popped into my head. Even before you said it. Is that messed up?"

"Totally."

He had no idea.

"Can you ask Maggie to call me?"

What? Hell no.

"What? Are you sure, man? It's going to complicate things."

"I know. I just wanna talk to her."

"Hang on."

What about his bride-to-be? I would be pissed if a month away from my wedding my fiancée was looking up old flings. Maybe he wasn't the person I thought he was.

Wait a minute, he had already deserted me. Why was I still giving him credit for being such a great guy?

Matt looked at me and pushed the phone in my direction. I must have still been under the influence of the Xanax, because I took it, with absolutely no idea of what to say.

Deep breath.

I cleared my throat. "Hello?"

"Oh my God, Maggie is that really you?" Ryan sounded relieved.

"Last time I checked. Although it could be a Russian spy crafted to look like me. I'm not sure."

He chuckled. "Still you. How are you? Are you okay?"

"I'm fine. Still pasty white, despite living in Florida. I just have a lot more freckles."

There was silence.

"Ryan?"

"Maggie, I am so, so sorry for not calling you. I just, I, um, I can't believe I'm talking to you again."

"Especially now. I seem to have really good timing when it comes to you."

"Oh, yeah. I guess Matt told you about being my best man and all." A small detail of omission. Made total sense, but an important detail, nonetheless.

"Yeah, sure. I guess congratulations are in order," I mumbled.

"I don't want to talk about that. How *are* you? What are you doing? Where are you? How are you? How have you been? I'm sorry. I should have called you. I was just, oh man. I'm sorry."

"Ryan," I interrupted. "You're rambling."

"Right. Right. You're right. I, um, this is just so unexpected."

"I'll say. Kind of came at me from left field too. Matt just showed up here. I've had a day or so, plus some Xanax to help me adjust."

Ryan chuckled again. He thought I was kidding. "Maybe I'll have to try some."

"I highly recommend it. So calm down and take a breath. I'm fine. I've been fine. I'll be fine."

"I'm glad to hear it." His voice was soft, almost like a whisper. It was silky, and it made me want to melt. Oh crap. "I worried about you. For a long time."

"Well, don't worry. We're fine here." Oh crap. Did I just say that? Maybe he didn't catch it.

141

"We? Right, you're ... right. To be expected of course. Only I would be stupid enough to let you go. So, okay then. Glad to know that you're okay. Um, keep in touch, through Matt. Maybe send me a Christmas card, you know if you feel like it. If you don't hate me ..."

"No," I said softly. "I don't hate you." I never could. "Bye, Ryan."

"Bye Maggie. Stay well."

I hung up the phone and limply handed it back to Matt, who was staring at me. I told him to stop and walked down the hall to the kitchen. I got myself a glass of ice water and stood there drinking, looking out onto the water.

"Well, that went well."

"About as good as could be expected."

"You didn't tell him."

"No, and I told you, I don't plan on it. He now has peace of mind that I am okay, and that's it. He can get married and live happily ever after, and we'll go on here, same as before." I plopped down in a chair at the table. Matt sat down too, tentatively.

"Ooohh" Matt exhaled. "I get it."

"Get what?"

"Okay, I don't know how to say this, and it might come out wrong or mean, but that's not how I mean it."

"Matt, just spit it out," I snapped.

"Okay, here goes. When I met you, one of the things that made me interested in you was your eyes. They truly are the windows to your soul."

"So my dad always says."

"Right, but don't interrupt. I wanna get this right. Okay, so your eyes. Your face and voice would be happy, but your eyes would always have a little, I dunno, hollowness in them. When something made you happy, it would get less and your eyes would light up and be full. I saw that in your eyes when we first met. Then I noticed when you were sad or talked about your mom and the accident, the hollowness got bigger. I watched you for most of college, and it was there."

Damn Matt for being observant. And here I always thought I hid it so well.

He continues, "Kind of an emptiness, but I thought that someday it would go away. And that's when you would be happy. And I saw it go away. I saw it virtually disappear that first night when we went to dinner with Ryan and Irene. And whenever you and Ryan hung out, it was barely even there. Your eyes were full of light and life. The night of your birthday, when you came out of your room expecting Ryan, in the second before you realized that he wasn't there, you looked so beautiful and radiant, and I realized that it was mostly because of the light coming out of your eyes. And then, in an instant, it was gone. The fire was out, and there was a blackness and emptiness behind your eyes that was darker and deeper than anything I had ever seen. And it never went away. And it's still there, except when you are with your kids. There is no hollowness there; your eyes are full of love with them. But they leave the room, and the light leaves your eyes."

"Very astute."

"I just saw the light in your eyes again. When you were on the phone with Ryan. That's why you won't tell him. You don't want to hurt him. No matter what he does, or has done to you, you can't bear to hurt him, because you ..."

"*Don't say it!*" I jumped up and turned around as if not looking at him would make it not real.

"Maggie, you are the most remarkable person I have ever met. You get hurt over and over, and you allow it willingly, just to protect those that you love."

I turned back around to look at Matt. My eyes were wide, and I felt consumed by the sadness and darkness in them.

He continued, "And you still love Ryan, don't you?"

I sank down in the chair and nodded. "It's why I can't ruin his life. And Elise's. It's not fair to them. I made these choices, so I will live with them. I won't ask him to be responsible for my decisions. End of discussion."

What I didn't say was that it was also why I didn't want to be with anyone else. I think I always knew, whether or not I admitted it. That there would never be someone who meant as much to me as Ryan did. It was kind of sad to think that those few months that we had were influential enough to forever direct my life.

I heard the door behind me open and close. Jake was home. Time to shift back into Mommy mode. Time to stuff all of my baggage and issues back into the deep dark recesses of my mind where they belonged. I had concluded a long time ago that I was irrevocably broken. When my body was shattered, something about my persona was damaged too. I couldn't be fully, totally happy.

Everything about my life had a negative attached to a positive. In the accident, I survived, but my mom and brother didn't. My survival was always a reminder of what was lost. And the survivor's guilt never left. I claimed to be over it, but it was a lot harder than I ever let on to anyone.

Anyone, except Ryan. I met him at the absolute worst time in his life, and it resulted in me being left alone and pregnant.

And I let him go so that his life was not sidelined for me. And I was doing it again. I was sparing him at the expense of me. I would let him think that I was married and let him marry Elise and be happy.

Matt shook his head. He nodded towards Jake, who we could see playing in the living room. "But what about him? Are you shortchanging him too? And I gotta tell you, he is one fantastic kid."

"I know, isn't he?" I agreed smugly.

"And Ryan deserves to know him and to recognize the sacrifices you have made. And to see what a great job you have done."

Matt watched Jake for a minute before turning back to me. "I know why he's so great. He's my two favorite people in one." I smiled at Matt through my tears and then looked lovingly at my son, building a tower out of Legos.

It was time for Matt to go sort out the rest of his life. Irene was waiting for him in the hotel, so he had to go face the music. I wished him luck and hugged him. It felt so good to have my friend back. I looked down at my feet and apologized for my behavior last night.

He laughed. "I've wanted to do that for a long time now. Ever since that night in the basement. You know, the night you stopped wanting to kiss me. Glad to finally know what it feels like. But I didn't make your eyes light up the way *he* can."

And I doubted anyone ever would.

CHAPTER FIFTEEN

There was no other choice but to put my life back together and move forward. Again. All I had to do was pretend the last few days hadn't happened and keep going.

Simple enough. I had work to do.

Jake finished up his homework. I made lunches for the morning. There were birthday presents to put away and remnants of the party to dismantle. By bath time Sunday evening, I was exhausted. My back and legs were screaming at me, and it was hard to stand up straight. At least the kids were clean and in bed. Sophia was still talking away, but she would settle down eventually. I could hear her prattling on about princesses and singing 'Twinkle Little Star.'

It brought a smile to my face. It always did.

I was truly blessed and focused my energy on that. I sat down on my bed and turned on my laptop. I had equipment parts to order and catalog and letters of medical necessity to file. I went to my email to see if a letter had been sent to me by a school therapist. Instead, I saw Matt's name flash in my inbox. I knew I should work first, so, being wired the way I was, I did.

My life falling apart didn't justify slacking off. It was nearly eleven when I finally opened Matt's email.

Hey Mags-

I talked to Irene. I told her that I'm done and it's over.

It was an uncomfortable plane ride back home, to say the least. She's staying with her sister now. Will be moving out this week.

Sorry for all the crap. You'll never know how sorry I am about all of this. I know I can't speak for why Irene acted the way she did, but I was the one with the poor judgment for keeping her all this time. I just keep thinking about how great it would have been for you and Ryan to have raised Jake together as a family.

Have a good week. Talk to you soon.

I sighed and shut down the computer without responding. I had never admitted to anyone, least of all myself, that what I wanted was the happy family scenario with Ryan. Why wish for things that were never to be?

I took out the picture of us from my bedside table. Matt was right. My eyes were happy. I looked young and vibrant. It wasn't a look that I was familiar with anymore. My reflection in the mirror hadn't shown that in a long time. I don't think I could have pinpointed what the difference was, until Matt pointed it out.

Part of me wanted to be mad at him for saying it, but I was more upset that it was true. I was hollow and dark, empty down in my deepest core. And it used to be okay with me. I had been content with the way things were. Until now. It wasn't that I was longing for anyone, I was longing for someone.

And that someone was Ryan Milan.

After a fitful night's sleep, Monday morning descended. I was up by six and in the shower so that I could be mostly put together by the time the kids got up. While drying my hair, it became quite apparent I needed a haircut. It was simply too long, with too much to manage right now. Maybe I could squeeze one in sometime this week. I gave up on straightening my hair out and twisted it up on the back of my head.

It would be too hot to leave it down anyway.

By the time I was putting my make-up on, Jake was up, and I asked him to wake Sophia as well. Jake put his Catholic school uniform on, and I dressed Sophia for daycare. My dad picked her up in the afternoon so she could nap at home. It made me feel less guilty about working.

With all the crap I was dealing with right now, working mother's guilt was lower on the priority list.

However, it remained.

The coffee pot kicked on automatically, and I said a prayer blessing the person who invented the automatic timer. It was fully brewed by the time we got to the kitchen, and I went straight for the pot to pour myself a cup.

The first of many it would probably take to get me through this day.

I took the lunches out of the fridge and packed the kids in their bags. Work mornings were always very hectic, but this morning, I didn't mind. I was so caught up in the routine, it didn't give me time to think about the last few days.

Once I was at work, however, it was a different story. I found it nearly impossible to concentrate. My productivity suffered and my to-do list loomed. I felt weighted down and like I was going to explode at the same time.

I needed to talk to someone. But who? I didn't want to talk to my dad or Marcy. This was the problem with living a walled-off existence. It left you alone in moments of crisis. I put my head in my hands for a minute. I was going to have to open up to someone. Michele, though a stay-at-home mom, had more meetings and appointments and seemed busier than I ever was. Today I was lucky, as she was available for an eleven-thirty lunch.

We met at a local café, close to my office. As soon as I walked in, she sensed my mood and immediately asked, "What's wrong, Maggie? I've never seen you like this."

"My life is about to implode, and I don't know what to do. I need to talk."

She realized the weight of this statement. I was never the one who needed to talk; I was the one who listened. She nodded and said, "Go ahead."

"It all began in organic chemistry ..." I started, going all the way back to that fateful class where Matt and I commiserated over covalent bonds. Then onto Irene, my crappy dating track record, and trust issues, finally admitting I had a hard time opening up to people. Her smile let me know that it was not news to her.

The Ryan story came next. I recounted the stories of the missed connections and crossed signals. How he was the one person I was able to be open with. But then his father and his torn obligations. Finding out I was pregnant and trying to get in contact with both Matt and Ryan. And how neither returned my calls.

"And now, *seven* years later, Matt shows up out of the blue. He and Ryan are still great friends. Matt's Ryan's best man because of course Ryan's getting married next month. Matt wants me to tell Ryan, and I still don't. It would ruin his life. And it would ruin mine if he tried to take Jake away. Not to mention what it would do to Jake."

Michele looked at me, "And you're still in love with him?"

I looked down at my mostly uneaten salad. "Yes. And I don't want him to be hurt."

"But what about you?"

"What about me?"

"You are hurting. You have been hurting. You don't deserve to have to go through this all alone. You *deserve* to be happy. Maybe it's with Ryan."

"But he's getting married."

"Didn't you say that he wasn't really in love with her? That's got to count for something?"

"I don't know what to do." I finally brought my gaze to hers.

"Honey, this just sucks."

"I know, right? Story of my life."

While I was no closer to an answer following lunch, having talked about it helped. I should remember that opening up isn't always a bad thing.

*****

Sophia's actual birthday meant one thing. The uncomfortable phone call with Lindsay. She could call any time she wanted, and I would not have had a problem with visits, but those were few and far between. She was a senior in high school, and it was still very difficult for her to deal with. I tried to be supportive and understanding. I hoped someday she would see this was for the best.

When the phone rang, I walked slowly to it. Jake raced me and beat me there, looking at the caller ID. "It's Uncle Dan!" He answered before I could stop him. "Hello? Oh, hi Lindsay. Are you coming to visit soon? Oh, yeah, here she is." Jake look disappointed when he handed me the phone. Before the pregnancy, Lindsay had loved Jake, and they had had a special bond. He didn't realize where Sophia came from, so the distance was hurtful to him.

I took the phone and talked to Lindsay while I cleaned up the kitchen. I filled her in on the party. "And thank you for the birthday girl statuette you sent. It's a wonderful collection. So thoughtful."

Quietly, Lindsay murmured, "Thanks for the pictures and flowers." Her voice was so low, I could barely make out what she said.

"How's school? Any thoughts about what you want to do next?"

"Prolly community college. I dunno." I could practically see her shrugging, head down. "Why do you care?"

Her surliness could be trouble. I didn't think I could handle any more drama.

Sure enough, the next night, the phone rang around midnight. It was Lindsay, and she had been drinking. The slur was obvious as she rambled about being legal now and maybe she could handle a baby. I was tired and still emotionally spent from dealing with my life. In other words, I was in no mood for her shit.

"Lindsay," I snapped. "This is neither the time nor the situation for this discussion. But we will have a discussion about this, *in detail*, in the very near future. I'm hanging up now, and I will see you this weekend."

First thing the next morning, I called Dan and asked him to take the kids to the zoo on Saturday so I could deal with Lindsay.

When the day came, the kids were so excited. They loved their Uncle Dan, and he was still as much fun as he had been when I was growing up. He never showed any preference between Sophia and Jake. He treated them both like spoiled grandkids and I, for the millionth time, thanked heavens for the great family that I had.

I picked Lindsay up, and we drove to Starbucks in silence. If I was a betting person, I'd lay down at least twenty bucks that she was hungover. She kept her sunglasses on, even inside. After getting our drinks, we sat at a corner table. She sighed impatiently and pulled out her phone to text. That was it, I had had it and I snapped.

I reached across the table and grabbed the phone and said, "Take those glasses off. I want to see your eyes to know that you are paying attention to me."

Lindsay did so sheepishly and looked at me. She was afraid to meet my gaze. I had never, ever yelled at her.

I took a breath and began. "I know that you were not happy at having to give Sophia up. But you made that decision. No one forced you to do it. You had the option to keep her, and you chose not to. She is a little girl, not a pair of shoes that you can buy and return and buy again. We are more than happy to have you involved in our lives. A child is blessed whenever someone loves them, and the more people who love a child, the more blessed they are. I am Sophia's mother. But you are a large part of her life, whether you are there or not. She will always know that she is so special that she has two mothers."

Lindsay grumbled.

"What's more, is that you need to get your shit together. You screwed up. And you got a 'get out of jail free' card. Most people don't. I certainly didn't."

Lindsay looked at me, "What do you mean, you didn't?"

I shook my head. Oh, the one-sided vision of teenagers. "Where do you think Jake came from? The stork?"

She shrugged. "Oh, I guess I never really thought about it."

"No, you probably didn't. And I was twenty-five, which is a lot better than fifteen, but I was still alone. Totally alone. For everything. Every doctor appointment. Even the delivery. Completely alone. The father left before he even knew I was pregnant. He didn't want kids anyway and never bothered to contact me again, even though I asked him to."

I paused, taking a breath.

Alone.

I still felt that hollowness in my chest. "I didn't want kids. I wanted to see the world. Now, all that I've seen is the World Showcase at Epcot. I gave up my whole life for Jake and now Sophia. And I'm glad that I did it, but believe you me, it has been a sacrifice. And I'm willing to do it. I am so happy that Jake and Sophia have each other."

Lindsay rolled her eyes.

I continued, "So take this time, and get your life together. Finish school. Figure out what you want to be when you grow up. Make something of yourself, of your life. Give Sophia a role model, someone to aspire to be like. Have fun, live a little. And stop being a brat. If you want to be an adult, then act like one. And that means taking responsibility for yourself and your actions and living with the results of your decisions. And part of that was to give up Sophia. Got it?"

She mumbled in agreement. I wasn't foolish enough to think this would be the end of the discussion, but I wanted her to know that I understood. However, she'd made a choice and part of being a grown-up was living with the consequences of one's actions.

I should know.

After bringing Lindsay back home, I used my spare time to do what all women do when depressed and overwhelmed—I got a haircut. My long hair was now about ten inches shorter and fell in an inverted, chin-length bob.

It actually felt like a fresh start.

And finally, I felt good about myself, until about a week later when I got a voice mail message from Matt.

"Um, Mags, it's me. Got a little problem. We're, um, supposed to go away for Ryan's, um, bachelor weekend. Just down to the Derby. But he says he changed his mind. He wants to go to Florida. To see you. Call me back."

Shit. Shit. Shit.

I called Matt back. "Tell him no, that it wouldn't be a good idea." I didn't even wait for him to say hello.

"I tried, he won't take no for an answer. He already bought plane tickets. He says he *has* to do this."

"Why?"

"When I ask him that, he won't answer. What are you going to do?"

"Jesus, Matt, I don't know. Maybe I can meet you out somewhere, so then I can feel it out. That's about all I've got."

"Shit. This is bad."

"I know."

Panic rising in my throat, I disconnected with Matt and immediately dialed Michele. Soon, the story of Lindsay and Ryan's impending visit spilled forth. Michele, demure and soft-spoken, was the consummate lady. "Maggie, this is seriously messed up."

"Michele, what am I going to do?" I pleaded. Like she could help me out of this colossal mess.

"Maggie, I have no answers for you, other than you need to look stunning. What are you going to wear?"

"Oh God, I didn't even think about it!" I laughed.

Michele laughed too. "Leave it all to me. Extreme Mom Makeover to the rescue!"

CHAPTER SIXTEEN

Friday finally arrived. I agreed to meet the guys at the bar in their hotel after work, and we'd have dinner there. It seemed like a safe place. Michele was taking Jake for the night, and Sophia was spending the night at Uncle Dan's. I felt like I was using all my over-nights for the kids so I could deal with my colossal screw-up of a life.

Nervous didn't come close to describing what I felt about seeing Ryan again. He was most likely going to hate me by the end of the weekend.

I took a deep breath. I could do this.

Aww, hell. I didn't even know what *this* was. It was like walking to the guillotine. I walked through the doors and turned left to go to the bar.

I saw them instantly. They were sitting on a couch, looking very comfortable. Glad someone was. My breath caught when I saw Ryan. He was as stunning as I remembered. I guess I was hoping that he would be fat, balding, and unattractive and that seeing him would repulse me.

I was not so lucky.

I clenched my fists tightly and tried to slow my breathing as I walked towards them. They saw me coming and stood up. I forced my gaze away from Ryan to Matt, forcing a grin. It probably looked more like a grimace.

Matt embraced me and kissed my cheek. He whispered in my ear, "Oh my God. You look amazing. Poor bastard doesn't stand a chance." I pulled back and smiled at my friend. I had missed him and was happy to have him back in my life. I hoped that at the end of this weekend, he would still be my friend.

I turned to greet Ryan. I hugged him, same as I had hugged Matt. "Oh my God, Maggie it is *so* good to see you." He didn't let go of me.

I thought I was going to spontaneously combust in his arms, heaven, and hell all at the same time.

I tried to pull back, and he finally released me, his hands sliding down my arms and stopping on my hands.

"You look stunning," he said.

I was caught in his eyes and could not look away. Finally, I pulled my hands away and turned to Matt. "So are we drinking here or what?"

Lord knows I needed a drink.

Matt motioned to the couch next to where he had been sitting. I sat down, and Ryan took his place on the chair, perpendicular to me. A waitress appeared and took my drink order. No one said anything until after the waitress reappeared with my merlot. I took a sip and then placed it on the small table in front of me.

Ryan finally cleared his throat. "Are we waiting for anyone else?"

I looked at him, confused. "No, I don't think so. Who were you expecting?"

"Um, I didn't know if your, if you were, ahh, bringing someone with you."

"Nope, just me."

Matt interrupted and started filling Ryan in on my career and the company that I was part owner of. He then turned to me and started telling me about how Ryan worked for the Solicitor General for the state of Ohio. I finally put my hand on Matt's, gesturing for him to stop. "We are adults here. I think we can manage to speak for ourselves."

"Right. Sorry, just trying to help."

"Matt, I appreciate it. Now, why don't you take a hike."

"Are you sure?"

I looked at him and glared.

"Um, okay. I'll go see when our table is going to be ready."

I sighed, took a long drink, and sat back on the couch. Ryan smiled at me. "Thanks."

I couldn't help but smile back at him. "So, you wanted to see me? Here I am."

"Here you are. You look stunning."

"You said that already."

"You look so good it bears repeating."

"Stop. You're making me blush." I looked at my feet. My face was on fire.

"But it's the truth. Plus, I like it when you blush. It's still very cute."

I looked up and met his eyes. "Please stop. You shouldn't be saying it."

Without realizing it, we were both leaning forward towards each other. I took another drink of my wine, and he took a sip of his scotch.

"Because your husband would get upset?"

"Because you're getting married. I'm sure your fiancée would not like to hear you talking to another woman this way."

He was looking at my hands, which were folded tightly in my lap.

"Maggie, I never thought I'd see you again."

"Same here."

"No, let me finish. I never thought I'd see you again. And if I did, you would be so mad at me for leaving you that you wouldn't speak to me. But here you are. You're sitting here and having a drink with me, and you're not even throwing it in my face. I would deserve it. I'd prefer if you'd do it with white wine, not the red though."

"Maybe," I shrugged, "but you know what they say ..."

"Don't make bacon naked?"

I laughed. "No, people in glass houses."

He looked at me, puzzled. He took a drink and put it down on the table. And then he put his hand on mine, resting top of my knees. It was almost like that first night, in the bar.

I cleared my throat. "So now, you've seen me, and I did not throw a drink in your face, and everything's all good. Closure and now you can go get married and live happily ever after."

"No, I can't ..."

At that exact moment, Matt came back. "Table's ready guys."

I stood up. "Um, I'm not hungry. I think I'd better go."

Ryan stood up too. "No, not yet. Sorry Matt, no dinner for me either. Maggie, will you come with me for a walk on the beach? There are some things I need to say to you."

I looked at Matt. I had almost escaped with my life intact. But I couldn't resist Ryan. I couldn't say no to a few more stolen minutes with him. I knew it was wrong and would only mean my heart breaking even further, but I could not say no.

I knew if I went for a walk with him my life, as I knew it, would be over. It was like a man making it through the Sahara and then refusing water. I couldn't do it. I needed to drink him in.

I looked at Ryan. "I'll meet you outside," I said, nodding to the patio doors. "I need to talk to Matt for a minute."

Ryan turned to walk away. I picked up my wine glass and drained it. "Okay, that, and about six more, and I might be ready to do this."

"Are you going to tell him?"

"I still don't know. I have to see what happens. He seemed really happy to see me, didn't he?"

"Of course he did. And I gotta say, I've never seen him look at Elise the way he looks at you."

"Don't say that."

"Why not? It's the truth."

"Because, even if he feels that way, or thinks he feels that way about me now, he won't, once he finds out."

"I hope you're not right. I'd like to see a happily ever after."

"Matt, have you met me? That's not how my life goes. But believe me, so would I." I hugged Matt and walked away.

I caught up with Ryan standing at the edge of the wooded pathway that led to the beach. He was holding his sandals and had rolled up his pants. I bent over to remove my shoes, wobbling on one foot like a drunken flamingo. Ryan reached out and steadied me, holding onto my elbow. I finally removed my sandals and straightened up. He kept his hands on my arm and gradually worked it down so that we were holding hands. We walked out onto the sand and down to the water's edge, side-by-side, and in silence for a few moments.

There was a sense of peace, walking along as the water lapped our feet, our hands together. I wanted to tell him, but I didn't even know how to start.

Finally, Ryan broke the silence. "Maggie, I don't even know how to start."

"Oh, good. That makes two of us." I dug my toes into the sound

"I, um, didn't think this would be so hard or awkward."

"Really? I didn't think it would be anything but.

"Ahh, but you're a better judge of character than I am."

"Usually." The word hung thick in the air.

"Okay, I guess I deserve that. But Maggie, I am so sorry for leaving you. I thought you understood why I had to go back home."

I look up at him, finally. "I did."

"I think this would be easier if you were angry. But if you were angry after all this time, it would mean that you still ..." he trailed off. Then I heard him whisper, "and I couldn't expect that."

"It's not that. It's just that I can't hold onto anger in my life. I've had a lot to be angry about, and it is very unhealthy for me. I have to let it go and move on. Otherwise, it eats away at me." I dig again, wishing I could disappear into the sand. I know what's coming.

"Sounds healthy. I don't know if I could do that. Let go of the anger, I mean. But I guess moving on is the way to go. And you've done well with that? Moving on?"

"As have you. Are you going to tell Elise that you came to see me?"

"Yes."

Wow. I didn't expect that kind of candid honesty. "How will she take it?"

"I'm guessing not well."

"I know I wouldn't."

"Well, especially since I'm calling off the wedding."

"*You're what?*" I stopped and turned to look at him. My knees felt like they were going to buckle.

Ryan looked at me and continued, "I can't go through with it. It's not fair to Elise. I care about her and what happens to her. But I can't marry her, not when I have these feelings about you. And whether or not I want to admit it, I do have feelings for you. I think they may have always been there, but I convinced myself that it was a long time ago and that you ... that it was all in the past. And that it was really no big deal. But hearing your voice on the phone, and now seeing you, I can't marry her when I think I am still in love with you."

My mouth fell open, and I stood there gawking at him.

He continued, "And I know that it's too late with you, but I'd rather spend my life alone and be free to think about you and to be available if you ever wanted me. I used to think about you all the time. I tried to convince myself that what we had wasn't real because if it was, then I was the world's biggest fool to leave you, no matter what my reasoning. But when I look at you, I know that it was the real thing. Do you know what I mean?"

I nodded.

"Maggie, do you ever think about me?" His voice was pleading, looking for affirmation about what he had just said. He reached out and touched my face. He wiped away a solitary tear that I didn't even realize was there.

If I hadn't been stunned by his declaration and his touch, I think I would have been able to come up with a better timed, more prepared answer. His candid declaration had my head spinning and I blurted out the first thing that popped into my head. "Every single day."

"Every day?"

I nodded. "Every day. I see your face every time I look at our son."

The world stopped.

His face froze for a moment, and then began to contort. "Our what?" He said. Then he yelled it again. "*OUR WHAT!?!?*" His hand fell from my face as if it had been burned.

This is what I knew was coming.

Somehow I thought his outpouring of feelings would prevent this type of reaction.

God, I was so stupid.

"Our son. He looks just like you, except he has my mouth. He's six and a half. His name is Jake. After my brother."

Ryan stumbled back a few steps and sank down into the sands. Was he in shock? I remembered how I felt, sitting on my bathroom floor, staring at the pregnancy test. I could relate.

I sat down next to him and did not say anything. I looked out onto the ocean and prayed for a happy ending. Finally, I realized Ryan was staring at me. He had a hard look on his face. I knew he was waiting for me to speak. So I did.

"I found out after you had left. I freaked out, of course. Matt was in Australia or wherever with Irene. I tried to get him to contact me. I didn't know what to do. The only time I heard from Matt while he was gone was when he emailed me to tell me that your dad ..." I trailed off. I took a deep breath before continuing. My voice was so low it was barely audible.

"You weren't returning my calls. So I sent you a note. I told you I would be there for you. But I wanted you to be there for me. And I asked you to contact me."

He nods, his movement barely perceptible.

I continued. "I kept trying Matt, even leaving him phone messages. But I never heard from him either. I had to do something. I needed help. So I left Boston, and I moved here. I bought a house and had the baby. Since I never heard from you or Matt, I wrote you both off. And believe you me, I was mad at you both for a very long time. But I had to keep moving forward for Jake. Three years ago, I adopted a little girl, so Jake has a sister. So that's it."

He still didn't say anything.

"When Matt showed up, we eventually realized that Irene had deleted all the messages from me. Matt thought I left without saying anything, and he had no way to get in touch with me. That's what the big blow-up was about. If Irene hadn't done that, then Matt would have made sure that you came back to me, at least to help out with the baby. She kind of ruined my life."

"Oh."

"Yeah, so Irene kind of screwed us all over."

"No wonder Matt kicked her out."

"It's about time."

"But I don't understand why you adopted the second kid." Out of all the questions I knew he must have had for me, this one was not expected.

"I told you, so Jake had a sibling."

"Can't you have any more?"

"I guess, but you kind of need someone else to help out with that."

"Aren't you married?"

I shook my head.

"When I talked to you, you said 'we' will be fine."

"I meant me and the kids."

"Oh, I thought ..."

"I know. It was easier that way."

"I still don't understand, why didn't you tell me?"

"What was I supposed to do? Leave you a message on your machine? 'Hi, Ryan. It's Maggie. You know, the girl you

163

dumped and won't call back. So, I know you want nothing to do with me, but, oh, by the way, I'm knocked up.' Seriously, give me a little credit."

"But if I had known ..."

"You didn't want kids. You made that perfectly clear."

"But neither did you."

"Yeah, but I wasn't left with much of a choice."

"But you didn't give *me* a choice."

"What? Yes, I did! Well, I tried to, anyway. I called you, how many times? I wrote to you. I told you that I would be there for you if you wanted me to, and I asked you to contact me. You didn't want me. You made your choice."

He was speechless.

I took a deep breath and continued. "I didn't list you on the birth certificate, just so it never resurfaced to ruin your career if you should be in public office."

He was incredulous.

I kept right on going. "Look, it obviously wasn't planned. It wasn't what either of us wanted. But it happened, and you made your choice, and I made mine."

I stood up and started walking back down the beach towards the hotel.

"Maggie wait!" I turned around, and Ryan was running towards me. "You don't get to walk away this time. You need to give me some answers!" He was yelling at me. It was the anger I expected.

Yet somehow, it seemed so out of place, considering his previous declarations. It took me by surprise, and I was shaking. Again. Why did I seem to be falling apart all the time?

The tirade continued, "How dare you? You can't drop this on me and run away! What the fuck? I have a kid? I cannot believe this! Here I am, about to throw away everything I have for you, and then you drop this on me!"

I stood there and took it all. He needed to get this out of his system. I owed him this for what I had done to him. "And Matt knew? You wouldn't let him tell me, would you?"

I shook my head and looked at my feet. I couldn't hold it in anymore.

"Look at me, goddammit. Look at me!"

I looked up and the tears were streaming down my face. I summoned my voice, but it only came out barely above a whisper, "Don't take him away from me."

"What?!?" Ryan was yelling as loud as I was quiet. Neither one of us seemed able to regulate the volume of our voices.

"I can't lose him too. He is my life. I've lost almost every person in my life that I love. Please don't take him away from me. Don't do that to me. Don't do that to him. Please."

"How dare you!" Ryan was yelling. "You have no right to stand here and ask *anything* of me! I cannot believe you! I cannot believe this!"

Matt must have heard the yelling. He ran up to us. We were almost back to the hotel, and people were watching the altercation. Matt stepped in between us and tried to make peace. "Hey guys, let's all calm down ..."

Matt was rudely interrupted by Ryan's right hook. Matt doubled over and grabbed his jaw. Someone was screaming. It was me. I bent over Matt to see if he was alright. When I stood up, Ryan was gone.

I looked at Matt, rubbing his jaw. I was trying not to hyperventilate. Matt looked at me. "Do I have something on my face? It doesn't hurt here or here so much, but right *here*." He quoted the line from Tommy Boy in an effort to lighten the mood. I started to laugh, and it turned into a hysterical cry. My knees started to buckle. Matt saw me going down and grabbed me.

"Maggie, stay with me. Don't pass out. Can you make it back to the hotel?"

I nodded and took some small steps. I was nestled into Matt's side, and he was supporting me. I felt like a shell of the person that I had been walking out onto the beach.

"Just take me to my car. I can't go back inside."

Matt steered me around the side of the hotel and into the parking lot. We crossed it, and I barely noticed the hard asphalt scraping the bottom of my feet.

"Is this the wrong time to make a joke about your awesome ride?"

I just looked at Matt, unable to even summon a smile.

"Guess so." He held the door open while I sat down. I just stared ahead at the steering wheel.

"Matt, I'm sorry that you got hurt. It should have been me. I wish he had hit me."

"He would never ..."

"I know," I cut him off, "but I wish he had so that I could feel the pain on the outside to match what I'm feeling on the inside."

"He'll come around, Mags. You'll see."

"He told me he was going to call off the wedding."

"He did? Did he say why?"

"He said it was unfair to marry Elise when he loved me. And then I ruined everything." I shook my head. "I gotta go before I lose it again. The kids are out tonight, so I think I have an appointment with some Xanax." I smiled a feeble smile.

"I'll call you in the morning. Hopefully, I can find him and talk some sense into him."

"I hope you can."

CHAPTER FOURTEEN

The jangling of the house phone woke me out of my drug-induced haze. I didn't know how long it had been ringing. It could have been the second ring or third round of rings. I rolled over and looked at the clock.

Eight.

Who could be calling this early? The events of the past evening came rushing back. Matt! Hopefully, he had news, and it would be good. I had no hope that it would be Ryan. I bolted upright and grabbed the phone.

"Hello," I said anxiously. I was not prepared for what I heard next.

"Maggie, it's Dan. We, um, have a little problem here." He sounded very serious.

"Is Sophia okay? Is she sick? I'll come and get her."

"Um, no, she's not sick. Has Lindsay called you?"

"Not that I'm aware of, but I was asleep. Lemme check my cell."

I got up and hobbled down the hall to the kitchen, where I had left my phone to charge. "Nope. No calls. What's up? Did she stay out all night again?"

"Yeah, um, she's not here. But that's not it."

The hair raised on the back of my neck, and I felt a full-on panic attack coming on. "Dan, what's going on?"

"Maggie, I don't know how to tell you this ..."

"Just spit it out!" I snapped. I had no patience for anything right now.

"Lindsay took off. And she took Sophia with her."

Oh my God.

"No!" I screamed.

"I think she'll be okay with Lindsay ... I think Lindsay will take good care of her."

"I have to call the police."

"I wish you wouldn't."

"How long has she been gone?"

"I don't know. I heard her come in around two a.m., and I didn't see her car when I got up around seven. I'm guessing she went up to Ocala."

Her mother, Dan's ex-wife, Vanessa, lived in a trailer park in Ocala. She lost custody of the kids when Lindsay turned up pregnant at fifteen. Sophia's biological father was Vanessa's twenty-five-year-old neighbor. Lindsay had been banned from seeing him in lieu of statutory rape charges, but she was not happy about it, and it was a great source of her surliness.

"Have you called her?"

"I did, but she didn't answer."

Okay, let me think. My first instinct was to call the police and have them issue an Amber alert, but I wasn't sure that it was necessary. "Lindsay wouldn't *really* take her, like, for good? She wouldn't be that stupid, would she?"

"I hope not. Sometimes, I just don't know with that girl."

I sighed. I wasn't even aware that I had that much air left in me.

"What if I text her and check-in? Then I can give her a time to get Sophia back by. If she doesn't reply or bring her back by that time, then I'll call the police."

I could almost feel my uncle's pain through his silence. His words came out slowly as if each one weighed a tremendous amount. "Okay, I guess. It's better than calling the police right away. God, I can't believe she would do something this stupid."

"Alright, lemme text her and I'll let you know when I hear from her. If I don't or hear something bad, I'll let you know before I call the police."

I picked up my cell and texted Lindsay.

Sophia ok? Let me know. She needs 2 b back by 5, or else I have to call police. Plz respond!

I sank down on the floor right in the kitchen and buried my head in my hands.

How could this be happening?

My life had entirely imploded in the last fourteen hours. I had to believe that Lindsay would do the right thing and bring Sophia home safe and sound. I had to believe that Ryan would not try to take Jake away. I had to believe that I would end this day with my family intact.

If I didn't, I wasn't sure that I could survive.

My cell beeped in my hand and startled me. It was from Lindsay. I hastily pressed the buttons with shaking hands to see what she said.

Sophias good, t8kng her to Disney w/caleb. B back by 5, kk.

I breathed a sigh of relief. She was going to come back. I tried to squash any thoughts of doubt that Lindsay was leading me on. I was uneasy that Caleb, the dad, was involved.

169

He was scum, and I didn't trust him. It worried me that he would try to pull something.

Oh shit.

I quickly punched in Dan's number.

"Hello?" he said anxiously.

"Lindsay texted me back. Sophia's fine. They're with Caleb. Apparently, they're going to Disney. She says she'll have her back by five."

Dan exhaled, "Oh thank God."

"Dan, does Lindsay know about, I mean, does she know that I have money? Do you think Caleb knows? What if he's cooking up a scheme to ask for ransom?"

"Crap, I didn't even think of that. I never told Lindsay about the money per se, but I can't say that she never heard it mentioned in passing. I don't even think I told Vanessa, but I may have said that there was a settlement after the accident."

"That's the only thing that makes me uneasy." It wasn't the only thing, but I could feel Dan's pain as it was. Lindsay was his little girl, just as Sophia was mine.

Her life was already a mess. This wasn't going to help things.

"I guess we'll have to wait and see."

It was the story of my life right now.

After disconnecting, I remained on the kitchen floor, unable to move. I don't even know how long I was immobile on the tile for when the doorbell rang. Unfortunately, my back and legs had tightened up, making it nearly impossible for me to stand without dragging myself up. I hobbled to the door and opened it slightly.

It was Ryan.

Matt was down the walk a little as if he were here to supervise. I didn't say anything and opened the door. I was wearing what I had slept in, only a tank top and little knit shorts. I didn't even want to think about what my face looked like. I stepped aside and Ryan entered. I motioned for Matt to come in too, but he shook his head.

Great.

I closed the door and turned to face a glaring Ryan. I limped by him and sat down on the couch. His expression softened as he entered tentatively, sitting on the opposite couch.

I should have said something, but I had no words. I waited for the demands and verbal attacks that would begin any moment.

Ryan finally cleared his throat. "I want to meet him."

I nodded, "Of course. He's at a friend's right now, but I expect him back in a few hours. I'll need to talk to him first, though, to prepare him."

"And I want visitation."

How the hell could I go through this right now?

My head was swimming, and I could barely focus, let alone assemble a coherent thought. I didn't have the strength to fight. But I had to. I inhaled sharply, trying to clear my head. "How exactly is that supposed to work?"

"I want the summer and holidays. All holidays."

The tears I'd been biting back began streaming down my face. "How am I supposed to send him halfway across the country with someone he doesn't even know? He's not even seven yet!"

"Well, you should have thought of that, shouldn't you?" Ryan's voice was cold and bitter.

At that moment, something in me snapped. All of the emotion of the past day came flooding out in a string of profanities.

"Fuck you, Ryan. Don't sit here and act all high and mighty on me. I called you. So many times. I wrote to you, asking you to call me. You did not, not once. I was not going to leave you a voicemail telling you about your child. You wrote me off, lock, stock, and barrel. And in the process, you wrote your son off too. Not my fault. Your decision, now deal with it."

I was on a roll and going with it. "I have spent the last seven years alone, fending for myself. I have never asked anything of you. I don't even have to legally grant you visitation until we have established paternity, as I'm sure you are well aware. And then, you would owe me support, retroactive, of course. But I'm not going to do any of that. But I know my son, and I know what he needs and how he needs to be handled. So, I will let you meet him today, although it is the worst possible time."

Now I was rambling, my voice high and screechy. "I will let you meet him, and then we will need to come up with a plan that is acceptable to both of us. I'm willing to meet you halfway, but you need to do the same. Otherwise, no go."

Ryan closed his eyes for a minute. "Fine. Should I stay here until he comes back, or just come back later?"

"As odd as this sounds considering the tone of this conversation, I need you to stay right now." I hope he didn't detect the desperation in my voice. "Now, could you go ask Matt to come in, while I try to put myself together?"

Ryan got up and went outside. I took the opportunity while his back was turned to haul myself up and hobble down the hall. I didn't want Ryan seeing me so weak right now. I took a quick shower and dressed. No amount of makeup would hide the bags under my eyes.

When I ventured back down the hall, I heard Ryan and Matt talking in the kitchen. I went in and sat quietly on a stool at the counter. Matt put a mug of coffee in front of me. "Still skim and sugar?"

I smiled weakly at him and nodded. I couldn't help but think about the morning that Ryan brought me coffee. I pushed the happy memory down and focused on the present, miserable situation.

I took a sip of my coffee. I had never eaten supper last night, only having the wine. Between the wine, Xanax, and stress, the coffee felt like it was burning a hole in my stomach. But I needed a clear head, so I took another sip.

Matt looked around. "Ry said Jake's at a friend's. Where's Sophia?"

I inhaled sharply and closed my eyes. "I don't know," I whispered.

Ryan let out a scoff. "Oh great, you're mother of the year, aren't you? Don't even know where your own kid is."

Matt cut him off, stepping in front of him and bending in close to me. "What do you mean you don't know?" His voice was full of concern and panic.

I exhaled, meeting only Matt's eyes. "She went to stay with Dan last night. Well, Lindsay took her during the night. She is supposed to bring her back by five, but I'm not sure she'll follow through."

Matt jumped up. "Whoa Mags. Do you mean Sophia's been kidnapped?"

"Legally speaking, I guess so. I just have to believe that Lindsay will do the right thing, enjoy their day together and return Sophia to where she belongs. If Sophia's not back, I'm calling the police and having an Amber alert issued."

Ryan interjected. "Who's Lindsay?"

"She's my cousin and Sophia's biological mother. I legally adopted Sophia from her. She was fifteen when she had her. She's eighteen now and her surly teenage attitude has only gotten worse. Her boyfriend, the baby-daddy, is twenty-eight now, and he's with them. I do not trust him. I'm afraid he's going to try and get a ransom."

"Just call the police," Ryan retorted.

"I wish I could, but I don't want to ruin Lindsay's life any more than it already is. Part of her didn't want to give her baby up, but she didn't have a choice. I have tried to include her in Sophia's life so she doesn't feel cheated. This way, she can live her life but still get to know her child. I'm trying to give her the best of both worlds, but she's too immature to realize it. I keep hoping that she'll pull herself together and make the most out of her life."

Matt said, "But why would you do that? You already bailed her out once."

"I want her to have the second chance at a life that I never did." My eyes met Ryan's for the first time. He looked away first.

"So, that's how my awesome day is going. Any more interrogations, or can I call Jake now and talk to him?"

"Fine" he grumbled, looking down. I could only imagine what he was feeling or thinking.

There were too many thoughts swirling around my brain. Michele was bringing Jake home. I knew she'd want details, but I couldn't think about that now. My mind kept going back to Sophia. Desperately, I tried to focus on the fact that Lindsay, although she'd done something tremendously stupid, was not inherently a bad or malicious person. She said she'd bring Sophia back, so I had to trust that she would.

Then I had to figure out how to handle Jake. And Ryan for that matter. I felt like I was running a marathon in my head while balancing plates on sticks. I thought back to the Chinese acrobats that had performed at Jake's school last year. I was a one-woman version of that show, trying to keep all seven plates from falling. A small smile spread across my face as I thought of that day with Jake. The contentment and happiness of the day carried me away from my own living hell for just a moment until I was startled by Matt's voice.

"Maggie, are you okay?" Matt's voice seemed overly cautious and scared. It took me a moment to be able to focus on him. "You have a really weird expression on your face."

"I'm just trying to compartmentalize my life and squash down all of the ... well everything ... so I can be put together for my kids. It's what I do."

Ryan had daggers in his glare. I was surprised at the intensity of his animosity, but it needed to be snuffed before Jake got home.

"Ryan, I want to ask you to leave." He opened his mouth to interject, but I held up my hand to silence him and continued. "You and Matt need to move the car down the street and then wait out on the dock. I don't want you in the house when Jake gets here. Otherwise, he might be overwhelmed. I want to talk to him first. I have no doubt that he'll want to see you right away, but this just gives him some room to breathe and make the decision for himself. I think he needs a little control over the situation right now."

I wish I had some control.

"Whatever he says, I'll call you and let you know. You need to give him a little space. He's just a little boy, and his world is about to change. Help him by doing this." I met his gaze and held it. I could not for the life of me believe that I was composed at this moment. But Ryan and Matt got up to leave, so they must have actually listened to me.

Wow.

Now, I just had to steel myself for facing my son. Michele, God bless her, dropped Jake off and let him run in on his own. He came banging in through the kitchen door

"Hey Bud, out here!" I called from my place on the living room couch.

Jake stayed in the kitchen. It sounded like he was playing with something.

"Jake, come out here. I need to talk to you."

"But Mom, I wanna play with my ..."

"*Jake*, it's important. I need you to come out here. Please work with me, Bud."

"Fine" he muttered as he slowly walked out. "Where's Sophia?"

"Um," *Don't lose it! Don't lose it!* "She's with Lindsay. She'll be back in a little while." *Please, God.* "But that's not what I need to talk to you about. Come sit with me." I patted the couch. Jake was an excellent snuggler. He cozied right up to me, and I held onto him tightly. "Jake, remember a little while ago when you asked about your dad?"

"Yeah," he pulled away to look at me and gave me a suspicious eye.

"Well, how would you like to meet him?"

"What do you mean? Does he live here in Florida?"

"No, he doesn't. He lives far away, and we didn't know how to get in contact with each other, until just recently."

"Why didn't you just call his cell?"

I smiled. "Oh, Buddy. I didn't have his number, and he didn't have mine. Anyway, we found out where each other lives, and he wants to meet you."

"What's his name?"

"His name is Ryan Milan. He is a lawyer, and he lives in Ohio. He even went to Ohio State."

"Cool, just like my great-grandpa! Can I tell him that? Do you think he's ever been to a real football game? Maybe he could take me. That would be even better than fishing! I can fish any time."

I interrupted before I totally lost him. "So, Jake, would you like to meet him now?"

"Sure," he shrugged. I could tell his mind was running in a thousand different directions. I extracted myself from him and went through the kitchen and out the back door. The guys were sitting on the edge of the dock, looking out onto the water. Their postures were stiff, and it didn't look like they were speaking. Ryan had his phone clutched in his hand.

I pulled my phone out of my pocket and called Ryan. I watched him press a button and hold the phone up to his ear without a greeting.

"Come on up. He's excited."

Ryan disconnected and started to rise. I watched him walk first towards me, then past me without so much as an acknowledgment. I sighed and turned around, stepping in front of him so that I could introduce him to his son.

CHAPTER FIFTEEN

The introduction went as smoothly as could be expected. Ryan extended a hand, and Jake looked so adorable shaking it. I should have taken a picture.

Then the questioning began.

Ryan visibly relaxed and did not seem to mind the interrogations. Jake wanted to know the most obscure things about him. I stood to the side and watched.

Part of me felt wonderful that this was happening and that it was going so smoothly, all things considered. Part of me was miserable that Ryan had not been part of Jake's life right from the get-go. Part of me was still wishing that Matt had never found me and that Ryan had never come back into my life because of all the complications. And part of me was terrified, thinking about Sophia. I stood there, fracturing into thousands of pieces, and needed to do something to pull myself back together. I went into my bedroom and grabbed my camera. However this turned out, it was still a momentous occasion and deserved to be photographed. Jake loved pictures, especially family ones. He needed this.

When I returned to the living room Ryan grimace at the camera in my hand.

But my son beamed. "Great Mom! Now I can take a picture into school to show everybody my new dad! And then they'll have to believe me. It won't be like Richie Hunt, who makes up having a daddy when everyone knows that it's not real, and the guy is just his mom's new boyfriend. But you never have boyfriends, so they'd have to believe me."

I laughed, and Ryan smiled, in spite of himself. "Well, we don't have to worry about that Buddy. Everyone will know that this is your dad. You guys look a lot alike."

They straightened themselves out and sat next to each other on the couch. Diligently, they smiled and let me snap away. Content that I had gotten a good shot or two, I put the camera down. I looked at Ryan and said, "I'll get your email and send them to you if you want."

He looked down, not wanting to meet my gaze. "That'd be good. It would be nice to have a picture of us."

Suddenly Jake jumped up. "I know!"

I looked at him, startled. "You know what, Buddy?"

"I know why Ryan looks familiar. He's that guy in the picture in your nightstand next to your bed. I saw you looking at the picture one time, and you were really sad. You put it away, but I found it. Right? It's him, right?"

Now it was my turn not to be able to look up. "You're right, but I wish you wouldn't snoop through my things, Mister."

I peeked at Ryan. It appeared that for a moment, just a moment, his gaze had softened towards me. Then, quick as a flash, the hardness was back again, and he turned away.

Jake resumed with the questions. It was occurring to him that he was going to have a lot more family, and it fascinated him. Ryan told him about his sisters, Jake's aunts, Jennifer and Kelly, and their children. Jake said, "Do I have a grandmother too? I only have one, sort of, Grandma Marcy, but she's not really related to me. But Mom says that it doesn't matter, but is this one really related to me?"

Ryan laughed again, amused by his son. Who wouldn't be? "Yes, you have a grandmother. Her name is Mary Louisa, and she is going to be so pleased to meet you. I bet she's going to spoil you rotten."

Jake said, in the matter-of-fact way that only a child can, "Well, my grandpa already spoils me rotten. Do I get to have another grandpa too? That'd be cool to have two grandfathers."

Ryan's smile faded. "No, I'm sorry to tell you that my dad, your grandfather, died seven years ago before you were born."

"Oh, that's too bad. What was his name?"

"His name was Philip. Philip Milan.

"Philip is just like me. My real name is Jacob Philip, but everybody just calls me Jake. Except for Mom. She calls me Bud."

Ryan froze. The air was so thick that I wondered if it actually contained any oxygen. It didn't seem to. I certainly couldn't breathe. I didn't know whether he was going to yell or cry. I didn't know if he was going to hug Jake or walk away forever. Before the question could be answered, the door opened, and Lindsay came trudging through, carrying a sleepy Sophia.

"Oh thank God!" I yelled, flying across the room to grab Sophia out of Lindsay's arms. I pulled my little girl to my chest and hugged her as tightly as I could.

My angel smiled at me and said, "Wow, that's a great big hug. Can I have another?" I obliged and kissed her repeatedly. She let me love on her for a moment more and then squirmed to get down. She ran over to Jake, before noticing Ryan. Instantly she switched into Shy Sophia.

After seeing my daughter was safe and well, my rage engulfed me until everything I was seeing was tinged with red. I grabbed Lindsay by the elbow and hauled her outside, letting the door slam behind me. I inhaled deeply, preparing to let her have it.

"Before you start," she interjected before I could even get going, "I just want to say how sorry I am. I thought I could do it. But I couldn't. I can't be her mom. She is so needy. Every five seconds it's 'I have to go potty! I can't walk! I'm tired!' " Lindsay began sobbing. She continued, "I couldn't even last one day with her. I don't know what she likes or how to stop her from being cranky. I couldn't understand some of what she said, and then she was getting mad and upset because I couldn't do what she wanted. And she just wanted you."

"Well, I'm the only mother that she knows."

Lindsay looked down. "I know. I guess I thought it would be easy, and that she would know who I was."

"She does know you, as her cousin, who she loves and adores. Someday, in the future, you can tell her the truth. You can tell her that you made a very hard decision, but it was the best thing for her and you. Sometimes, being a mother is all about making the hard decisions. Now call your father."

I opened the door and peeked in on my children. Jake was still sitting on the couch and was playing with a car. Sophia was taking out her tea party paraphernalia and had already donned her dress-up clothes. Ryan was sitting on the couch next to Jake and appeared to be absorbing the scene. Matt had come in and was sitting on the other couch, getting served a gourmet meal of pretend cake and tea. He looked at me, and I nodded. I closed the door and sat down on the step. Lindsay came and sat down next to me.

"Am I in trouble?" she asked sheepishly.

"I don't know. You certainly aren't going to be allowed to be alone with Sophia for a while. Any visits will be strictly supervised. You have to rebuild my trust."

"Okay," she mumbled.

"To be honest, Lindsay, I don't even know what I'm doing with my life right now, so it's going to be hard to figure out what to do with you. Jake's father showed up, and I'm not sure how that's going to play out."

"That hot guy in there is Jake's dad? Score one for you!"

I looked at her, unamused.

"Sorry," she mumbled again. Then she looked at me. She opened her mouth as if to say something and stopped. I motioned for her to continue. "The worst part of the day was Caleb. He didn't want anything to do with Sophia, or me really. I think I had this dream that he would see us and fall back in love with me and her, and we would all live happily ever after. But he has a new girlfriend, and I wonder if he ever loved me." She was starting to cry. "And my whole life is ruined, and he doesn't care. Even if I had kept Sophia, well, he wouldn't have helped at all, and my life would have been a dead end."

No duh.

Finally, she said, "I guess that's what people have been telling me all along. Even my mom said I didn't want to be saddled with a kid. Kids are just there to ruin their parent's life."

That's great parenting advice. Vanessa's a strong candidate for Mother of the Year.

"Well, that's not exactly true. Children can be the best part of your life when you are in a place to provide for yourself and them. And preferably, with a committed partner who is willing to share in the responsibility and fun. But you have to be able to take care of yourself first."

"I guess so. Maybe someday I'll be ready to do this."

"I'm sure you will, in the future. I've got to go back inside. I'll talk to you later." I got up and turned to walk into the house.

"Maggie?"

"What Lindsay?"

"I'm sorry."

I couldn't even acknowledge her. I nodded and went back into the house. Ryan and I had a lot to hash out. I didn't see any way that it was going to be pleasant. But Sophia was safe and sound and home where she belonged. Now I just needed to make Ryan see what a bond the kids had and how it would be wrong to pull them apart.

CHAPTER SIXTEEN

Somehow, reason prevailed over emotion, and Ryan and I were quickly able to come to an agreement about how we would work visitation that evening. Not surprisingly, it required a lot more work on my part, but it, at least for now, removed the threat of a custody battle. I was willing to pay that price.

Our arrangement had the kids and me packing up and driving to Ohio for a few weeks as soon as Jake got out of school. It would require me either taking a leave of absence from my job or arranging to fully telecommute. Best case, I had to cut my hours dramatically. It would probably be feasible, considering I worked from home much of the time anyway. My dad would check in on the house and keep things under control in Florida while we were away.

Lodging was more difficult to figure out. Staying in a hotel would be tricky with the kids unless I could find one with a kitchen. I didn't want to be eating out three meals a day for weeks on end. And I would want it to be near Ryan's so that I wasn't trekking all over an unfamiliar city daily.

The next few weeks were busy and flew by. Ryan called about every other day, just to talk to Jake. He did not speak to me, other than a cursory greeting if I happened to answer the phone. Pretty soon, Jake anticipated the call and ran to get the phone each night. I tried not to take it personally. Ryan had a lot on his plate too. I was unsure about whether or not he was going to go through with the wedding. It was pretty obvious that his previous declarations of love were now null and void.

However, I was ready to get off the emotional roller coaster, so I set about planning, which was always a comfort for me. Excessive planning and micromanagement was a coping mechanism that I used to combat the utter loss of control that I was experiencing. At least I got *something* out of all that therapy.

Being busy was the only way I survived the day-to-day. My calendar was so full, I didn't have time to sit and think. Jake's schedule was packed with end-of-the-year festivities and field trips, which he loved telling his dad about. I was trying to pack and organize to be away for several weeks. At work, my partner, Paul and I tied up loose ends and moved all my work to an online platform for the summer. I wasn't sure how long we were going to be staying in Ohio, so I prepared for a long stay.

In preparation, I spent more hours at the office. As a result, Sophia spent more time in daycare and with my dad. I assuaged my ever-present guilt with the thought that we'd be spending lots of time together over the summer. I also needed to make sure the kids spent lots of time with Uncle Dan before we left since he'd miss them too. Lindsay remained distant and was only allowed to be with Sophia with supervision. She seemed remorseful about her stunt, and I tried to put it in the past. I was no less guilty of poor judgment at times, so I was trying to be forgiving. I was not successful, but I tried. I hoped the summer would help with that.

My "spare" time was spent researching Ohio online, trying to plan things to do. I'd found a hotel that rented out long-term, that didn't seem too seedy. The best part was it was only a few miles from Ryan's address. I wasn't sure about his living arrangements. He and Elise had been living together, but I didn't know if it was a house or apartment. I still wasn't even sure about the wedding. Ryan never said, and I couldn't bear to ask the question.

There was no reason for him not to get married. He wasn't going to give me a chance. I had to accept the marriage, but I was concerned about the introduction of another new parent into Jake's life.

I had emailed Ryan my plans to embark on the drive the Thursday after Memorial Day. It was about a sixteen-hour drive, so I was planning to drive as much as I could in one day and then stay overnight somewhere. I don't think it ever occurred to him that such a long drive with two young kids would be difficult. I was hoping he would offer to fly down and drive up with us, but he didn't. I don't know why the thought even occurred to me. It was pretty obvious that he would rather amputate a testicle than spend sixteen hours in a car with me. So, I did the best I could, and I managed.

Alone.

The story of my life.

Armed with dual DVD players, tons of snacks, new CDs, and other mystery bags of new toys, as well as a van packed to the hilt, the kids and I set out on our trip northward. We got a later start than planned and didn't get going until after lunch. I called Ryan once we got on the road, just to let him know. He was out of breath and seemed excited. I suppressed a thought about what I could have been interrupting, especially with his wedding only a few days ago. When he answered, I rambled on, talking about the late start and my plans to drive until I couldn't any longer. I said that I had all the stuff in the GPS so I should be all set.

Then there was silence on the line.

"Ryan, are you still there? Ryan, can you hear me?" Damn spotty cell service.

He cleared his throat and said, "Well, actually, um, I have a new address. Moved into a bigger place this week."

Okay, what did that mean? I asked him to text me the address so I could update my GPS the next time I stopped. Thanks to tons of bickering and fighting, the drive was longer and harder than I'd anticipated. Sophia, I expected it from, but Jake's behavior was hard for me to accept. He was such a good kid that the constant mouthing off and loud volume in the back seat surprised me. I stopped when I could find a fast food place with a play area so the kids could blow off some steam. What should have taken eight hours took about ten, and I was wiped out when I finally checked into a motel for the night, just north of Charlotte.

I carried a sleeping Sophia in and had to wake Jake up to get inside, as he was now too big for me to lift. The kids fell right back to sleep, but slumber eluded me for a while. While I blamed it on too much caffeine, it was more due to anxiety over what this visit would bring. I was very nervous about what was to come.

I used my GPS to look up the new address that Ryan gave me and found that it was outside the city, as opposed to downtown, where the previous address was. I called the motel and canceled our reservation. I wondered if Ryan would let us stay with him when we got in, at least until I could find a closer hotel. I didn't know where to look, and this luxury three-star motel didn't have internet access.

We would get on the road early in the morning, putting us into Columbus around dinner. Maybe I could find a hotel for the night on the drive into town. Finally, with a plan in place, I drifted off into a deep but shortened sleep.

It felt like it was only about five minutes later when a little person was poking me and sitting on my chest and asking for breakfast. I looked at the clock, and it was already seven, which was about when I wanted to get up anyway. I put the TV on for the kids while I took a quick shower and got them dressed. Within minutes, our belongings were repacked in the overnight bag, and the cooler was once again stocked with ice. We ate a quick drive-thru breakfast and got back on the road. The kids were more in the routine of traveling and did better on Day Two. We made good time and hit Columbus, unfortunately, just in time for the evening rush hour.

So close, yet so far.

My phone rang again on the seat beside me. It was Ryan again.

"Where are you?" he said, not even saying hello.

"Umm, getting onto 270 from 33. Traffic is kind of heavy."

"Okay, so you're about twenty minutes out. You're gonna take exit 41B, which is Route 40, or East Main."

"Okay, I'll look for it. Lemme get off the phone so I can pay attention to traffic and signs. I guess we'll be there soon."

He hung up without saying goodbye either. I sighed a little. It was going to be a long couple of weeks. After our walk on the beach—just prior to me blowing it—we'd confessed our feelings. I couldn't stop missing him and longing for him, no matter how much of an ass he was being. He was angry and had a right to be. He needed time to work through it.

But that talk had reignited the tiny little shimmer of hope that I'd buried deep within. And then it blew wide apart, flaming and burning everything in its path. I was trying to grasp at the flecks of light to hold onto that hope, but they kept slipping through my hands.

And now here I was, driving a thousand miles to share our son. With him. And his new wife. The thought of his *wife* made my stomach flip and the bile rise. I could only imagine what he'd told her and her opinion of me. There was no doubt it was anything but favorable.

I'm guessing he left out the part about deciding he was still in love with me until he found out about our love child. I'd probably omit that too. I wondered how the whole discovery (look at me using legal terms!) had gone down. Oh, well, I was sure that at some point in the next few weeks, I would find out.

The kids' excitement level rose the closer we got to our destination. As I was exiting, I was relieved to see a hotel right there. The GPS had us about five minutes away from Ryan's house, so that would be a good place to stay tonight. I'd call for a reservation after we checked in with Ryan. There were a lot of chain restaurants right off the exit too. While I longed for home-cooked food after two days on the road, I knew that I was in for another night of chicken fingers and mac 'n cheese. As I turned off into the subdivision and approached the house, my anxiety spiked to an all-time high. There were five or six cars in the driveway and in front of the house.

Uh oh. What the hell was I walking into?

I parked the van in the one vacant spot and got out. I stretched my back quickly, trying to smooth my wrinkled clothes. I was wearing gym shorts and a t-shirt and flip-flops. Comfortable traveling clothes, but not exactly appropriate for meeting a whole host of people who probably already thought poorly of me. I also tried to ignore the feeling that I really, *really* had to pee. In my haste to arrive, I'd already been ignoring the feeling for much too long.

I straightened my shoulders. I could do this. After all, this wasn't really about me, it was about Jake spending quality time with his father. And a whole lot of company, it seemed.

Before I could get around to open the door, Jake's door slid open, and he flew out. He had an ear-to-ear grin on his face. "Is this it? Is this my dad's house? Is he here? Can I go see him?"

"Settle down, Bud. Lemme get Sophia out, and we'll go in."

I looked at him and noticed he was fidgeting, doing the tell-tale pee dance. Great. He never liked to stop doing something interesting to go to the bathroom, and now we had to walk into a house full of people and have a fight about the bathroom.

I knew I should have stopped one last time.

"Jake, as soon as we get inside, I want you to go to the bathroom."

"Mom, I don't have to go."

"No arguments. Think of how embarrassing it would be to have an accident as soon as you get here."

He grumbled "fine" as I extracted Sophia from her car seat. With Sophia balanced on my hip and Jake was next to me, we headed toward the entrance. Jake was about to ring the bell when the door flew open. It was a girl, about ten, with long dark hair and even longer legs. She was almost as tall as I was. "They're here!" she squealed and turned and ran back into the house. Jake followed her in and was met in the hall by Ryan. Jake ran to him and gave him a big hug. It was touching, and I wish that I had my camera to record the moment. A flash caught my eye, and I saw a room full of people on the other side of Ryan, some of whom were taking pictures.

I was relieved and made a mental note to track the camera owners down so that I could get pictures for Jake.

Sophia squirmed to get down and ran to Ryan too. He picked her up and hugged her as well. He turned his back to me and led the kids into the living room where all the people were. I spotted a hallway with a bathroom next to us and motioned for Jake to go in. He gave me a look but then ran in and shut the door. Ryan looked at the door and laughed, keeping his back to me. I hoped that this was not a sign of how things were going to go, but I did not hold out a lot of hope either.

Once Jake came out of the bathroom, Ryan took him, with his hand on his back, and started introducing him to the room full of people. First was to his mother, Jake's grandmother. Mrs. Milan was about my height, and still probably a size eight. You could picture her going to the Y and swimming daily. Her short hair was a golden blond, fading into silver that made her look dignified and regal. Then Jake was introduced to his aunts, Kelly and Jennifer. Kelly was the sister who was two years older than Ryan. Kelly was tall and thick with a long braid hanging down her back and a baby strapped to her front. The baby girl looked to be about six months old. She was married to a short, squat balding guy named Jeff. Their older son, Marc, was twelve, and their younger son, Billy, was seven. Marc had Ryan and Kelly's dark coloring but was built like his dad, while Billy was built like Jake, long and lean. Jake and Billy looked like they were brothers.

Jennifer was the oldest of the Milan siblings, and the mother of Kylie, the girl who had opened the door. A husband or father wasn't present or mentioned, so I figured I would find that out later.

I felt like I was walking into a firing squad. People's eyes kept shifting to me and then quickly away if they accidentally made eye contact. I was mostly hanging back, watching Jake work the room. He was a bit shy, but his curiosity won out, and he at least said hello to everyone. There were a few cousins there too, and Ryan's grandmother, his dad's mother, was sitting in an overstuffed chair in the corner. She had to be closing in on ninety and looked frail. Jake, when introduced, looked her over and gave her a great big hug, probably a little too exuberant for her wispy frame. Good thing she was sitting down. A smile spread over her face and up to her milky eyes until she looked up at me. The smile faded abruptly, and she turned away.

That about said it all.

I took Sophia's hand and made my way to the bathroom. I took care of my needs and then Sophia's, washed up, splashed a little water on my face, and went back out to join the fracas. I tried to hold my head up and retain some sense of dignity, but it was hard. I looked around but did not see anyone who could be Elise. People were moving in and out of the house and into the backyard, where I could smell the grill. Maybe she was out there. I knew in my head, I was picturing a well-put-together woman, not unlike Liza from Ryan's work all those years ago. I couldn't picture him with any other type. Or me.

Mrs. Milan came up to me. "You must be Maggie. I'm Mary Louisa Milan. It's so nice to meet you."

"And this is my daughter, Sophia. Sophia, say hello to Mrs. Milan." Sophia turned towards my legs shyly.

"Oh, call me Grammy, just like all the other kids do," she said, squatting down in front of Sophia. "I bet you like princesses, don't you?" Sophia nodded, taking her fingers out of her mouth. "Kylie set up some princess tents in the backyard for you. Do you want to go see them?"

Sophia nodded and smiled, and Kylie came over and led Sophia away, holding her hand. Mrs. Milan smiled and stood up, with only the slightest of groans. "The knees aren't what they used to be, but the little ones keep me moving."

I just nodded. I was so overwhelmed and just wished this day was over so I could be in the quiet of the hotel room with the kids. Mrs. Milan must have sensed my unease. She put her hand on my arm and said, "I hope this cookout is alright. I told Ryan it was probably not the best idea to ambush you with these people. He rarely listens to me though. I did think that you might like some home cooking after being on the road, but I thought you would like to put your feet up and relax a little more."

I smiled and nodded. "The food smells wonderful. Much better than the fast food I've been eating for the last few days."

"Okay, then, let's get you some food. It looks like the kids are occupied with the other kids for a few minutes, so why don't you get something to eat and sit down."

I took the woman's wise advice and made my way out onto the deck. No one else was out there. It gave me a minute or two to catch my breath. My back was killing me from the drive, and the stress of the gathering did not help. I closed my eyes for a moment and tried some deep breathing relaxation techniques. I calmly opened my eyes and looked around. It was about three steps above the level of the fenced-in yard. The kids were running around, Jake playing ball with Billy and Marc, Sophia mesmerized by Kylie in the princess castle. I made my way over to the table and started making myself a plate. There was chicken, bratwurst, and hot dogs for the kids, as well as a variety of salads and sides. I made myself a plate and sat down gingerly on a chair in the corner. I could hear the voices coming out of the living room through an open window.

"She has *two* kids?"

"The second one isn't Ryan's is it?"

"Not at all what I expected."

"No wonder Elise flipped out."

That made me wonder about Elise. I had not been able to identify anyone who could be her. Maybe she was staying away so she wouldn't have to meet me. I was sure I would find out soon enough. I looked down at my plate. There was nothing left on it. Years of eating on the run gave me the incredible talent of virtually inhaling my food, and I'd done it again. I just wanted to leave and be by myself with the kids. I had thought, in painstaking detail, what it would be like facing Ryan.

I had never truly considered what it would be like to be ripped apart by a defensive and angry family.

I looked down at my empty plate and wanted to cry. Only the sound of the chair moving next to me pulled me out of my pity party. It was Jennifer. She plopped down in the chair and sighed. "So this is totally weird, right?"

"Right."

"I couldn't believe it when Ryan told us that he had a random kid out there in the world. Then, he wouldn't even answer any of our questions, just that there was this kid and that you were coming up for a while."

"Yeah, bet that went over like ..." I broke off. I couldn't think of anything that didn't sound crude and crass. Since no one liked me without even speaking to me, I didn't need to give them any more ammunition.

Jennifer smiled. "Like a fart in church. But Ryan has been so weird and erratic lately, that we don't know what's coming next. Like he only told us about the little girl today. What's her name again?"

"Sophia. She's three."

"She's adorable." Jennifer watched the kids play for a minute or two. "Sophia must look like her dad," she said finally.

I felt like she was searching for information. I decided to oblige. "Actually, she looks like her mother."

Jennifer looked at me quizzically. I continued. "She's adopted. Long story, but I felt like I could help make a bad situation better, so I stepped in. This way, Jake gets a sibling, and I get a daughter. Win-win."

Jennifer looked amazed. "Wow. And I take it your husband was supportive of it?"

I shook my head. "Not married. Never have been. It's just me and the kids."

"So what's the deal with you and Ryan?"

"Other than I'm pretty sure he hates me, I have no idea."

She laughed a little, and then the kids came running over. They were hungry. We sent them into the house to wash their hands while we started fixing plates and putting them on the table. Kelly came out and started making plates for her boys, still with the baby strapped to her chest. She plopped down in the corner next to us. "This is the weirdest thing. It's like seeing Ryan as a kid all over again," she said, gesturing to Jake.

"So I'm told," I said. "He and Billy look like they could be brothers."

"How many times do you think they'll get asked if they are twins?" Jennifer asked.

Kelly replied, "A lot. But Sophia, she must look like her dad."

I looked from Kelly to Jennifer and back again. It must have been a hot topic of conversation.

Jennifer interrupted, "She's adopted. Already got the scoop. Had to get it from the source since Ryan is absolutely no help."

Kelly looked at me, "Ryan has always been difficult, but this whole thing has made him impossible. Mr. Perfect has really tarnished his record this time."

I didn't understand what she meant by that.

Jennifer laughed. "I guess I don't look so bad right now." She looked at me and must have seen the puzzled look on my face. "Ryan has always been the golden boy. We call him Mr. Perfect because that's how he is. Now, though, it looks as if ..."

She was interrupted by Ryan, standing in the doorway. "That's enough Jenn. I'm sure Maggie doesn't want to be concerned with our long-standing sibling rivalry."

I stood up. "Um, we need to get going anyway. Ryan, can I use your phone book for a minute? I want to call the hotel before we drive over, just to make sure that we can get a room."

Ryan turned around and went back into the house. Stormed off was more like it. I shook my head and sat back down. "I guess I just can't win here."

Kelly said, "I'd be pissed too if I were him. He went through a lot to get into the house before you got here, and now you don't even want to stay?"

I turned my palms up and shrugged my shoulders. "I don't know what you mean. He just told me yesterday, as I was already on my way, about this place."

"He wasn't sure he could pull it together, so he didn't want you to be disappointed."

"Disappointed? Why would I be disappointed? It's not my place to be disappointed if the house wasn't settled. I leave that up to him and Elise. And I know that if I were her, the last thing that I would want as a newlywed is my brand new husband's baby mama staying with me. So, please don't think even worse of me than you already do, but I just want to get out of here before she gets home. It's been a long few days, and I don't think I have the strength to meet her right now."

"Maggie, what are you talking about?" Kelly asked. "Elise doesn't live here."

Now it was my turn. "What are you talking about? Didn't they buy the place together? I mean, I was kind of surprised that they would spend the week after the wedding moving instead of on a honeymoon."

Jennifer just laughed. "Oh, this is rich. I mean this takes the cake. It's even better than the long-lost child news. He didn't tell you? That's great."

Kelly interrupted, "Jenn, I'm sure Maggie doesn't find this at all amusing. Maggie, Ryan called the wedding off. Well, I guess technically he tried to postpone the wedding. He told Elise he needed time to process the whole situation, and she called it off. Ryan bought a place that was bigger so there would be room for you guys to stay here."

"Oh. He never said anything to me, one way or another, so I just assumed ... I feel like such an idiot. He never asked or mentioned that he wanted us to stay with him ..." I didn't know what else to say.

"Why else would he want you to come all the way up here?" Kelly asked.

I shrugged my shoulders. "I dunno. This whole situation is, well, not good, from any way that you look at it. I didn't think it was possible, but I feel like even more of an ass."

Jennifer smiled, "See, Mr. Perfect strikes again. He has excelled at making the little people like us look bad. I guess you're one of us now."

I got up and called the kids to come inside. Whatever the arrangements were going to be, I needed to make them quickly. It was almost bedtime, and my kids needed desperately to be bathed. And I needed to pass out for about twenty hours. I walked into the house and found Ryan in the kitchen. The house had an open floor plan, so the kitchen counter provided the only barrier between the two rooms. He was just on the other side of the counter, washing something off in the sink. The living room was still full of family, so it looked like I would have an audience for this. Just shoot me now. I walked up to him. "Ryan," I said softly. "Did you want us to stay here?"

"What the hell did you think?" he growled at me under his breath.

"I didn't know. It's fine. It's good. I need to get some stuff out of the van and get the kids washed up. Um, where are we staying?"

"Rooms upstairs" he grunted with a nod of his head in the direction of the stairs.

"Thanks a lot," I said, placing my hand on his elbow. He jerked it away with such an abrupt movement that I recoiled as if he had swung at me. He stalked off through the doorway into the dining room. I turned to look to see every pair of eyes in the living room on me.

Great.

I made about six trips out to the car to bring stuff in. My inkling that no one liked me was confirmed by the fact that not one person offered to help me carry anything in. Not even Ryan. By the last trip, my back was screaming, and I wasn't sure I was going to make it without dropping the load I was carrying. There were three bedrooms upstairs. The two smaller ones were decorated for the kids. One was in blue, and in addition to the bed and dresser, it also had a desk, some books, and a collection of Legos. The room across the hall was done in pinks and purples, and it had a princess blanket and a large stuffed giraffe on the bed.

I couldn't help but smile. Ryan had put a lot of thought and effort into getting these rooms ready. I wondered if his sisters had helped him. I walked down the hall into the other bedroom. It was a large master bedroom with a huge bathroom. It was decorated in soft beiges and blues. It was tailored and masculine yet warm at the same time. It had to be Ryan's room. I was thankful that I had packed the baby monitor so that I would be able to hear Sophia from wherever I was sleeping. And where exactly was that?

I didn't have time to worry about that. I showed the kids their rooms and unpacked a few of their things so they would feel more comfortable. I bathed Sophia while Jake checked out the Legos in his new room. I heard Ryan come up and could hear them talking in Jake's room. I finished washing up Sophia and carried the towel-clad little girl into her new room. I deposited her on the bed to get dressed and went back in the bathroom to start the tub for Jake. I poked my head in his door and told him it was time for his bath. He sulked as he went into the bathroom. I showed him the bin for dirty clothes could go and let him get in the tub.

Sophia came out into the hall in her nightgown, and I ushered her back into her room so I could comb her long blond hair out. I tucked her into bed, assuring her that I would be here in the morning. I plugged her CD player in and put on her favorite lullabies and closed the door. I saw Ryan still sitting on Jake's bed. He appeared to be playing with a Lego truck. I poked my head into the room.

"Thanks for the rooms. They look great."

Ryan looked up startled. He looked tired. "No problem."

"I've made enough erroneous assumptions for one evening, so I'm going to come right out and ask you, where am I staying?"

He looked confused like he couldn't believe that I was asking the question. "Well, up here."

"Oh, okay. I thought that it was the master bedroom, so ..."

"I thought you'd want to be close to the kids. I have the room downstairs."

"No, that's good. I mean, it's good that I'm close to the kids. I need to get Jake through the tub, and then I need to crash. Is there anything planned for tomorrow?"

"Not really. I didn't know if you'd need time to recuperate. My mom wants you to come over for dinner."

"Sounds good. Your mom seems really nice. Your sisters were nice too."

He grumbled something under his breath and got up. He brushed by me without even looking and went out into the hall. He poked his head in the bathroom, told Jake good-night, and went downstairs without speaking to me again.

After I got Jake into bed, I moved my bags from the hall and into my new bedroom. I was absolutely exhausted. I tried to reflect on the day and how Ryan was acting. *Ryan didn't get married.* What would that mean for us? Not much if he didn't change his attitude toward me. Why was he acting like that? But, before I could figure anything out, I was asleep.

CHAPTER SEVENTEEN

The eight weeks spent in Ohio were interminably long. The days unfolded, one after another, in the same uncomfortable fashion. Ryan had arranged his schedule so that he worked a four-day week so he could take a day to do something fun with Jake. If it was something appropriate, like the zoo or a museum, Sophia and I tagged along. Ryan often took Jake fishing and just out and around. They went to the batting cages and mini-golf and other father-son-bonding type expeditions.

Jake was having a blast. It was great to see.

However, the price of his happiness was my misery. But I did what I thought a good mother should do and kept my head down and my mouth shut.

Ryan and I never really talked about how things would work. We barely spoke at all. If he was making plans, he would tell me what he was working on. He never asked, only informed me. He would likewise inform me if it was something that Sophia might like. I assumed that if she was invited, I was as well since he had no true responsibility to care for her.

We did a lot of assuming.

Every so often, he would call or let me know that he had other plans, only so I could let Jake know. It wasn't out of concern or respect for me. He never said where he was going nor what he was doing. I never asked either. Part of me was afraid to speak up—I didn't want him to yell at me again.

Since Ryan and I didn't communicate, we never discussed how things would work financially. I wasn't going to be accused of being a freeloader. I gave him cash at the beginning of each week to cover rent and what my usual utility expenses would run. I put the money in an envelope and put it on the desk in his office. He never said a word about it. Whether it was too little, or too much. But the envelope was gone each time I put it out.

Even so, I felt like it wasn't enough. I felt like our presence was a burden, so I did everything I could to alleviate that. I cleaned the house because keeping it neat was no easy feat with two small kids. I did the grocery shopping so I could cook supper nightly. Ryan came home from work, ate with us. I cleaned up after dinner while Ryan and Jake spent quality time together. I didn't think much about it initially, but after a few weeks, I started to become resentful.

I felt like the hired help, except I was paying to help.

He had to notice the fact that the house was cleaned and that the cupboards were stocked. He never even commented on the food, unless one of the kids asked him about it.

In the evenings, while the men bonded, Sophia and I stayed upstairs. I would catch up on emails and correspondence for my company, and then I logged in two to three more hours of work on the computer after both kids were tucked in.

The days were exactly the same.

The Ryan that I had idealized for so many years was barely visible. I caught glimpses of him when he interacted with Jake and even Sophia, who he seemed to adore. Although

I had no expectations of a relationship between them, he did seem very fond of her. It was hard not to be. She was a charmer and seemed to be working her magic on Ryan, as well as the rest of the Milan clan.

I was miserable.

The underlying stress made my appetite vanish. That was a new one for me. I could eat small meals during the day, but at dinner, I had to force myself to choke down each bite while I waited for him to say something. Anything.

A few times during the week, we would go to the pool at Kelly's house, where Jake and Sophia would get to play with their cousins. Kelly watched Kylie while Jennifer was working. It turned out that Jennifer was a single mother, but no real explanation was given for the absence of the dad. We would chat by the pool but mostly it was about the kids. What they were interested in. Anecdotal stories about their lives.

She didn't ask a lot about me, and I didn't volunteer a whole lot. It was apparent that Jennifer, Kelly and Ryan were all very close and protective of each other. The feeling of not belonging persisted. Still, Kelly was cordial to me, and that was probably all I could hope for from this family.

One day while out by the pool, it became apparent that it was going to storm. And quickly. We raced to pack up our belongings as the sky darkened, and the winds whipped. The older kids got right out of the pool and began toweling off. Sophia, being her stubborn three-year-old self, refused to get off of the steps. As a flash of lightning lit up the sky, I bent quickly and grabbed her, hauling her out. As I went to stand up, something in my back cracked, and flashes of pain shot through my back and into my left leg. I managed to put Sophia down on the concrete but could not stand upright. Involuntary tears came out of my eyes in response to the pain. I told Sophia, in not a very calm voice, to get into the house with Aunt Kelly. Kelly, up on the deck, turned to look at us. She called to Sophia and ushered her into the house. I was taking very slow and painful steps, climbing up the steps of the deck. Kelly looked genuinely concerned. "Are you okay? What happened?"

"My back went out. I'll be okay in a few minutes."

I continued my laborious pace up and finally made it into the house. I leaned on the furniture until I reached the den, and then I let myself down to the floor. Kelly, followed by the kids, came in to check on me.

"Can I get you something or do something for you?"

Jake piped up, "Her back is broken, and it does this sometimes."

Kelly, startled, turned to look at him, "What do you mean broken?"

"It was from her accident when she was seven. Everyone else died, but her back just broke. I'm almost seven. Anyway, it still hurts her sometimes and makes her cry. She cries a lot, but mostly it's because she is so sad, not because of her back. But right now it is because of her back."

"That's enough, Jake" I sniped. "Just give me a moment."

I rolled onto my back and did a move to help the pain ease. My back was still throbbing as if it had a hangover from the pain, but the acute pain was no longer there. I closed my eyes and laid still for a few moments.

Kelly shuttled the kids out of the den and got them changed into dry clothes. She set them up with a snack and a movie in the family room and came back to check on me. "Can I get you anything?"

I managed to sit up and smile at her weakly. "I'm okay. I just have to pay attention to what I am doing when I try to lift the kids." I stood up slowly and walked out into the kitchen with her. She put a cup of coffee down on the table for me and smiled at me when I gingerly sat down.

"Um, what was Jake talking about?"

I filled her in on my accident and what I had been dealing with ever since. I hadn't told many people about the pain I experienced. She listened and murmured words of sympathy and then encouragement.

"About what Jake said," she glanced at me, and then down at her coffee. She continued, "Are you really sad? Because, no offense, but you seem it."

I nodded. "This whole situation is really difficult for me. But, it's, ahh, I don't know if I can talk about it."

She smiled. "Just pretend he's not my brother, and I'm just a friend. I won't hold it against you, promise."

I returned her smile. "Okay, well, I guess I never really got to know Ryan. I mean, I thought I did. I thought I knew him, and I thought I loved him. And even after he stopped talking to me and everything with Jake, I," I faltered. "I still held a torch for him and had this crazy dream that someday we would find each other again. I knew it wasn't realistic, but I think deep down that's what I hoped for. And when we did see each other, he was happy, until he found out about Jake. Now he hates me."

"Oh, I'm sure he doesn't hate you," Kelly interjected.

"No, I really think he does. He doesn't even speak to me. Nothing. I'm, um, I'm very lonely. It's really hard being in a room with someone else who doesn't even acknowledge you. And this silly dream I had of happily ever after is stomped and crushed out every single day that I'm here. But I have to stay because I owe it to Jake and Ryan."

I felt like I had said too much. "But enough about me."

Luckily, we were interrupted by the baby crying, waking up from her nap. I stood gingerly and found that my back and legs were able to hold me. I put my cup in the sink and collected my kids and their belongings. I thanked Kelly again, not only for her hospitality but for listening. I only hoped that I hadn't said anything that she could use against me. No matter how she'd reassured me, Ryan was still her brother. I hoped she wouldn't tell him about my back—or my feelings. My chest felt tight with anxiety. Somehow, talking about my feelings only made them more intense and painful.

As our last week in Ohio unfolded, I could not wait to get home. *My home.* I wasn't looking forward to the drive, but I'd had enough. I needed to be able to be me again, not just this robotic shell of a person.

I needed to be in my own space again. I needed to be alone in my house. In the entire time up at Ryan's, I had not had a single hour without at least one of the kids. I'd been spoiled by my dad and Marcy and Uncle Dan, plus other friends who pitched in and watched the kids for me so I could get out. I had not been to the market without the kids or even gotten a cup of coffee by myself.

I felt like crying all the time. I was so rundown. So low on energy and motivation. I looked terrible, with bags the size of steamer trunks under my eyes. This trip had not been good for me.

Especially when, on Monday night after the kids had gone to bed, I decided to take a quick work break to get a drink. Without taking my iPod and headphones off, I filled my cup with ice and water. Then I heard it. not it, a voice. I pulled the earbuds out and listened for a minute. It took me a minute to realize Ryan was on the phone. His voice carried out from his office, located right next to the kitchen. I froze when I realized he was talking about me.

"I know I need to get over it, but I just can't. For instance, she wears these pajamas. Really unattractive. They are absolutely the ugliest thing I have ever seen a woman wear."

I looked down. I was wearing my pajamas. They were too big on me, especially now, and were quite unflatteringly. They were black with hideous purple paisley, but they were so soft I loved them for their sheer comfort. It wasn't like many people—or anyone for that matter—ever saw what I slept in.

I put the earbuds back in and ran back upstairs. I shut the door to my room and turned the iPod off. I shut my computer down and collapsed onto my bed. It was so hurtful to hear him say such a mean thing about me. I closed my eyes and buried my face in my hands. I could not hold the tears back. They stayed, burning a trail down my face until sleep claimed me.

The pajama incident stayed with me, but I had to power through the rest of the week. On Wednesday, I finally faced Ryan. Okay, it wasn't about his hurtful comments but to discuss plans for future visitation.

I took a deep breath, vowing not to let my composure slip. "What do you think would be a good time to visit again?" I led off.

"Oh," he said like he had never thought about it. "Fall?" He grunted. Even now, he could not muster up a full sentence for me.

"I think Jake would like to see a football game. Is it possible to come up for a weekend and go to a game? If it was for a few days, I could leave Sophia with my dad to make things easier."

"Um, okay. Matt said something about coming in for a game, so figure it out with him."

"Oh, uh, okay. Sounds good. Um," I shifted nervously, picking at my fingernails. "I cook Thanksgiving every year. It's my thing. Would you like to come down for that, and then we can come up for Christmas? That way you and your mom can see Jake for the holidays this year."

He shrugged. "Don't see why not. Oh!" he said sitting up a little straighter. "I have a work picnic tomorrow afternoon. It's a family thing. I want to bring the kids. Both of them."

I had wanted to pack, as we were leaving the day after. But, as with everything else, I did not feel that I could turn Ryan down and deny him an opportunity to spend time with Jake. It was touching that he wanted Sophia to come too. I had even heard him say "my kids" to his mom one time. So, I knew that I would bring them.

I was curious too about his colleagues. And how he acted around them. It had to be better than how he treated me. Though I'm guessing no one at work ever had a secret baby that he didn't know he'd fathered. This picnic was the first social thing he'd asked me to do in the entire eight weeks that I had been there.

"Can you leave me directions, and what time to be there, and I'll meet you?"

He shifted uncomfortably. "Um, I can come and pick Jake and Sophia up. You don't need to come."

I just looked, trying to make sense of what he was saying.

"It's for the whole office. Everyone will be there. I wanted to introduce the kids to Elise before they left."

"Oh," I breathed out. I felt like I had been kicked in the gut. All the air left my body.

"And it would be weird with you there." He continued as if I was too slow to understand, "You might make her uncomfortable."

"Of course. I'll have them ready for you."

"Maggie?"

I stood up to leave the room before I fell apart. "What?"

"I need to bring something for the picnic. Can you make me something?"

"Sure," I mumbled without even thinking.

I started to walk out of the room. What the hell was wrong with me? I was turning into a spineless Stepford Wife. It made me sick. I stopped and turned around and stared him right in the eye. "No, I don't think I can make something for you. It would make me too *uncomfortable*," I hissed and left the room.

With those two events, I was ready to leave Ohio and never return. I never wanted to see Ryan Milan again. He had smashed my heart and will to smithereens, and I needed to get away. I focused on cleaning and packing, determined to leave the house in the brand new condition it was when we arrived.

On Thursday, I had gotten the kids ready and was waiting for Ryan to pick them up. They were watching TV, and I was packing more toys up. I'd spent the day, in between cleaning and washing nine billion loads of laundry, getting gifts together for Ryan's family. I had made a photo book for Mrs. Milan of Jake throughout the years. She was fond of both of the kids and had shown me a kindness I had not expected. I had wanted to do something for Kelly too, so I got her a gift card to the Cheesecake Factory, which she had commented about being her favorite. I wondered what she thought about me. On the surface, she was nice to me. But Kelly never mentioned the heart-to-heart we had had during the thunderstorm that day.

Late afternoon, I heard the door and expected Ryan to walk in. I was surprised to see Mrs. Milan and Jennifer. I smiled at them, but it fell upon seeing Jennifer's scowl.

Jennifer had never seemed to warm up to me. She was often short and made snide comments to me. I couldn't understand. I thought that she, out of anyone, would understand. She was a single mother, working hard to make things work. Her ex-husband was a deadbeat and left her for good when Kylie was five. Apparently, there was family gossip that Jennifer had had a fling with her ex's friend, and he was never able to get over it. I never got the details, but I overheard Kelly talking one time.

"Oh, good. I'm glad you stopped by. I have something for you," I said as I went to the foyer to grab the present.

"I'm dropping off German potato salad for Ryan to bring to his picnic," Mrs. Milan said as she went into the kitchen. I hadn't noticed the large aluminum foil pan in her hands.

"Oh" I was speechless.

Jennifer piped up. "Yeah, Ryan asked Mom because he said that you wouldn't help him out."

"Of course he did," I muttered without even thinking. I glanced up and saw them both looking at me. Jennifer was smirking.

I closed my eyes and bit my lower lip. I exhaled slowly. "I'm sorry, that was a rude thing to say. Ryan did ask me, and I said no. I am trying to get packed and cleaned so that we can get on the road before dawn tomorrow. I'm hoping to make the trip in one day."

"Of course, Honey. You have your hands full here. This is a big place, and you've done a nice job keeping it up this summer." Mrs. Milan smiled genuinely at me. At least she'd noticed.

"It is a bigger place than I'm used to, and I didn't want the kids trashing it before Ryan really had a chance to live here."

Jennifer piped up, "Yeah, you must have loved living in the lap of luxury this summer. Big house, all expenses paid. Must be nice."

I stared at her, my mouth agape. Obviously, Ryan had not said anything about me paying for rent, utilities, all of the food, and for myself and the kids on every single outing we had gone on. I knew that she thought I was a gold-digger, or at least looking for a free ride, and there was probably little I could do, short of showing her my financial statements (which were quite impressive, by the way) that would change her mind.

But I was fed up.

I could no longer hold back. I launched into her and said what was on my mind. "You know, Jennifer, I really thought that you, out of anyone, would understand where I am coming from. You don't like me. That's fine. You don't have to. I am doing the best I can here. You can think what you want about me, but I have not spent my entire summer up here with any malicious intentions."

Mrs. Milan interjected, "Of course you haven't, Maggie. This has been an odd situation, to say the least, for all of us. You have handled yourself with nothing but dignity and grace. I do not question that you have had all but the best intentions here."

"Thank you," I whispered. I started to get choked up. I handed her the present. "Just a little something. Trying to make up for lost time." I smiled at her through teary eyes. "Thank you again, for everything." And I hugged her. And she hugged me back, which is more than I ever expected from Ryan's mother. As we were standing there hugging, Ryan came in. He rolled his eyes at the sight of us hugging and called for the kids. They came running and dashed out to the garage to get into Ryan's car. He turned without speaking to me, got the salad, and tossed a "Thanks, Mom!" over his shoulder as he walked out. Just as he had all summer.

It was the first time I was alone all summer. I used my solo time to pack up the van, and we headed back South on Friday without looking back. My soul was deflated, and I did not think that I could recover from this. How could I ever bounce back?

CHAPTER EIGHTEEN
Fall 2008

The kids were happy to be back home and acclimated well. They were happy to see their grandparents and told them tales of their summer up in Ohio. By mid-week, I was relatively unpacked and back to work two days each week, plus what I did from home nightly. I was comforted by returning to my regular life. But I felt like I was a shell of the person I had been before going to Ohio. I robotically went through the motions of my life. I had not felt this low since the January that Ryan left and I found out I was pregnant.

I missed being happy.

I missed laughing and having a sense of humor. In other words, I missed being me. I was realizing that I was going to need professional help soon if I could not shake myself out of this funk.

I had a lot of work to do to make up for my leave of absence. There were numerous wheelchairs to be specked out and ordered. I worked on letters of medical necessity. Most people didn't understand that when a person with disabilities needed equipment, their insurance and Medicaid didn't just pay for it. When I was a practicing physical therapist, I spent hours upon hours writing up letters of justification for wheelchairs and other pieces of equipment. When I joined the company, my role was to evaluate and justify what the client needed. It was time-consuming, often frustrating, and I loved it. I oversaw two other therapists who did the same thing. I had some other administrative duties as well. Our company was very involved in the community, sponsoring teams and various fundraisers for children with disabilities and diseases. I was lucky, I had a job that I not only liked doing but that was rewarding and made a difference too.

Soon after we got home, it was already time for Jake to go back to school. Sophia started a pre-school program three mornings each week. My dad picked her up from school, and I was working three days in the office and nightly from home. We resumed our regularly scheduled programming and being busy helped me a little. Jake turned seven right after Labor Day. A package arrived from Ryan for his birthday, which made his day. It contained the tickets for the Ohio State game over Columbus Day weekend, along with a whole Ohio State wardrobe. I bought plane tickets for Jake and me and coordinated with my dad and Marcy to take Sophia for the weekend. I talked to Matt on the phone about the weekend. I was excited to see him but overall dreading the whole thing. I didn't want to see Ryan again. As per our usual, we didn't speak to each other. He called weekly to talk to Jake, and that was it.

Somehow, as I always did, I just kept plowing through. I think I was too stubborn to do anything else. The October weekend was fast approaching. I dreaded it. I would catch myself staring morosely at the calendar, wishing that the notes denoting our travel would somehow disappear. I thought that it would be nothing but unpleasant. Jake was another story. He was so excited to go to the game and talked of nothing else for the weeks preceding it. The only thing that would make the weekend bearable for me was Matt.

Matt flew into Port Columbus from Logan and got in about thirty minutes after we did, so we greeted him at his gate. I ran up and hugged him tightly. Matt smiled at Jake and ruffled his hair. Ryan was waiting for us in baggage claim.

Jake smiled and ran up to his father. Ryan picked Jake up and hugged him. It was truly touching, and I couldn't help but smile. Ryan met my gaze and his grin fell instantly. Only a look of cold bitterness stared back at me. Matt saw it too. I broke the stare first and walked over to the baggage carousel to get my suitcase. I hugged my arms tight to my body as I watched the suitcases pop up from underground somewhere. My head was down. I was willing the tears to stay in my eyes. I felt warm hands on my shoulders. "Hang in there, Mags. It'll get better."

I leaned back into Matt and sighed. "I don't think it will. I don't think he's ever going to get over this. Oh, there's my bag." I went forward to grab my bag. Matt stepped forward and lifted it off with ease.

We stopped at Steak and Shake on the way home. While we waited for our burgers and fries (and of course, milkshakes), we listened to Matt and Ryan tell Steak and Shake stories from their high school and college years. "So, they make everything to order, even in the drive-thru, and the drive thru is open twenty-four hours" Matt started. "And we had been out, um, drink—" he glanced at Jake, "really late. Ryan was driving."

Ryan started laughing and picked up the story. "I probably shouldn't have been driving because I was, um, so tired." I glanced at Jake, who was paying more attention to his DS than to the grown-ups talking. "And there we were about three cars back. We both fell asleep. Next thing we know, the

KATHRYN R. BIEL

manager is banging on the window, yelling at us to wake the F up." We all laughed. I looked at both Ryan and Matt sitting across from me. This was the most relaxed I had seen Ryan.

Come to think of it, it was the most relaxed I had been. As long as Matt or Ryan was talking, Ryan stayed relaxed. However, when Matt and I began trading college stories, Ryan became tight-lipped and tense again.

I just couldn't win.

We got back to the house, and I got Jake settled. I went right to "my" room and changed into my pajamas. Somehow, just being around Ryan drained me to the point of exhaustion. I had bought new pajamas just for this trip—I didn't need to give him any more ammunition against me than he already had.

I sat on my bed, curled up into a little ball with my knees against my chest, watching a movie on TV. Matt came wandering in. "Whatchya doin' up here? Hiding out?"

"Nothing, just watching a movie."

"Are you hiding out?" he asked pointedly.

I shook my head. "No, I just prefer it up here."

"Mind if I hang with you for a while?"

"Nope." I shifted so I was turned more towards Matt, who was now sitting next to me. I leaned my head back on the headboard.

"You are looking mighty fine this evening," Matt said playfully, wiggling his eyebrows at me. I followed his eyes and glanced down at my chest, which was threatening to spill out of my top.

Stupid new pajamas with a stupid camisole top.

I never had this problem in my ugly pajamas.

"Oh jeez!" I quickly reached down to the end of the bed, where I had thrown a sweatshirt. It was a Flashdance throwback, with a wide neck that hung off of one shoulder, but at least my chest was covered. I liked to sleep in it because it was not too constricting.

"Why you gotta do that? I was enjoying the show. I was even going to get some singles out pretty soon." Matt teased.

"Show's over folks," I laughed. "But it's nice to know that at least someone out there doesn't think I look hideous in my pajamas."

Matt just looked at me, quizzically and raised an eyebrow. "Explain," was all he said.

I told Matt about *the incident*. "Now I know that I'm not this hot young sex kitten, but he was just being mean."

"Was that all you heard?"

"Well, yeah. I left the room before I could hear him rip me apart anymore. Hearing that was bad enough." Something occurred to me. "What do you mean, was that all I heard? Was he talking to you? What else did he say?"

Matt sighed and looked down. He looked like he was trying very hard to figure out what to say next. I could practically see his internal wheels turning.

Oh no, it must have been bad.

Ryan must have really gone off about. I didn't think I could handle hearing anymore. I held up my hand as if to silence him. "Know what? Never mind. If it's that bad, I don't think I want to hear it. He's already done a number on my self-esteem and just about everything else. I know how he feels about me. I don't need to hear an itemized list of all my faults."

Matt and I were staring each other down. I could tell he was still wrestling with telling me. I couldn't figure out why. It was obvious how much Ryan despised me. Did Matt need to beat me over the head with it? Matt opened his mouth to say something but was interrupted by Ryan clearing his throat from the doorway.

"You two look cozy. Am I interrupting?" His voice sounded like he was trying to keep it light and joke, but his underlying tension cut right through.

"Nah, just watching a movie. Maggie is, for some reason, obsessed with Pulp Fiction," Matt said casually. I tightened up into more of a ball and put my head down towards my knees.

"Mind if I watch with you guys?" Ryan said, moving into the room. He looked around for a place to sit.

"Not at all. Maggie picked the movie but, knowing her, she's gonna fall asleep in about twenty minutes, and then we can watch whatever we want."

I smacked Matt playfully. "I will not fall asleep. And anyway, it's a good movie, you know it."

"Maggie, unless something drastic has changed, you are physically unable to watch an entire movie after nine p.m. without falling asleep. Am I wrong?" Matt taunted.

"I, well, um, shut up Matt. Just watch the movie."

Ryan settled down on the floor by the foot of the bed. I was glad he couldn't see me from where he was sitting. He never sought out my company and being in his presence made me nervous. It was truly awful. He no longer even liked me as a person, and despite his rude and mean behavior, I still had this messed up fantasy about living happily ever after. I couldn't let that dream go. Being in the same room with him caused me agony.

Somehow with Matt there as a buffer, and with Ryan not able to see me, it wasn't as bad as it could have been. I relaxed a little and slid down into a semi-reclined position.

Sure enough, within about twenty minutes, I started getting very tired. It was a struggle to keep my eyes open. I was pretty sure that my blinks were getting kind of long. From somewhere that sounded very far away, I heard Ryan say, "Be careful, she'll kick you pretty soon. She likes to sprawl out. I have never seen someone so small take up so much room in a bed before."

Matt answered quietly, "And how would you know? From what she says, you never even speak to her."

"Oh, yeah. Well, I used to come up and check on the kids. I like to see them sleeping. So, sometimes I peek in here, to make sure she can sleep and that she's okay. She cries in her sleep."

I wanted to open my eyes and join the conversation, but I simply couldn't. I was too exhausted, emotionally and physically. I don't know if it was a moment later or an hour later, but I heard them talking again. I heard Matt first this time. He was still on the bed next to me, and he was running his fingers through my hair. "What's it gonna take? I mean, it can't go on forever."

"I dunno, man. I just, I mean, I can't get past the anger yet. I want to let it go, but I just can't. I feel like I have enough anger to last forever."

With that, I felt darkness closing down on me. I was sinking into sleep, but it seemed like a perfect metaphor for our situation. He was going to stay angry at me forever, and it would always sit in between us. Any chance for us to be together had closed.

I'm not sure how I made it through the next day. I know I did it for Jake. He was in seventh heaven. We bundled up and headed out early in the morning to get to campus before the noon game. There were crowds and tons of people, and it was hard not to get caught up in the enthusiasm of the day. The few beers that I'd didn't hurt either. Ryan and Matt ran into a few old friends before the game, and Ryan took pride in introducing Jake around. I tried to stay in the background. I'm sure it looked like I was there with Matt. Ryan did not introduce me to anyone. I saw the surprised glances between the girls when Ryan introduced them to his son. I was sure that it was going to be hot on the gossip mill for a while. Fortunately, it slipped my mind as soon as we entered the Horseshoe, and I never really thought about it again.

When we got back to Ryan's after a long and exhausting day, his mother stopped by to see Jake. Matt had gone to his mother's to visit for the night, so Ryan's mother was another needed buffer. Mrs. Milan was, as always, pleasant to me, and even invited me to a baby shower brunch the following morning for one of Ryan's cousins. I didn't know what to think. I mean, I wasn't family, but I thought it would come off very rude if I said no. I agreed and did a quick mental inventory of what I had packed to see if I had anything appropriate to wear. Of course, I didn't. I knew this meant that I was going to have to go shopping, which was the last thing I felt like doing.

While Jake was visiting with his grandmother, I sheepishly pulled Ryan aside into his office. "Um, I, um" I nervously stammered, looking at my feet, "I need to go out and get a shower gift and card. And I didn't bring anything to wear so I need to get something. Is it okay if I leave Jake here? It's been a long day, and he needs to get to bed on time." I looked up at him, just hoping he wouldn't yell at me. I felt like a teenager asking my dad for permission to use the car. Ryan rolled his eyes. "Don't you trust me with him?"

"Um, yes, of course," I stammered. "It's just, I mean, I don't expect you to babysit him for me."

"He's my kid too, Maggie. It's not babysitting. Jesus." He turned abruptly and started to walk away.

I hated to have to do this, but I called after him. "Ryan?"

He stopped. "What now?"

"Um, thanks. And do you know what your cousin is having?"

"Yeah, no. Not really into the baby thing. Ask my mom." And with that, he disappeared back into the living room.

I found out that the gender of the newest addition was yet to be revealed. Armed with that, I headed out to get a gift card and a decent outfit to wear. While I normally enjoyed shopping, I was tired and frazzled. Being around Ryan simply sapped all of my energy away. I finally found a conservative, yet flattering, black cowl-necked sweater dress. I could never wear anything this heavy in Florida, so it was a welcome change to my wardrobe. I also picked up some outdoor winter clothing for the kids while it was out. We were scheduled to be here at Christmas time. If my memory served correctly, by the time winter was in full swing, all of the hats and gloves would be gone and the shorts would be coming out. I hoped Ryan would let me keep some of the stuff at his place so I didn't have to haul it back and forth. I hated that I had to walk on eggshells like this. It was tearing me apart inside, and I knew that someday I would snap and that would be that.

The next morning, I got up and got ready for the shower. I was able to pair my new dress with my boots and thought I looked quite respectable. Ryan simply gave me a blank look when I walked into the kitchen. It made my heart sink.

The definition of insanity is doing the same thing over and over and expecting a different result. So, it was becoming evident that I was insane, since I somehow expected, or at least hoped, that Ryan would comment on my appearance.

Mrs. Milan picked me up. When we got to the restaurant, I realized the expectant cousin was one of the people who had been there on my first trip to Ohio. I guess I hadn't realized then that she was expecting, but I was so wrapped up in my own inner turmoil that I hadn't noticed. Apparently, Mrs. Milan had called ahead about my attendance, because the cousin, Lucy, didn't seem surprised to see me. And neither did Kelly and Jennifer, with whom we were sitting. Jennifer gave me her usual surly look, while Kelly gave me a reserved smile.

As per the usual shower conversation, the topic turned to our respective children and their deliveries. The fact that Lucy had not found out the gender of her child was hot in debate. The older women at the table, Mrs. Milan included, had been of the generations when it was not possible. Kelly asked me, "Did you find out?"

I had been mid-bite on my quiche, so I quickly held my napkin in front of my mouth while I nodded. I chewed as quickly as I could. "Yes, I'm a planner, so there was no way I could wait to find out. I don't have that much patience." I took a sip of my water. "I was pretty sure it was a boy, and I think I would have been shocked if I had been told anything different."

Jennifer, who was in the camp of not wanting to find out (of course), replied, "Well, there are so few surprises left in the world."

I'm not sure where my gumption came from, but I spoke up. "Well, I know, at least for me, I was moving into a new house. I couldn't paint myself because of the fumes, so I had to hire a painter. I didn't want my child in a green or yellow room for years, and it would be wasteful to have to repaint a room so soon after. Plus, it was what I wanted."

Jennifer tensed and looked ready to re-load. Kelly, sensing the imminent possibility of a scene, tried to step in and intervene. "Well, finding out certainly makes it easier for shower planning. You get a lot cuter clothing when you know what sex to buy for." Mrs. Milan and her contemporaries started nodding and talking amongst themselves about what they had given and how difficult it is to shop for a baby "these days" without knowing the gender. The conversation shifted to the large gift pile that Lucy was going to receive and some of the women started talking about what their favorite gift was that they had received. I had a pit in my stomach and hoped no one would ask me. I looked down at my empty plate and considered getting a refill, just to avoid the conversation. I could not meet anyone's gaze at the table, lest I be included.

Jennifer, always watching me with a judgmental eye, must have sensed my aversion to this conversation. "What about you Maggie? Since no of us attended *your* shower, what was your favorite gift?"

All eyes on the table shifted to me. You could have cut the tension with a knife. I cleared my throat and sat up as straight as possible. "I didn't have a shower."

Jennifer's eyes were ablaze with amusement. "Oh really. Why not? Not a lot of people want to celebrate the whole unwed mother thing?" My mouth fell open.

Mrs. Milan looked sternly at her, "Jenn, enough."

I closed my mouth, met Jennifer's gaze and replied, "No. That wasn't it. I didn't want one. My father and his wife bought me a crib and bedding set, and my uncle bought me a stroller. That was all I needed."

Kelly was dumbfounded. "But that's not all you need! Didn't you want all the goodies and the party and everything?"

"My dad's wife, Marcy, is great, but she and my dad got together after I went to college, so we weren't that close back then. I didn't really think I could ask her to go to all of that trouble for me. She has been a great help along the way though, and the whole thing brought us a lot closer. And with my own mother being gone and all, and I had left my friends in Boston, there was really no one ..." I trailed off, trying to fight back the tears that were welling up. I cleared my throat again and continued, "So, I've been flying a solo mission from the beginning. And it's been fine."

Of course, anyone listening to my voice could tell I wasn't fine.

Mrs. Milan patted my hand and asked someone across the table about some other topic just to get the heat off of me. After an acceptable amount of time, I excused myself and went to the ladies' room to pull myself together. I thought about not even going back in, but I didn't want to embarrass Mrs. Milan that way.

When I got back to the table, the conversation had shifted to labor and deliveries. Oh great. Another chance to put myself out there and be criticized. When it became apparent it was my turn to share, I just shook my head. "I'd rather not talk about it." Lucy had come over and sat down at our table. "I don't want to scare Lucy, since she still has to go through it. I just wish her a quick and pain-free experience." I tried to make my refusal light instead of defensive. A few women chuckled. A painful hour later, the shower was over, and I was back in the car with Mrs. Milan.

"Maggie, I don't want to make you uncomfortable, but someday, when you're ready, I would like to hear about how my grandson entered this world. I would also like to hear about how Sophia came about too since I consider her my granddaughter as well."

I almost started crying at her kindness. "Of course, I just didn't want to get into it at the table. I didn't want to scare Lucy. I know my story would have scared the bejeezus out of me. I had a terribly long labor. Like seventy-five hours long. Back labor. It was the first time in a long time that I just wanted my mom to be there with me and make it all better, but of course, that wasn't possible. When I finally went to the hospital, on day four, I was so scared that they would send me home. I didn't know how long it was going to take, so I sent my dad and Marcy home. I had to stay in bed the whole time because they were monitoring Jake. He was in distress, and they didn't know what was going on. They gave me an epidural because they were sure that they were going to have to do a C-section. Suddenly, Jake's heart rate dropped and they were going to open me up right there, and they realized that he was coming out the traditional way! I pushed a few times and there he was. The cord was around his neck a few times. He was okay, but I was worried. I kept yelling for them to give me his APGAR's."

We were in Ryan's driveway by this time, and Mrs. Milan made no move to get out of the car. "Were you alone, dear?"

"I had some great nurses, but yes." The tears finally escaped and ran down my cheeks. "My dad doesn't do hospitals well. It's too hard for him since the accident, so I didn't want him there until there was something to be happy about. Even with having a grandson, it was hard for him to be there. He tried to keep it from me, but I could tell. Since Jake was born just before midnight, he was less than forty-eight hours old when I took him home. And the first morning that he was home was September 11, 2001. I sat there, with a brand new baby, no clue of what to do with him, and watched the world change. It was kind of surreal."

Mrs. Milan reached over and hugged me. "I can't believe all that you have been though."

"Just dealing with the hands I get dealt." I sighed. "Although one of these days, I could really use a better hand."

"Maggie, I know that this situation is odd and to be frank, difficult. Ryan has never been the same since he came back from Boston and his father died. It doesn't excuse his behavior then, or now for that matter. I am displeased with the behavior of two of my children at this moment. It is obvious that this is an issue where we have not heard the whole story. But please rest assured, honey, you and your children are part of my family. And you always will be."

I hugged the kind woman again and got out of the car. I wiped the tears off of my face as I walked in the front door. Ryan stopped and looked at me. I may have had cloudy vision, but it almost looked like he was concerned about me. In a neutral voice, he asked, "Did everything go okay?"

I almost didn't know how to respond to a non-curt comment from Ryan. "It was fine. Just talking with your mom and all. She's really great. I'm not used to having a mother. You are very lucky to have her."

He nodded, "I know." He paused awkwardly. "She likes you."

I nodded in response.

He continued, "Maybe if you were here all the time, everyone could get to know you better."

"All the time?"

We stood there, just looking at each other for what seemed like an eternity. I waited for him to say something else. A thousand thoughts seemed to run behind his eyes.

For once, there was no anger. Only uncertainty.

This is the moment in movies where the man realizes that he cannot live without the woman and rushes to her and sweeps her up in his arms. See, this is why my heart is constantly breaking around Ryan. I was still waiting for my movie moment. But life is not scripted with a happily ever after in mind. However, what came next no one could have foreseen.

As Ryan and I were standing there, unable to speak, unable to move, and unable to move forward, the door flew open and before I knew it, Matt had rushed in, grabbed me, dramatically dipped me back and kissed me. Hard and firm on the lips. I grasped tightly onto Matt's shoulders to avoid being dropped on my head. I glimpsed Ryan out of the corner of my eye. The walls were up. The anger was back.

Matt returned me to upright as abruptly as he had pulled me into the dip and spun me around. As I was trying to regain my balance, I wiped my mouth off and said, "What the hell was that?"

Matt virtually skipped and gaily yelled, "I'm free! Ding dong the witch is dead! I'm free!"

Ryan turned away and walked into the living room, and Matt virtually ran after him. Matt grabbed Ryan's shoulders. He was like a giant exuberant St. Bernard. "Did you hear me, man? I'm free. The divorce is final. I never have to deal with Irene again! I'm so happy I wanna kiss you too!"

Ryan shoved Matt back onto the couch. "Kiss me and you're a dead man." There was a smile on Ryan's face, but it was a plastic one that certainly did not reach his eyes and did not reflect the joy his best friend was feeling. I walked quietly into the living room and sat down in the comfy, cozy overstuffed chair.

Matt turned towards me. "Don't you understand Maggie? It's officially over with Irene and me. I'm free to start my life over. I know I can never make up for what she did to you guys, but I want to start with a clean slate. What do you think?"

"I think that Irene was ancillary to this situation. Mistakes were made by people other than her. Her actions were out of spite and malice, but she was not the only one at fault. And the sooner we all realize that, the sooner we can all move on." I could not believe that I was almost defending her.

But it was the truth. Ryan and I were culpable too. The only innocent party was Jake.

Ryan mumbled something about going up to check on Jake, who was playing with his DS in his room. I covered my face with my hands. I had wanted Matt to be away from Irene for as long as I could remember. I was happy that he was going to get a chance to start over. He would make a great dad and deserved the chance to find someone to build that life with.

I was jealous. He was getting to wipe the slate clean and start over, while I seemed to be on this hamster wheel from hell. Stuck in limbo with a man I still loved, even though he despised me. Living between two houses, a thousand miles apart. Giving up my life for my children, instead of having a cohesive life together.

Ryan took Jake out for the rest of the afternoon and for dinner, leaving Matt and me together. In a way, it was kind of like old times. I'd missed my friend and the comfortableness of being with him. When I was with Matt, no matter what we were doing, I was relaxed and could be myself. I didn't truly realize how uptight Ryan made me until the tension slid away with Matt. We had seven years of catching up to do.

Ryan and Jake returned, and my son's bedtime was rapidly approaching. I gave Matt a hug goodnight and kissed him on the cheek. I accompanied Jake upstairs and sat with him for a while, getting filled in on his day. Once he drifted off to sleep, I quietly got up and went down the hall to my room, and went to bed. I waited for Ryan to come up and finish the conversation we had started. But he didn't.

We left in the morning. Ryan was not only back to not speaking to me, but he was downright pretending that I wasn't even there. It made me think I had imagined our little emotionally charged stand-off in the foyer.

Was he really about to ask me to move up to Ohio permanently? Perhaps I had been so off-balance from the talk with Mrs. Milan that I read more into it than was there. Maybe he was just blaming me for the distance between him and his son.

That was the most likely reason.

Ryan dropped us off at the airport. He got out to hug Jake but didn't even bother to help me get the bags out of the car. I winced as I pulled the bag out of the trunk and took a moment, still bent over before I could catch my breath. I walked around the car and stood before Ryan and waited until he had the decency to meet my eyes. "We're going to drive up for Christmas. I'll be in touch with details. Thanks for the weekend."

He just stood there, not saying anything. Okay.

"See you at Thanksgiving? I make a mean stuffing, so bring your appetite." I hesitated. "And I think that we need to finish our talk. We need to discuss where and how things are." I'd had enough.

It was time to call Ryan out on his behavior. I'd do it as soon as we were on my turf.

CHAPTER NINETEEN

The October trip changed me.

While my life was not what I had planned, I had always found peace and contentment with my life with the kids. We were very routine-oriented and had our schedule for everything. Work, family, school, and fun were carefully balanced to maximize our quality time together. Now, despite the full color-coded calendar hanging in the kitchen, a feeling of emptiness and loneliness hung around like the most stubborn of cobwebs. No matter how many times I swatted them away, I turned and saw them hanging in another corner. On another wall.

On the rare nights that we were home in the evening with no scheduled activities, I found myself waiting and watching the door, almost expecting Ryan to come in. Worse than the feeling of hope and longing was the ever-growing feeling of self-hatred. How could I care for a man who was cruel? I was setting such a poor example for my children, especially my daughter. Here was this guy who treated me like crap, yet I knew I would go to the ends of the earth for him. I could rationally process that I should not be acting like this.

But I could not change my feelings towards him.

Not even when he bailed on Thanksgiving. He called me the Tuesday before to tell me that "something had come up," and he wasn't coming down. The call totally blindsided me, and I could barely respond, other than to croak out "okay." He called Jake on Thanksgiving, but of course, he didn't talk to me. I tried to play it off that I was disappointed for Jake, which I was. I couldn't admit out loud that I was disappointed at not getting to see Ryan myself. With every visit, I still held out hope that he would soften, and the Ryan I met in Boston would resurface. Part of me wondered if he was avoiding talking to me about how things were going. We had seemed on the brink of a real conversation, but then the moment was gone and we were back at square one.

I talked to Matt every few days and asked if he had said anything. Matt's answer was as puzzling. Ryan was barely talking to Matt now too. I hypothesized that Ryan thought Matt was siding with me on things, and it pissed him off. I couldn't figure out any other reason why Ryan was acting like this. But on the other hand, I'd never really been able to figure out what did and did not motivate Ryan in life. Or, better put, what motivated Ryan enough to act.

The irony of this whole situation is that Ryan re-entering my life had made me feel alone and isolated. However, as a result, Michele and I had become much closer, and she was now a trusted confidant. I needed her humor and hypochondriasis to keep me from taking my situation too seriously. I always felt better after talking to her, even if it couldn't change the situation. Somehow, her friendship helped me change my perspective.

Matt and I talked regularly too, and it was good to have him back in my life. Despite the addition of these friendships, I couldn't help but feel the emptiness of not having a life partner. Even Matt was already dating again. Nothing serious, but he was out there, meeting new people. I knew I should date, but I just couldn't pull the trigger yet. I had more baggage than an American Tourister store, and I just didn't have the energy to deal with anything else.

With Christmas fast approaching, another Ohio trip loomed ahead of me. I ordered Christmas gifts online and had them shipped to Mrs. Milan. We had arranged this ahead of time since she was at least speaking to me. I emailed Ryan our travel plans, which were to drive up (so we would have room to bring gifts back) about a week and a half before Christmas. It meant pulling the kids out of school a few days early, but it would make for a longer, less hectic trip. I had to have all of my Christmas shopping done ahead of time, which, in addition to the usual flurry of holiday activities, made the time zip by. However, the early travel also meant that I would have to spend my birthday in Ohio. Ryan had never even asked me when my birthday was, so I was sure that he was not aware of this occasion. It brought back memories of our time together, as well as our night that wasn't when he left Boston.

When we arrived at Ryan's, he was as distant and cold to me as usual. And, as usual, he was great with Jake and Sophia, which further confused my feelings about him. I didn't want to love him, but I didn't want to hate him either. I wanted to feel indifferent. To not care about him. It was obvious that he felt that way about me.

As much as he appeared to love my kids, he was that uninterested in me. How one person could be so dichotomous was beyond me. The day after we arrived, I'd planned nothing but recuperation time, since I'd managed the full sixteen-hour haul in one day. Ryan informed me that he had "something" going on that evening and would not be around. I knew the kids would be disappointed, and I was grouchy. I didn't want to have to entertain them all evening.

I was dozing on the couch in the late afternoon while the kids were playing in front of the TV. Ryan told me that he was leaving, and I nodded to him without even opening my eyes. I'm not sure if I had been asleep for one minute or ten when I was woken up by the door opening and someone coming in. I bolted upright, disoriented to my surroundings. In doing so, I managed to fall off the couch. I sprung to my feet and found myself face to face with Matt. I squealed and hugged him. "What are you doing here?"

"I came in for Christmas. We're having a high school reunion this weekend. Everyone, no matter what the year, kind of gathers down at Tony's Tavern the week before Christmas anyway. I'm taking you with me."

"Oh, Matt, sounds great, but I can't." I gestured to the kids, who had resumed their trance-like state in front of the boob tube. "Ryan is out for the night, so ..." I just kind of shrugged. It figured, the one time while I was in Ohio that someone wanted me to do something was the one time that Ryan was not around to stay with the kids.

"Not a problem," Matt replied smugly. We had sat back down on the couch, and, now that the shock of waking up so abruptly had worn off, I was feeling drowsy again. I rested my head on Matt's shoulder while he punched some numbers into his cell. I closed my eyes, just feeling comfortable for the moment. "Mrs. Milan, it's Matt." I bolted upright and stared at him.

"Yes, ma'am. Here for the holidays ... Oh, yeah, she's happy I'm here. I'll tell her and my dad you said hello. I was wondering if I can ask a big favor of you? I'm here with Maggie and the kids, and Ryan is out somewhere for the night. Maggie's birthday is in a few days, and I wanted to take her out for some fun tonight."

I stared at Matt, my eyes as big as dinner plates. How dare he? I punched him in the arm and tried to get him to stop his conversation. He easily pushed me off and continued, "Is there any chance that you could watch the kids tonight? You know, Maggie never gets a break when she's up here ... Oh, okay ... Sounds good ... No, makes perfect sense ... Trust me ... Yeah, I'm sure that will be fine ... That's great ... They will love it ... Yeah, sounds good. See you then. Thanks again, bye!"

It was maddening only listening to one side of the conversation. "I cannot believe you did that Matthew!! What did she say?"

"She said fine. She wants to have the kids over for a sleepover. She's picking them up in an hour, if you can give them dinner."

"I can't ask her to do that!"

"You didn't, I did. She said she wanted to have them for an overnight, but she wasn't sure you were ready for it. I think she's more excited than the kids will be. It will be fine. I need to take you out and show you some fun."

Who was I to disagree?

I got the kids packed up and fed. They were excited about the sleepover and so happy to see their grandmother. She was equally as ecstatic.

She hugged me tight as well. "Maggie, thank you so much for letting me take them overnight. I've wanted to do this for a while, but I wanted you to feel comfortable with me first. I hope you have fun tonight."

"Thank you so much, Mrs. Milan. I hope you know that I didn't expect this."

"No, of course not dear. But you are too serious, and you need to relax a little. Think of it as part of your birthday present. And speaking of which, why did you never mention that it is coming up? We need to celebrate."

"Oh, no, please don't do anything for my birthday. Any time that I've planned something big, it has gone catastrophically wrong." I tried to laugh it off, but it was true. My dad, although well-intentioned, wasn't great with the celebrations. Or presents. For my sixteenth, instead of a big party, or even taking me to get my driver's permit, he had scheduled a dentist appointment for me. On my twenty-first, my roommates got drunk before we went out, and I spent the night taking care of them. Matt had a final the next day, so he couldn't even come out and celebrate with me. I was also thinking, of course, of the night that wasn't with Ryan. It was my twenty-fifth, which was a milestone for me. It really should have been an occasion, getting stood up aside. Even though my dad had to sign some papers, he never even remembered that milestone. I had let most of my birthdays pass without much notice, although now Marcy usually got a card for me from her and my dad. I had no intentions of letting this one be any different.

I packed up the kids and sent them off. I took a long, hot shower and prepared myself for a night on the town. I could not even remember how long it had been since I had been out, just to have fun. And, since I was going out with Matt and his high school friends, I had absolutely no pressure. No one knew me, and no one expected anything of me. I could relax and let Maggie come out.

I decided to wear my skinny black pants that hugged my curves with my high-heeled black knee-high boots. I was obsessed with these kinds of boots and had been through several incarnations over the years. I put a flowered peasant top on that gathered at the top of my hips. My hair, since I had not had time to get a haircut since last spring, was now a bob, with the front longer than the back. I pulled the top back to let the sides frame my face. I added some sparkly chandelier earrings that went with the flowered top. I actually had time to put on some make-up. The results were pleasing, if I did say so myself. You wouldn't even know I was a depressed, confused single mother of two. Even Ryan would have to admit I still cleaned up well.

Matt picked me up, and we were off to meet up with some high school friends. I'd met some of them over the years, or I felt like I had from all the stories Matt told over the years. Apparently, the feeling was mutual, and I felt right at home. Dinner was fun, with lots of anecdotal tails and even gossip on some classmates who had made less prudent decisions along the way. I mean, what's not funny about someone getting arrested for DWI on a motorized bar stool? We ate awesomely unhealthy bar food and kept the beer flowing. The bar also had a trivia league, and I still could not resist a challenge. After a few rousing rounds of trivia, in which I kicked serious ass, I excused myself to visit the ladies room. The two other women at the table, Kari and Meredith, accompanied me. They were high school friends and had married their high school sweethearts, who were also friends of Matt's.

While touching up our make-up, Meredith threw her arm around me. "Kari and I were talking," she said, only with the slightest trace of a slur, "and we decided we like you."

Kari piped in, "Yeah, you're much better than that Irene. Glad Matt divorced her ass. What a bitch!"

I just giggled. I had never heard someone echo my thoughts so clearly. "I agree!" My voice, too, held the faintest trace of a slur.

We were all laughing as we headed back to the table. Something about their comments was triggering something in my head, but I was too fuzzy to fully process it. It was something about them thinking I was better than Irene. The music was starting to get loud, and it was obvious that dancing would soon begin. Kari continued, "So other hot gossip ..."

"Do tell!" I encouraged as we huddled together so that we could all hear over the music. "I love gossip. I don't care if I don't even know the people. And the juicier the better!"

Meredith laughed. "See, we knew we liked you. Okay, here's the scoop. So, Tiffany Pulson, who was in our class. She was the cute cheerleader, who all the guys loved. Well, she married Greg Kessler, who went to the Catholic high school in town."

Kari took over, "So they've been married for a while and have a kid. Anyway, it's been pretty apparent from the beginning that Greg has been cheating on her with anything that walks."

Meredith resumed her story, "But the kicker is that Tiffany looks up her high school boyfriend, Brock Riley, on Facebook, and they start having an affair. Except he lives in like Iowa or something. And Greg finds out, and *he* kicks Tiff out for being unfaithful.

"Oooh, that is good. See, another reason to avoid Facebook. As much as I love the gossip, it's not worth the trouble." I said. "Plus, I dated nothing but losers in high school and college, so looking them up would not exactly improve the quality of my life." They both laughed. Kari continued, "Okay, another good one. Ryan Milan, he was a year or two ahead of us. Matt and he are good friends, so maybe you'll meet him while you and Matt are out here."

I just swallowed hard and tried to keep a neutral expression on my face. Taking a large sip of beer seemed to help. Or at least, I thought it did.

"Okay, so he was about to get married last spring to this frosty chick that he worked with."

Kari interrupted, "What is it with Ryan and Matt being with total bitches? They're such nice, down-to-earth guys, why do they pick these awful women? And not to mention good-looking. Especially Ryan. Not to disparage Matt or anything."

Meredith cut Kari off. "Anyway, Ryan was about to get married, when some chick that he had had a one-night stand with tracked him down and told him that he had this random kid out there. Totally messed up, right? So Ryan's fiancée, Elise, totally freaked out and ditched him."

Kari sighed. "But he's still so hot. Always has been but never dated much. Kind of flaky in that respect. I think we were all surprised that he had gotten his stuff together enough to get married, let alone father a kid with someone."

I thought I was going to be sick. I leaned back and tried to get some air. I concentrated on breathing in and out so that I didn't vomit all over the table. Matt noticed my expression and was beside me before I knew it. His arm was around my waist and he pulled me up. "Come dance with me."

"Matt, I'm not in the ..."

"Just bear with me. I heard the end of the conversation. They don't know that you're the infamous baby mama. Relax."

"Don't call me that. Maybe you should take me home."

"Maybe you should shut up and listen to the music and dance, and just have fun for once."

I opened my mouth to argue with him but realized that it was a song I liked from our college days and that I was still kind of— okay, pretty— drunk.

"Oh, screw it. It's not like I'm gonna see these people often. This is my one night of parole."

Matt and I danced for a song or two until "Wake Me Up Before You Go-Go" came on. At that point, and having had another beer, I let loose and danced to the best of my 'I was a child of the 80s' ability. Matt, likewise, was feeling no pain, and we were having fun. It was kind of odd. I definitely had beer goggles on, but the thought of Matt as more than a friend started to cross my mind. I remembered how attracted I was to him when we first met and how we used to flirt shamelessly. But, I was more invested in having fun tonight than thinking deeply, so I just kept dancing and singing. Loudly.

Matt was right, I just needed to let loose. At the end of the song, we walked off the dance floor, his hand still around my waist. I leaned into him, shaking with laughter. I could not remember the last time I'd had this good of a time.

That is until I heard Matt say, "Ahh, shit."

I lifted my head off Matt's chest and looked at his face. He was looking across the room. I tried to see what he was looking at but couldn't see through the crowd. He looked down at me and just shook his head. Kari was suddenly at my side. "I guess I stand corrected. Ryan, Mr. Hottie-Hot, Milan is here, and he is apparently back with his fiancée. They just walked in! Oooh, this is getting good. I gotta find Meredith!" And off she went.

I craned my neck to see, and it became apparent, even in my drunken haze, that this was what Matt was looking at. Ryan and what had to be Elise had just come in, obviously from a dressy event. Must have been a Christmas party. Ryan was looking breathtaking in a dark suit with a pale green shirt and a darker green tie. Elise was a Nordic beauty. She was about five-foot-ten, which was much better suited for Ryan than my petite status. Her blond hair was flawless, as was her skin. She was wearing a basic black cocktail dress that left little to the imagination in terms of her bust size (at least a D cup) or the length of her legs (to her neck). And they were headed in our direction.

"Shit, shit, shit." It had been so long since I had been drunk that I had forgotten that I tended to lose the ability to censor what came out of my mouth. Not a good combination right now.

"It'll be fine."

"Shit. No, it won't. Shit! They're coming over here. Shit!" Shit was the only word I knew anymore.

"Maggie, relax. We're all adults here. Nothing is gonna happen."

Famous last words.

We all kind of converged on the same central location at the same time. Ryan, of course, looked pissed.

"What the hell are you doing here? Where are the kids?" He'd been drinking too. Oh, this was not a good combination.

Since my internal censor had gone on sabbatical, I said the first thing that popped into my head. "Aren't they with you?" I asked with the most innocent, wide-eyed expression I could muster.

Matt chuckled. I elbowed him and giggled.

"Maggie, seriously. Where are the kids?"

"I thought they would be fine by themselves. I locked them in their rooms and tied them to the beds so they can't get into any trouble."

Ryan did not find me amusing.

"They're with your mom, relax."

"Oh great, you dump the kids on my mom so you can go out and get shit-faced. Nice."

Matt jumped in. "Jeez Ryan, relax. You had no problem going out. I just thought it would be nice to take Maggie out for her—"

I elbowed Matt to shut him up. I still didn't want Ryan to know my birthday was coming up. On the one hand, it would just give him another opportunity to make me feel small and insignificant in his world. On the other, if he ever thought about the past, he would realize that he stood me up on my birthday. Then I had to laugh as if he'd remember that much detail.

Either way you looked at it, I was rapidly becoming fed up with Ryan's shit and was not going to give him any more opportunities to shit all over me.

"Your mother wanted to take the kids overnight for a sleepover. I assume that since you have such a low opinion of me, you would view this as a step up in the world." Wow, beer gave me balls. I should have taken up drinking a *long* time ago.

Matt interrupted, always trying to be the peacemaker. "Let me get you guys a drink. Elise, what're you having? Maggie?"

"Maybe just water for me; otherwise you're gonna be carrying me out of here, and I cannot be held responsible for what happens in your car." I smiled at Matt. He winked back at me. God bless my friend. I would have been lost without him.

Ryan offered to go and get Elise's drink for her. A chardonnay. Of course. I mean, really? It was a sports bar. Who orders wine at a sports bar? I stood there, watching Ryan and Matt walk to the bar. Anyone on the outside would assume that they were as close as they had always been. But I could see that a wedge had been driven between them, and I knew that I was that wedge. Kind of ironic. This had been my fear of getting involved with Ryan all those years ago. It just took the total imploding of my life to finally have an impact on either of them. I only hoped at the end of the day, their friendship would survive.

Too much had already been lost.

I turned my focus to Elise and tried to make polite conversation. "Were you at a Christmas party? You look very nice."

Elise stared at me with the iciest glare I've ever been the recipient of. If this had been a science fiction movie, laser beams of fire would have shot out of her eyes and rendered me burned up and dead. "Don't you play nice with me you home-wrecking slut."

Didn't expect that one. My mouth fell open. "Excuse me?"

"You hear me, you piece of white trash, gold-digging whore. Who do you think you are, coming here? You have ruined my life, and I have no intention of letting you act like you belong here. You don't."

I could not believe what I was hearing. Where was this vitriol spewing from? It certainly could not be coming out of the mouth of this elegant-looking, well-polished, highly educated woman standing in front of me.

"Elise, perhaps you are under the impression that I did something to you?"

"*Under the impression*? Um, yeah. You come out of the woodwork with this mystery kid days before my wedding and expect Ryan to step up and be father of the year, and that it wouldn't affect my life. Stupid bitch."

"Whoa! That's not exactly what happened, and I never expected Ryan to call off the wedding once he found out about Jake." Of course, I omitted that Ryan was ready to call off the wedding before he knew about Jake, to be with me. But that argument would probably not help my case. And why was I still protecting him?

"How could I marry him? I'm not gonna let my hard-earned money go to support your money-grubbing ass. And I don't want any fucking brats to raise, let alone some Florida cracker trash. You ruined our plans for our perfect life with our careers."

"Well, I never wanted anything from Ryan." I put my hands on my hips. I felt like a child next to her.

She scoffed. I continued, "You cuddle up with that career at night, and see if it keeps you warm. And if you say one more thing about my son, I will kick your skinny little ass into tomorrow."

"You so much as touch me, and I will have you in jail on assault."

I looked around to see where Matt and Ryan were. I needed to get out of here. Elise saw me looking.

"Looking for your screw of the night to rescue you? What do Ryan and Matt do, pass you back and forth? Are you here tonight to service all their old friends? Are you worth so little that they share you like a garden tool? It was bad enough knowing that he had screwed you in the past, but I can't even imagine what diseases you're spreading around now. I am going to burn every piece of furniture that your skanky ass has touched in that house."

That was it. I had had enough. I shouted at her, "That's it. Stop right there." By then Matt and Ryan were back. It was obvious that we'd been having words.

Ryan, naturally, assumed that I was at fault. "Maggie, what did you say?" One look at his face told me that he was worried that I had told Elise something that would ruin his reconciliation with her.

"Ryan, I'm done. I am not doing this anymore."

"What do you mean, done?"

"I mean, done. I'm taking *my* children home and not coming back. Elise, have a good, perfect life with your perfect careers. Good luck picking out new furniture. Matt, I'm sorry to make a scene. I'm leaving. I'm done!"

And with that, I walked out and hailed a cab back to Ryan's place.

CHAPTER TWENTY

So, it's totally anti-climactic when you storm out on a guy but then have to return to his house. But I had no choice. Ryan was such a spineless piece of shit. He spent his life surrounded by domineering women who didn't require him to think for himself. No wonder he didn't want me. I forced him to think for himself. Of course, years of non-practice left him ineffectual at this skill. It probably explains why he had been so passive all those years ago in Boston, and why he left without ever talking to me.

So, needless to say, he did not come home and certainly did not chase after me.

This confrontation was undoubtedly one of the most clarifying moments in my life. There was the part of me that wanted Ryan to come running after me and profess his undying love. But I knew that Ryan did not exist outside of my warped, too-many-Hallmark-movies head.

Ryan was not who I wanted him to be. He never was and never would be. He let me chase after him and waited for me to initiate everything. He couldn't be upfront with me that he wasn't interested in Samantha. He couldn't even bring himself to initiate hitting on me or sharing a bed with me for months. Then, when his dad's condition deteriorated, he

245

couldn't ask me to be with him. He couldn't even answer my phone calls or letter.

Now, he was letting his family, especially his sisters, and his ex-maybe-current fiancée assume that I was a gold digger who was looking for him to pay my way through life. Ryan was an inactive spectator in his own life, and I was sick of trying to get him to play. After eight years of being on hold, I was ready to participate in life again.

I emailed my dad, asking him to set up our Christmas tree in our house, so it would be ready when we got home. I packed all our things and loaded them up in my (yep, still awesome) mini-van. I'd go over to Mrs. Milan's first thing in the morning and explain to her that we had to leave. I knew that I would do everything possible to include her in our lives if she still wanted to be included, but I was done with Ryan. The flurry of activity helped burn through the rest of my adrenaline quickly, and suddenly I didn't feel so good. I went into the bathroom, threw up, and fell asleep on the bathroom floor.

Which is where I was when Matt found me a few hours later. Go figure, it was Matt who came after me. Maybe he was my knight-in-shining-armor, not Ryan. I woke up to the sound of him laughing.

"Shut up Matt."

"I'm sorry, I just ..." he broke off, still laughing.

I tried to get up but only managed to get to a sitting position. "Shut up. You are entirely too loud."

From behind his back, Matt whipped out a McDonald's bag. "Still Egg McMuffin and a Coke, no ice?"

"Have I told you how much I love you?" I smiled at him and reached for the bag.

"No," he replied, "but I'm willing to hear it anytime."

"Matthew Slavin, you are my bestest friend in the whole wide world, and I love you. Now gimme my food!"

I managed to somewhat stand up, but I could not fully straighten up after the night on the hard floor. I perched myself at the edge of the large spa-like tub and unwrapped my greasy goodness. I was chowing down, as one should never do in front of another human being when I became aware that Matt was watching me intently.

"What?"

"Um, what happened last night between you and Elise?"

"Oh, that."

"Um, yeah, that. I have never seen you so mad. I thought I was going to have to pull you off her."

"Let's just say her exterior does not match her interior. But it helped clarify things. I was finally able to figure out some things."

"Like what?"

"Like, I'm taking the kids and going home."

"You're *what*?"

I nodded, still with a mouthful. "I, no, we're leaving. I know Mrs. Milan will be disappointed, but I cannot live my life for someone else any longer. I'm done with this house. I'm done with Ohio, and I'm done with Ryan."

"Done?"

"Yes, done. I don't need him. Hell, it's not like I need his financial support. That's laughable. Yet, most of his family, and certainly Elise, think that I'm a gold-digger who is going to rob him blind. Did you know I paid rent this summer, as well as for utilities, groceries, and for all the activities that the kids did? I have never asked him for, nor ever seen one single cent from him. Yet everyone seems to think I'm getting a free ride. And Ryan never corrects anyone or sets the record straight."

I took a long sip on my soda and continued. "I don't need to be treated like shit anymore. He's mean to me. I mean, who criticizes someone's pajamas? Who does that? He's barely civil. I know he hates me. He obviously can't stand to have me around, so problem solved. I won't be around."

Matt had a weird, uncomfortable look on his face. He probably didn't want to hear me malign his friend. Or maybe he was worried that I was going to end things with him too?

"Matt, you are my best friend. I really mean that. I didn't realize how much I missed you over these years until we started talking again. I need you to be in my life. I'm just not sure how. Do you get what I'm saying? We can figure out how later. Maybe you can make a fresh start down in Florida with us?"

"Maggie, what are you asking me?"

I put my head down on my knees, suddenly queasy again. "I don't know. I don't know what I want."

Matt was kneeling down in front of me. "Then we will save this conversation for another day. We will have lots of time to figure out where we stand."

I smiled and hugged him goodbye. He felt so warm and comfortable. It would be easy to be with him. I felt myself relax in his arms. I had not even realized the amount of tension I was holding in. He was my friend first and foremost. He knew me for all I was. He loved my kids. He was my best friend. And he would be there for me in the future. Maybe he was my future.

But now, I had to do something very difficult. I showered and packed up the rest of our stuff. I drove over to Mrs. Milan's, rehearsing for the whole twenty minutes about what I was going to say. How was I going to take these kids away from her, especially after I had promised her Christmas? What kind of person did that make me? My previous reaction would have been to stay, so as not to hurt anyone else, regardless of my feelings. But, it seemed that all of my other previous responses had been dead wrong. If I wanted to truly take care of my children, I needed to take care of myself first.

Mrs. Milan was surprised to see me there so early. "Maggie, what are you doing here? I would have brought the kids back. I wanted to give you a chance to sleep in."

"Oh, that's nice. I, um, couldn't sleep."

"Dear, don't take this the wrong way, but you don't look very good. Is everything alright?"

"No, it's not. That's why I'm here. I cannot apologize enough, but we need to leave. To go back to Florida."

"Is everything okay? What's happened? Is your father ill?"

"No, everything is not okay, but I hope it will be. My father is fine, everyone down there is fine. It's not that at all. I just," I faltered. "I just need to leave. I know it is not fair to you, but I will find some way to make it up to you. I promise. I just can't be here anymore."

"And I assume my son is somehow at fault?"

"Yes, well, I mean partially. We're both to blame. I've let this go on for entirely too long, and I mishandled things right from the beginning. I don't wish to speak badly about him to you but being around him is not healthy for me. He does not treat me well. I can't have it any longer. I need to leave and raise my children in a happy, healthy environment. And with the exception of you, I have realized that that environment does not exist up here. I have lived my whole life trying to please other people and doing what I thought they wanted me to do and being who I thought they wanted me to be. I just can't do it anymore."

"I'm sad, but I feel like I need to give you an atta-girl."

I threw my arms around the woman. She was more of a mother to me than anyone had ever been since my own mother had died. "I'll find a way to make it up to you. I can fly you down every month if you want. If you want to become a snowbird, we can manage that too. I want you to be a part of Jake and Sophia's lives. But I cannot expose them to Ryan and certainly not to Elise."

"Elise? What has she got to do with it?"

"I think they are back together. Maybe. Who knows? It's certainly not that he tells me anything. And it's not that I mind that Ryan is with someone. He has made it crystal clear that he has no desire to be around me. But not Elise. She is a hateful person, and I do not want her anywhere near my children."

"I'm sorry you feel that way."

"I am too. I had thought that Ryan and I could be adults and find a way to co-parent and provide a warm, loving, and happy environment to raise the kids in. But it is abundantly clear that, well, I just can't do it here."

Mrs. Milan hugged me again. "I wish things could be different."

Through my tears, I said, "So do I. Oh, so do I."

I gathered up the kids and started driving. I was tired, and we didn't make it too far. I found a hotel a few hours south that had an indoor pool where the kids could play and I could assume a semi-vegetative state. After a decent night's sleep, we were back on the road and back home by evening. Marcy—God bless my stepmother—had stocked the fridge and pantry with some essentials, including milk, juice, and bread. I called to thank them and to let them know that we were okay. They immediately came over. I don't think they believed me that I was okay, and they had to see for themselves. After a short while, they were assuaged and left me in peace.

I spent the next few days making the house look festive for Christmas. It helped me to keep busy, thinking about menial tasks so that I didn't have to think about anything deeper. Jake, especially, was disappointed at having returned to Florida early but was trying to make the best of it. What a trooper.

After a day or so, I called Michele to tell her that I had left and was done with the whole situation. She expressed her congratulations and pride at my finally taking a stand. Since we did not have a lot of holiday plans, she invited us over for Christmas Eve to spend with their family.

It turned out that a large, loud, boisterous gathering, with lots of delicious food and drink, was just what I needed. I camped out in the kitchen, helping Michele plate and prepare the next round of food while Jake and Owen played, and an older cousin entertained Sophia.

"So what has he said?" Michele finally asked.

"What has who said?"

"Ryan," she said with exasperation. "What has he said to get you to come back?"

I shrugged. "Nothing."

"What do you mean, nothing? It's not like he would let you go and not try to get his kid back."

I just looked at her with a raised eyebrow.

"Really?" she said incredulously.

"Really. I've neither seen nor spoken to him since I stormed out of the bar. A total replay of eight years ago. I guess he wants to be done with me as much as I want to be done with him."

"So, it's really over?"

"Guess it looks that way. But the weird thing is that I haven't heard from Matt either. I mean, I haven't contacted him, but I thought he would call me at least. Especially, since," I broke off ...

"Since what? What are you leaving out?"

"I dunno," I shrugged. "I guess, I don't know how to put it." I sighed. "I guess I kind of maybe started kind of thinking that maybe I should think about seeing if things might happen between me and Matt."

"Way to sound committed."

"I know, right? See, I just don't know. I don't know if it's because he's my," I saved myself quickly "other best friend, so I can feel open to him. I mean, he knows all the stuff, and he's okay with it, and I know his baggage too. Maybe it's because he actually touches me."

Michele raised her eyebrows and gave a little "bow chicka bow bow."

"No, not like that. Get your mind out of the gutter. It's just, I dunno, human contact. He hugs me and stuff. We sometimes cuddle on the couch. He played with my hair one night. It's just the kind of thing that I didn't even realize I was missing or needed. Oh, I don't know, I'm so confused."

"You need some fresh meat. Leave it all to me. I'll find someone fabulous to set you up with."

"Oh, Michele, I don't know that I'm ready to do that."

"No, you are ready. Time to put on your big girl pants."

"So someone can take them off?"

She laughed. "Exactly."

CHAPTER TWENTY-ONE
January 2009

*S*eriously, *I'm old enough to be his mother.*

That's what I was thinking, reading the latest text from my friend. Michele kept to her word and was scouring the community (and when I say community, I mean Planet Earth) for eligible bachelors for me. Daily, she texted me a picture (usually shirtless) of some movie or TV star, asking if they were my type. It was hard not to laugh, especially when she was sending pictures of teenage heartthrobs, who happened to be the pick of the day. But it kept the mood light, and it was just what I needed.

The holidays had been rough. I never heard from Matt or Ryan. It was such a repeat of eight years ago, and it made me angry more than anything else. The only one who bothered to contact me was Mrs. Milan when she sent a late Christmas present. When the package was delivered, I was totally surprised. There was a beautiful card that read, *"Maggie, You are first and foremost a wonderful mother. I hope you find the peace that you deserve. May God bless you and your children. Love, Mary Louisa Milan."*

The small box revealed a beautiful white gold mother's ring with sapphire for Jake and diamond for Sophia stones surrounding a center blue topaz (for me). It was the most thoughtful gift I had ever received. I cried for a long time after opening it.

But I was determined that this year would be different. I was moving on. I was no longer waiting for Ryan. And I wasn't going to sit around and wait for Matt either. They both failed me. Again. I could not believe that, for the second time, I left them, and neither one came after me. It was ten times worse this time, because Ryan not only abandoned me this time but his son as well. This time, it was all on him.

Jake was hurt that his father no longer called. How do you explain to a seven-year old when I, at thirty-two years old, couldn't understand? I wasn't sure that Jake believed that it was not his fault, and I was sure we were looking at years of therapy to get over this. Sophia too noticed the absence. She liked having cousins and a grandmother. Things that I could not give her.

I did my best.

Lindsay was back in our lives. She was attending college in northern Florida, and we saw her over the holidays. We were in phone and email contact, and she actually seemed to be getting her life together. So, all in all, life seemed to be falling into place. Which, usually for me, meant the bottom was about to drop out.

But for right now, I had good things to look forward to. My company had purchased a table at a gala to raise money for the Spina Bifida and Neural Tube Defects Association. I had a lot of clients with spina bifida to whom I sold wheelchairs and equipment. It was, as the name implied, a fancy, black-tie event. I loved the idea of getting all dressed up. I invited the Suarezes to be my guests, and Michele and I were consumed with getting ready. We took Sophia shopping with us for our gowns. We did manicures and pedicures and made sure that we had new shoes and purses and jewelry. I desperately needed a haircut, but somehow never got around to it before the gala. But Michele was hell-bent on finding me a date for the night. Despite my repeated pleas to leave well enough alone, she continued to scour her world for someone who could escort me. She checked out her accountant (too nerdy and socially inept), the oldest child's school principal (in the process of a nasty divorce), and Owen's drum teacher (most likely gay) before homing in on her orthopedic doctor, whom she was seeing for a foot problem. And who she referred to as Dr. Feel-good.

I respectfully declined her generosity.

Getting ready for work one morning, the week of the gala, Michele had called me in a panic. "Jeez Maggie, I did something so awful. It's so embarrassing! I'm gonna die! What am I gonna do?"

"Slow down, what did you do?"

"Oh God, it's so awful. I'm going to die of embarrassment. I wish the floor could swallow me up right now."

She finally stopped ranting and swearing long enough to tell me the story. Without my permission, she told the ortho doc, Dr. Feel-good, about me and asked to take his picture. Now, I have dealt with my fair share of orthopedic surgeons in my life. They are all arrogant, and most lack even cursory bedside manner, but Michele was smitten with this guy.

I'm pretty sure she'd leave Juan for him.

So humble doc posed, letting Michele snap a picture for me. Which she then captioned, "OMG, so f-ing hot!" And then, she proceeded to text it. But instead of sending it to me, she sent it to Owen's drum teacher. Michele didn't even realize she'd done it until he sent her a reply text that, while she must be well-intentioned, his love life was private, and he would appreciate it if she would mind her own business. And that it would be best if he no longer had anything to do with teaching her son.

"Can you believe it? I got the boot from my kid's music teacher. I'm supposed to be the one firing him because he's the weird one. Now, *I'm* the weird one!!"

I was laughing so hard that tears were streaming down my face. Tit was so nice to be crying from laughing instead of being sad for once. My cheeks hurt, and I was seriously in danger of peeing my pants.

"And, not only that, but Juan is threatening to take away my phone for inappropriate texting!"

That brought about another round of laughter.

"Okay," I said, gasping for breath. "Maybe this will stop your fruitless quest. I'll talk to Juan and make sure you get to keep your phone. What is he, your dad or your husband?"

She swore at me.

I continued, "Such language. Look, I appreciate all the hard work, but I don't need to be set up with anybody. Not that I don't appreciate the pictures though. Although, apparently, not everyone appreciates them so much." I started laughing again.

"Shut up! I still cannot believe I did that. Now we're gonna have to move far, far away."

"Oh, you'll live. And you can't leave me now. I have managed to alienate myself from everyone else in my life. I can't lose you too! Who would entertain me this way? Seriously, my cheeks hurt!"

I was still laughing when I got off the phone with her. It was so nice to laugh again. It made me feel that for the first time since Matt showed up on my door last April, I was going to be fine. Jake was still sad, and I needed to work on that, but I couldn't help him when I couldn't even help myself. I viewed this as the first step in reclaiming our happy life, just the three of us.

So, in the movies, the night of the gala is when someone shows up on my doorstep and professes his undying love. Except, as I've discovered over and over, my life is not like the movies. I went to the gala, unescorted, and came home, unescorted. There was no Cinderella ending for me. But, in all reality, it was fine. The most important thing was that the charity raised tons of money for a worthy cause.

Dr. Feel-good (of the infamous text) was there. He was an attractive, if not slightly cocky gentleman in his early forties. We bumped into each other—when you-know-who gave me a little shove—and did spend a brief amount of time talking. He alluded to calling me "when his surgery schedule permits."

Whatever.

A night out for fun would be nice, but Lord knows I was not looking for anything more than that.

Since all my appropriate movie moments had passed, I was then totally unprepared for what happened next. On President's Day, almost exactly two full months since I had left Ohio, Ryan showed up on my doorstep. The kids were with my dad. I was home alone and using the time to clean. I was wearing a wife-beater and Capri leggings. Not my finest look. My hair was back in a messy, quasi-pony tail, and I had my iPod on. And I was belting out songs. Loudly. And badly. Not my finest moment. I turned around, and there was Ryan, standing there in the foyer. He scared the ever-living crap out of me. I screamed.

Pulling the earbud out of my ear and putting my hand to my heart, I said, "You scared the ever-living crap out of me!"

He replied, "I knocked a few times, but you, ah, apparently couldn't hear me."

I looked at him. He looked awful. His hair was shaggy, and it looked like he hadn't shaved in a few days. His eyes were red-rimmed, and he had bags under them. Even his usually olive complexion looked sallow and drawn. "Wow, you look like crap," I said, still half in shock.

"Well, you sing like crap. Are we even now?"

"Um, I guess. What do you want?"

"You left."

"Two months ago. Are you just noticing now?"

"No, I just ..."

"Just what?" Man, I was really on the defensive. I was done taking his crap. Finally.

He looked down at his feet. He mumbled, "I don't know. I just thought Matt would have made you call me or something."

"*Made* me call you? Are you kidding me? Look, I may have been acting like a lovesick puppy dog for way too long, but no one's gonna make me do anything. Especially not after how I was treated." My voice rose to a yell.

"What do you mean how you were treated?"

Are you freakin' kidding me?

"Really? Do I have to spell it out for you? Okay then. You may want to take some notes because you seem pretty slow on the uptake these days." And then almost an entire year of repressed feelings and hurt proceeded to pour out of my mouth. I did nothing to hold it back.

"Let's start with you showing up here and declaring your love for me, only then to turn it to hate seconds later. Did it ever occur to you that I still had feelings for you too? That, by turning on me so relentlessly, you were crushing my heart over and over again. But I got that you were angry at me and needed time to cool down. Except you didn't. You stayed angry at me. Your anger not only didn't dissipate, but it *increased*. You never once took into account how *my* life had been altered by all of this. First, by being left by you, then finding out I was pregnant. I had to do everything on my own. But I made the best of it and continued on. Then, I turned our whole lives upside down to come to you last summer. Did you ever *once* think about what I had to go through to pack up the kids and move them north for eight weeks? You couldn't even be bothered to help me carry their suitcases in! And the whole time I was there, you never spoke to me. We did not have one single, solitary conversation that didn't involve the kids."

I paused and waited for a response. Always the passive observer, Ryan said nothing. He just sat down on the couch and looked at me. So I continued. "And I have never asked you for anything. Never asked for one single cent. In fact, you probably made money off of us being there this summer, what with being paid for rent and utilities, having your house cleaned, and food bought and cooked. Yet, you let your sisters and your fiancée and God knows who else think that I came out of the woodwork simply for your money. If you even knew how laughable that was!" Okay, I was getting a little manic. But this had been building in me for a very long time. I was powerless to stop it. I needed to get this all out so that I would finally be able to move on.

"And I get that you're angry with me. You have to know that I didn't plan this whole situation. It was not my fault. It was *our* fault. And for you to maliciously attack me, from what I wear to bed, to how I sleep in my own bed, to how I parent, to what my 'ulterior motives' are is just wrong. I don't deserve any of this. And what I certainly don't deserve is to have your fiancée calling me a gold-digging whore, and that you and Matt pass me around to all of your friends because I'll open my disease-ridden legs for anyone. It's way, way over the line, and I'm done. With all of you."

"Elise said what to you?" He seemed dumbfounded and like he was struggling to keep up.

"It doesn't matter exactly what she said, although I do want you to know the words 'whore, slut, gold-digger, white-trash, cracker, and skank' were popular. So, I can only imagine what you had been saying to her to help her form that opinion of me."

Ryan didn't reply, which to me was a confirmation.

"But you may want to know that she called your son a," I held up my fingers for air quotes. "Brat and Florida cracker trash."

"Are you done?" He finally asked.

"For now," I shrugged and sat down abruptly on the couch across from him.

"Where's Matt?"

"How the hell should I know? I haven't heard from either of you."

"What do you mean?"

"DO YOU WANT ME TO SPEAK SLOWLY? I HAVE NOT HEARD FROM MATT. THE PIECE OF SHIT DESERTED ME, YET AGAIN."

"Oh."

"Oh? That's all you have to say for yourself is 'oh?' You're a real piece of work."

"Maggie, I don't know what you want me to say. What do you want from me?"

"Are you serious?"

"Since you seem to be in a sharing mood, I want to hear from you what you want from me? I cannot figure out what you want. Do you even know?"

He was getting irritated. Good. It's about time he had *some* kind of reaction.

"Frankly, no I don't."

I sighed. "I just don't want to be fighting all the time. I don't want you to be mean to me. You need to stop being angry at me. Get over it."

"I'm not angry at you."

"Well, you could have fooled me. Especially when I heard you tell Matt that you would never get past your anger. I wasn't quite asleep that night, you know."

"You heard that?"

"Yep. You said you would never get past your anger. What am I supposed to do with that? I've bent over backward to bring Jake to you. To stay out of your way. I was pretty much a live-in servant. I don't know what else I can do."

"I don't think you heard all of the conversation. My anger is not about you, Maggie. It's about me. I'm so angry at myself for letting all this happen in the first place. If I had just called you back when I came back to Ohio. I wanted to, I really did. But it would have been hard, so I took the easy way out and look how that turned out."

"So, you're not angry at me?"

"Well, maybe a little, but I know that I brought it about. As soon as Matt said that he found you, I knew that all I wanted was for you to be back in my life. It became crystal clear that Elise was not the right person for me, and marrying her would be taking the easy route. Like I always do. I let people direct my life because it's easier than standing up and making hard choices. But it's difficult for me, and I'm not good at it."

"No shit, really?" I snarked.

"But I stood up to Elise and told her that I couldn't marry her then. Not with everything I had to figure out."

"But you didn't even tell me that Ryan! I thought that we were coming up, and you were already married!"

"I told you I couldn't marry her. On the beach."

"But that was before you found out about Jake and got so angry."

"But deep down, it didn't change how I felt about you. Just me. I was so mad at myself. And then ..." he broke off.

"And then what?"

"Well, I was trying to work through my, whatever, stuff. I knew I had these feelings for you, but I was so full of self-loathing that I didn't see how I could pursue anything with you until I dealt with that. I felt like I didn't deserve you. I would come home every night, and there was a delicious meal. And the house was clean. You kept doing all of these things that made me feel like I could never be good enough to deserve what you had to offer. But I told Matt. About how being around you was driving me crazy because I just wanted to be with you so badly."

"Yeah," I scoffed. "You wanted me so badly that you told Matt how ugly I was in my pajamas." I rolled my eyes. "You know, when you're not the only person in the house, you shouldn't speak on the phone without making sure the person you're talking about is not in the next room."

"What exactly did you hear?"

"Enough. That I was the ugliest thing you had ever seen. I didn't stick around to hear any more. I'm not a glutton for punishment."

"Maybe you should have stuck around. Because what I said was that even though your pajamas were the ugliest things I had ever seen, I could not stop wanting to touch them. And you."

Now, it was my turn to be dumbfounded. "Oh. They are really soft."

He laughed. "I knew it!"

After a moment or two, Ryan grew serious again. "So ..."

"Yeah, so. It still doesn't change that you have done a lot of things to hurt me. I don't know if I can get past that."

"And it doesn't change the fact that I waited too long, until you found someone else."

What?!?

"What are you talking about?"

"You and Matt," he said glumly.

"I really can't say that there's anything between us. Why would you say that?"

"Because, even though I told him that I wanted to find a way to be with you, he got you in the end."

"I am so confused. What are you talking about?"

"It's obvious that you two are together. You're not sly about your PDA's."

"No, you're wrong. We're not together. Never have been."

"What are you saying?"

"I'm saying that the more of a dick you were to me, the more I began to think that maybe Matt is the better guy for me. But nothing ever happened between us. And now he's left me high and dry too. So screw him. Screw you both for that matter."

Ryan buried his face in his hands. "I blew it again."

"You're just figuring that out?"

He just sat there. Watching the agony on his face, it all became clear what had happened. "So let me get this straight. All this time, while giving me the cold shoulder and being mean and cold and cruel, you were confessing your undying love to your best friend. Then, because you continued to treat me like shit, you thought your best friend swooped in and got the girl. And you, rather than opening your mouth and saying anything, got back together with Elise, who, by the way, is a total bitch, but you can't figure out why you're still unhappy?"

"I'm not back with Elise. We were at a work function that night and decided to go out. But then I saw you and Matt dancing, and you were obviously together ..."

"Jesus Ryan, why are you so dense? We were having fun. He was being nice to me. He wasn't putting the moves on me. I get touchy-feely when I drink. Nothing happened."

"I didn't know how Matt could be with you when he knew how I felt."

Something else dawned on me. "So, when you were telling Matt these things, what did he say back to you? Did he tell you to go easy on me or to be nice or what?"

Ryan looked confused. "Um, I don't remember him telling me anything helpful. He was just kind of quiet. Why?"

"Well, because I was telling him as well about how, despite your deplorable treatment of me, I was still in love with you."

"You are?"

"No, I was."

"Oh."

"But the point is that Matt knew we were both spinning our wheels out of sync. He knew we both wanted to be together but didn't know how to get there."

"Huh."

"Yeah, huh is right. If you and Elise hadn't shown up that night, I probably would have ended up with Matt."

"But he took off."

"Giving him the benefit of the doubt, which is difficult right now, because I'm pissed that he didn't say anything, I wanna believe that maybe he is distancing himself from me so that we don't end up together. End up hurting you."

"Okay, so the fact remains that you and Matt are *not* together."

I was excessively frustrated at this point. If I had had a frying pan in my hand, I would have beaten him over the head with it, just to emphasize my point. "NO! And we never have been. And never will be. I told him when he first found me that he could not be friends with both of us without betraying one of us. I had no idea that he would betray us both."

"So where do we stand?"

"Oh God, Ryan, I have no idea. I'm pretty sure there is not a 'we' or 'us' anywhere in the near future. You have been a passive observer in your own life for way too long to think that you could be an active participant in our lives. Right from the get-go, you sat back and let everyone else do the work. Having a relationship means that both parties have to try. You can't even speak up enough to tell me that you want to be around me or your son. Do you know what he has been through these last two months? He thinks, no matter what I tell him, that it is somehow his fault that you don't want anything to do with him. So congratulations. You have broken not one, but two hearts in this house."

CHAPTER TWENTY-TWO

O f course, I let Ryan see Jake that night. As crappy as he'd acted, Ryan owed it to Jake to try to make it up to him. I gave them some privacy and went out to sit on the deck.

I owed Matt a phone call. I yelled for a while and cried a lot too. I mean, how could he know that Ryan had feelings for me and not tell me? How could he know that I had feelings for Ryan and not tell Ryan? He was almost as bad as Irene in this whole situation.

Matt was quiet for the longest time. Finally, he told me that, even though he knew it was wrong, he stayed quiet, because he wanted his chance with me. But he felt guilty about betraying his friend, and so he removed himself from the situation before any irreparable damage was done.

It was probably too late.

I had eight years of anger toward him. I still couldn't understand how he didn't try to contact me all those years ago when I left Boston. If we were such good friends, then how could he have accepted that I was gone without leaving any contact information? It bothered me that he just let me go. He replied with some lame-ass excuse about trying to "respect my privacy" and that if I had wanted him to know where I was, I would have left him a way to get in touch.

"But I did!"

"But I didn't know! How was I supposed to know that Irene would do something like that?"

"How could you not know? She staged a whole sleeping with someone else scenario just to make you jealous. Did you really put it past her? I mean, did you think she was going to let us stay friends if Ryan was out of the picture, and I was still a threat to her?"

"I dunno. I guess I never really thought about it."

"You mean to tell me that in over seven years, it never once occurred to you to think about me or what I was doing or how I was?"

"Yes, I thought about you, but I thought that you wanted nothing to do with me because of Ryan. So I figured that that's how it should be. But once I saw your picture, even without seeing Jake, I just knew I had to find you again."

"Seriously, what is it with you guys?"

"Do you mean the male gender as a whole or me and Ryan?"

"Mostly you and Ryan, and because you are such stellar representatives that I have not felt the need to share company with any other members of your gender."

"Okay, so what exactly is your complaint?"

"Both of you—you take this passive, backseat approach to life, and you let life pass you by. You're both so afraid you're going to miss something or hurt someone or do something wrong. But neither one of you understands that doing nothing is an action too. It is a choice not to respond. And by choosing not to take action you are still making a choice. And you both have chosen poorly."

"Wow, I never thought of it that way."

I heard Ryan's voice from behind me. "I never thought of it that way."

I turned to look at Ryan. I held up my finger—no, not the middle one even though I was tempted—so he could give me a minute.

"Look, I gotta go have a similar conversation with Ryan."

"Maggie, will I ever hear from you again?"

"Yes, Matt, I'm sure you will. I just can't say when. I need a little time to figure things out. It's more than just about me. I've got a lot to consider."

"Maggie," he whispered, "I'm so sorry. Even if you decide never to speak to me again, you have to know that I never wanted to hurt you."

"I know that," I said, choking on my tears. "But you know what they say—the path to hell is paved with good intentions."

"I'm seeing that now."

I wiped my eyes with the back of my hand, the phone still clutched in my hand. I was freezing cold. "I need to go inside before I get frostbite."

"It's only about fifty degrees out here Maggie."

"Really? You're gonna fight me on this? I'm cold and I'm going in."

I stormed past Ryan and into the house. I made myself a cup of decaf coffee and specifically did not ask Ryan if he wanted any. I'd had enough of being the perfect hostess. A lot of good it did me.

We sat at the counter at opposing bar stools. I just sat and waited. Ryan was going to have to speak first. I was done letting him cruise through these things. No more EZ-Pass for him.

Finally (thirteen minutes later, but who's counting?), Ryan spoke. He cleared his throat nervously and said, "So where do we stand?"

"With what?"

"I dunno, stuff?"

Okay, really? I mean this guy was an educated, articulate law school graduate with a job in the Solicitor General's office for the State of Ohio, and all he could come up with was 'stuff?' Give me a break.

"Okay, well, what kind of stuff?" I was not going to help out on this at all. I was done leading the horse to water and waiting for him to drink (but apparently I was not done with the clichés and metaphors).

"Jake. What do we want to do about Jake?"

"Jake lives with me. He goes to school here. He has friends and is very well adjusted."

"Can we discuss some kind of visitation?"

"We can."

"Do you feel comfortable having him spend part of the summer with me? I mean, now that you've been up there and all."

"Who will take care of him while you're at work?"

"Oh, I hadn't thought of that."

Of course not. "You see Ryan, this parenting thing is hard work. It's twenty-four, seven, three-sixty-five. All of these things need to be considered before we can decide anything." I couldn't help sounding a little sarcastic.

He thought for a minute. "I guess I could ask my mom and Kelly to split the time, and I would take some vacation then too."

"Okay, fair enough, if that works for them."

"Would you let Sophia come for some of the time at least too?

Okay, didn't expect that one. I sucked in a breath. She was only going on four, so traveling would not be as easy for her.

Had all this stuff really happened since last April? Unbelievable.

"I don't know, just because of her age. I'll have to think about that one."

"Can I come down at least a few times a year to see the kids?"

"Yes, with ample notification. Next."

"Support."

"No."

"What do you mean no? I think legally I'm obligated to pay child support."

"I don't want it."

"Why not? You're entitled to it. And it doesn't make you a gold-digger or anything like that. You've supported Jake for the last seven years without any assistance. And this will help defray your travel expenses."

"No."

"Now you're just being proud and stubborn. I'm not saying that you have not done a great job providing so far, but I don't want my child doing without because you're too proud."

I started laughing, but it had a mean edge to it. "Oh, that's good. Ryan, I don't want your money. I don't need your money."

"Well, I know you don't *need* it, but it would help." He was getting patronizing. I was getting fed up.

"No, it really wouldn't. Ryan, I'm loaded."

"What?" I could see him looking around my modest house. I still lived frugally and did not waste money on lavish things. I kept the house up nicely, but it was still a smaller house. To me, a larger house just meant more to clean. But I couldn't expect him to understand.

"I've been working and have a very successful company from which I not only draw a salary, but I'm a co-owner, so I get some of the profits. Plus, I inherited a boatload of money the day I turned twenty-five."

"You what?"

"You heard me."

"But how?"

"It was a settlement from the accident. My recovery was uncertain, and they didn't know if I was even going to walk again. My dad wanted to make sure that I would be financially set if I was in a wheelchair or if I could not work. He arranged for me to get the money when I turned twenty-five since he thought I would be mature enough to handle it by then."

"How come you never mentioned it?"

"I don't tell anyone about the money. First of all, I don't want to be seen as someone's meal ticket. Secondly, I never wanted the money. To me, it was blood money, and it didn't change the fact that I was motherless and brotherless. I had always planned on keeping the trust intact and donating it somewhere when I died. I had to use some of the money to get on my feet and get my business going once I had Jake. My dad reassured me that it's what it was there for and that my mom would want me to be comfortable. Of course, that is what got me. And thirdly, you didn't stick around long enough to make it to my twenty-fifth birthday."

He ignored the dig and thought for a moment. "I guess you got pretty lucky. You're fine."

His glib answer bothered me. "Lucky to be alive, yes. Fine, far from it. I don't think you understand what I go through daily. But how could you—you've never once asked.

And you can't even claim ignorance on this one. You are one of the few people that I've even talked to about the accident in detail. You've never even asked me how I'm doing. So you don't know: How much pain I'm in. How hard it is just getting up and moving every morning. How, if I don't exercise, I can't move. But how hard it is to take the time out for myself to exercise when I'm a working single mother. How I had to create a new career niche for myself because I physically couldn't be a PT, not even for little kids—that it was too hard on my body to do the job. How I'll need more surgeries and more rehab, but I'm putting it off, hoping for a better answer. Hoping that I can wait until my kids are older so they're not so traumatized by me being incapacitated for a while. And how you just illustrated the very reason that I don't tell people about the money. You said it yourself: I'm so lucky, even though the quality of my life is crap."

"And now you have to deal with a ..."

"I believe douchebag is the word you're looking for."

"Yeah, I guess. I," he faltered. "I want to help you. I want to make up for all the colossal ways that I have let you down before."

"I don't know if you can make it up to me. I don't think you have any idea of what I've been through and what I go through every day. I don't know why I put such faith in you. I think you proved right from the beginning that you weren't dependable. I was an idiot to think that you would somehow wake up one morning and be this stand-up guy who wanted to be a father and a partner. I know it was never your life plan."

"But this wasn't your life plan either."

"No, it wasn't. And it wasn't Lindsay's plan to be pregnant at fifteen either. And it would have been one-hundred times worse for her to keep Sophia. Life doesn't go according to plan. You have to adjust and change with what gets thrown at you. I think you just sit there, waiting for the perfect pitch to come along. Sometimes you just gotta swing."

Again, he ignored the dig. God, I was turning into a shrew.

"Okay, so no support, although I would gladly pay it."

I realized how mean I sounded. I was not much better than Elise. I needed to try to soften my attitude. I didn't like being consumed by anger and hate. In the past, I'd always been able to let things go. I needed to start doing it now. I took a deep cleansing breath in and out. "I realize that you would, and I appreciate the offer. Far be it for me to tell you how to do things, but you could put the money away for Jake's college."

"That's a good idea. I'll create accounts for Jake and Sophia."

"You don't have to do that."

"I know I don't have to. I want to. I love that little girl too."

I didn't know what to say. Suddenly, the Ryan that I had met and thought about for eight years was resurfacing. Maybe it's because I had decided that I needed to let things go. I started to soften towards him. Just because he loved my kids. It didn't change how he had treated me, but I was having trouble seeing past that. Before I knew it, Ryan had stood up and walked around to me. I swiveled my stool around and looked up at him.

"Can I give you a hug?" he asked.

I paused. How do I respond? Was this a pivotal point between us? And why the hell didn't he just hug me without asking?

I nodded, and finally, he put his arms around me.

CHAPTER TWENTY-THREE
Summer 2009

L ife continued on as it has a habit of doing.

Matt and I resumed our friendship, long-distance of course. Our friendship would forever be defined by missed opportunities and what-ifs. Somehow, our timing had never been right. We had known each other for almost half our lives. It was apparent that, if we had not managed to get together in the fourteen years we had known each other, it was not meant to happen. After years of starts and stops, Matt's friendship meant more to me than anything else. I had lost enough over the years, that I would rather have his friendship than try for something more.

Our final friendship deal included flirting privileges and veto status for any new girl that he became serious about. I grudgingly granted Matt the same. At least one thing was settled.

Ryan was another story. We had let go of our anger and were working on rebuilding communication. If we'd been in the same state, we would have gone to couples therapy or something. Regardless, we managed to achieve some peace. There was no more hostility and no more yelling, which was a victory in and of itself. We were trying co-parenting, with actual conversations and all. But the uneasy edge remained just below the surface.

Ryan wanted us to move to Ohio. I didn't want to. We'd tried that already. As much as communication had improved, I was still doing a lot of the work. Ryan was still incapable of meeting me halfway, and I was no longer settling for that.

As much as I wanted to have things work out between us, I knew he would not make me truly happy. I would be doing what everyone wanted me to do, rather than what *I* wanted. It's what I've done since the accident.

I wanted to be myself. I wanted to be taken care of. I wanted someone to sweep me off my feet. I wanted to be consumed by love. Ryan wasn't capable of giving that to me. I think he knew it too, but he kept trying. It was ironic. The more disinterested I was, the more interested he became. It was irritating. After all this time, now he tries to act?

So, life in the Miller house continued as a party of three. There was talk about getting a dog, mostly from the kids. Jake finished up second grade and Sophia finished pre-school. Jake was going to go up to Ohio for the summer again. I would fly up with him, get him settled, and fly back home the next day. Sophia and I would fly up again for a week at the end of the summer to spend time with everyone up there. I would miss my little boy dreadfully, but Ryan needed this too.

In general, I was happier. We had settled back into our groove, and I felt like a weight had been lifted off my shoulders. I was re-building a better Maggie.

But dropping Jake off for six weeks was so hard. I would miss him so terribly. I would miss how he still crawled into bed with me every morning, at precisely 7:10 a.m., no matter what time he went to bed. I would miss our conversations. It had been us for eight years, and I had never spent any real time without him. So, with a tearful goodbye, Jake and Ryan brought me to the airport. I wasn't sure if I'd be able to get on the plane, leaving my little boy behind in Columbus.

"Don't worry Maggie. I'll take good care of him."

"I know, it's not that. I'm just gonna miss him so much."

I knelt down to hug Jake. He threw his arms around me. He whispered in my ear, "I love you, Mommy. I'll be good, I promise."

"I know you will, Sweet Boy. I just don't know that I'll be okay without you."

"Well, you have to be. You have to take care of Sophia. We can talk on the computer."

"I know. I just won't be able to do this over the computer." I tickled him. He squealed and squirmed away.

"Mom!"

Ryan and I started laughing. It was enough to break the heavy mood. I slowly straightened up. I looked at Ryan. "You better take good care of him."

"Maggie, you know I will. We'll call you." He moved in to hug me. As he held me, he said, "I can't thank you enough for this, for him. I missed so much, I don't want to miss anymore."

I pulled away. "I know, and I don't want you to miss any more either. It's just hard for me."

"You don't have to go. You can stay."

"No, I can't, and you know that. Ryan, we're no good together. We bring out the worst in each other. But we made a beautiful boy over there." I nodded towards Jake, who was checking out the arrivals/departures screens. "He's what matters now."

"I know, but you should really reconsider, um, me."

I shook my head and walked through security. I managed to keep the tears at bay until I boarded the plane. I felt sorry for the lady sitting next to me. Finally, I looked over, "I just left my son with his father for the summer."

She looked at me like I had three heads and went back to reading her book.

Okay.

I had pulled myself together by the time I changed planes in Baltimore. Perhaps the cocktail that I drank (it was one o'clock, totally respectable, right?) on the layover helped. I kept my sunglasses on to hide my puffy eyes and turned my iPod on. I closed my eyes and listened to the music, trying not to read too much into all the song lyrics. It seemed like every song could be applied to the situation between Ryan and me. I think I might have been dozing off, or at least free-associating while on that flight. Conversations were replayed in my head, set to the music I was listening to. I felt like I was watching a movie montage of the two of us. Did I want to be with Ryan? I wanted the Ryan who existed in my mind. But that wasn't the real Ryan. Did he deserve another chance? Could he make me happy? Could we make each other happy? I had thought about being with Ryan for so long, and now, here it was, mine for the taking. Why couldn't I just reach out and take it?

Because deep down, I knew what the answer was.

Yet still, trying to convince myself, I made a list of pros and cons about the situation. The pros included: Ryan was Jake's father. Ryan loved my kids. I loved Ryan's mother. Ryan had a reliable job and was an upstanding member of the community, and oh my God, he was still hot.

He had a lot going for him.

But then I got to the cons: Ryan lived in Ohio, so someone would have to move. Ryan had been a colossal ass to me and treated me like crap. Ryan had proved over and over that he could not step up in a crisis and could not take care of me. Ryan and I seemed destined to fail at communicating with each other. Lastly, I didn't think I could trust Ryan not to break my heart again.

By the time the plane was starting its descent, whether I wanted to admit it or not, I knew what my answer was. I knew what choice I had to make. For so long, I'd felt like I was reacting instead of choosing. Now, it was my chance to choose.

Even so, I was unsure of myself. This was not a muscle I'd ever flexed before. I needed a sign to let me know I'd chosen correctly. With that decision, the plane landed. Standing up after sitting for a while was always interesting for me because of my back, as was reaching my baggage in the overhead bin. As I tried to stand up straight, which was not an easy feat at the moment and then stand on my tiptoes to reach my bag which had shifted to the back of the compartment, an arm reached over me as a voice said, "Let me help you."

I turned to thank my Good Samaritan. He looked familiar and recognition flashed in his gaze. We looked for a minute, and he handed me my bag. Finally, it dawned on me. Before I could stop them, the words flew out of my mouth. "Oh, you're Dr. Feel-good!"

Dear God, shoot me now.

My hand flew over my mouth.

He laughed. "And you're Michele's friend from the gala. Did you like the picture she took for you?" He posed slightly.

I had to laugh.

Then, he took my bag out of my hand. "Let me. It's almost as big as you are."

We deplaned together, falling into step. He still carried my bag. I felt obligated to tell him the story of the music teacher and the text gone horribly awry. We could not help laughing at the predicament of our crazy acquaintance.

"So, what brings you traveling today? Business or pleasure?"

I thought for a minute. "Um, I don't know."

"How can you not know? Either it was fun or it was work," he challenged.

"Well, that's the thing. It was neither fun nor work. What about you?"

"Continuing education course."

"Ahh, gotta love those. Learn anything interesting?"

"Yes, actually, it was about improved techniques for minimally invasive knee replacements." He said, trying to sound technical. I didn't think he remembered that I was a physical therapist. Or maybe it hadn't come up.

"I thought you were a foot guy?" I asked.

"I handle all body parts," he answered smoothly.

I just laughed. "Oh, you've gotta be kidding me. Really? That's your line? You can do better than that!"

By now we were approaching baggage claim. He handed my bag to me. "Did you check anything else? I'll wait with you."

I shook my head. "I'm good. I travel light."

He laughed. "I wouldn't describe that bag as light."

I shrugged. I wasn't used to someone swooping in to assist me. I gave him a little smile and wave. "Thanks for the help with the bag."

"No problem. Any friend of Michele's has got to need some help," he jested. "And let me know if you need any more pictures."

I walked away, chuckling. It was just what I needed to ease my re-entry into my Jake-less summer.

*****

Sophia and I got our groove on for our girls-only summer. We did lots of fun things, all super girly, and we were able to spend some quality time with Lindsay too. She came over on Sunday mornings for a cup of coffee and to visit. She had matured a lot over the past year, and I was very proud of her. I could see that it was difficult for her not to be Sophia's mother, but she managed it well. She was thinking about being a social worker or child psychologist. She had a long way to go but at least she had a direction now.

"You know, Honey, sometimes it's not the initial action that is so important, as is your reaction to it. Sometimes, things are set in motion by things outside our control, and the only thing we can control is our response. And that is what defines us."

She nodded. "I guess. So, it's not that I'm destined to be a teenage pregnancy statistic. I can be something and not let," she nodded her head towards Sophia, who was playing across the room, "that be the story of my life."

"Exactly. It's why I'm torn about Ryan. I always kind of understood why he walked away in the first place. Well, actually I don't. We had something really great, and I can't understand how he could leave and not look back. But I understand, in his head, that his rationalizations made sense. What I cannot get past is his reaction after he found out about Jake. He didn't know how to handle *anything*. He wouldn't stand up for me, as the mother of his child. He sat silently as people made assumptions and jumped to conclusions. He didn't want to get into fights with people who he cared about, and he thought correcting them would do that. So he said nothing. I think that says more about him than anything else. I know he loves Jake and wants to be in our lives. But I can't accept how he had virtually no emotional reserve to handle the situation and how he is totally incapable of communicating his wants, needs, and fears."

"So what are you going to do? He is super hot."

I sighed. "I know he is. But believe it or not, it's just not enough. I still don't know what I'm going to do. I'm waiting for a great cosmic sign."

"What kind of sign?"

"I don't know. A billboard with an eligible bachelor's phone number on it?"

Lindsay laughed. "Not if I drive by it first!"

"I always say, 'If you don't listen to your guardian angel whispering in your ear, then he'll hit you over the head with a two-by-four.' I'm hoping to hear the whispering because I think I've already gotten hit enough for this lifetime."

Lindsay stood up to leave. "What are you guys doing for the rest of the day?" she asked.

"I think we're gonna go with my dad on the boat for a little while, and then we'll be back here for naptime. What are you up to?"

"I've gotta work in a little while. Thanks for the coffee and the advice. You've been nicer to me than you should have, and I appreciate that." She looked like a little girl, apologizing.

"Remember, sometimes the reaction is more important than the cause."

She smiled, hugged Sophia and left.

Sophia and I met my dad out on the dock. We had a good time, going out on the river. When we got too hot, we jumped in the water and cooled down for a few minutes. Sophia wore a swim vest, and it cracked me up how she bobbed up and down in the water like a buoy. We arrived back at the dock, and I climbed out of the boat. The seat that I stepped on to get out of the boat was wet, so I turned to give

Sophia a hand, rather than letting her climb out on her own. I reached for her and grabbed her left wrist. I gave her a little tug to pull her up, but as I did, her foot slipped on the wet seat, and she fell with me still holding her wrist. I felt her arm pop, and she began crying. She immediately pulled her arm into her abdomen and just started yelling, "Owie, owie, owie!" over and over.

My dad scooped her up and handed her to me. I clutched her to my chest for a minute. Then I put her down and tried to take a look. She was still screaming and didn't want me to touch her arm. I was guessing that it was a radial head dislocation, and it could be easily reduced. But I didn't want to take the chance that there wasn't more ligamentous damage or even a fracture, so I knew that meant a trip to the ER.

My dad looked a little queasy when I mentioned the hospital. I assured my dad that we would be fine and that I would call him as soon as I had news. I didn't think it was a big thing, but I just wanted to be sure. I picked her up, carried her to the house where I grabbed my purse and her pink blankie and her pink "Pammy the Lamby" and loaded her into the car. I ran back into the house and grabbed an ice pack and put it on her arm before we drove to the hospital. My poor baby just kept crying and saying that she needed a band-aid.

My already fragile heart shattered.

I carried my still sobbing child into the ER waiting room and found it virtually empty. I could have cried with relief. Of course, I still had to check her in. And then wait. And talk to the triage nurse. And then wait. And then be brought into the back and talk to that nurse. And then wait. What was so frustrating was that I knew the problem and the solution. I just wanted a quick x-ray to verify that there wasn't a fracture. So, I'd lost a little—lot—of patience by the time I told the on-call pediatrician who came in. I explained, with very thinly veiled manners, "She slipped and fell down while I was holding her extended, pronated wrist. There was a pop. She has a radial head dislocation, but I just want to verify that there is not a buckle fracture before I reduce it, if you don't mind."

The patronizing Doogie Howeser-type resident, who, if he wasn't careful, was going to get punched, just looked at me. "Ma'am, we can't know what it is until she is examined."

"Do you wanna bet money?"

"Ma'am, I know you're worried, but we know what we're doing here. And we do not advise anyone but trained medical professionals to treat this type of injury. You did the right thing by bringing her in." Then he patted my hand. Like I was some demented little old lady. And did he really just call me ma'am?

Seriously, he was about to eat my fist. "Can you just get the ortho on call? I'll deal with them."

Sophia was quietly watching the exchange with wide eyes. She was curled up into me, her blanket wrapped around her. She was still wet and in her bathing suit. I hadn't wanted to put her terry-cloth cover-up on because I didn't want to have her put her arms through the sleeves. Which reminded me, I was still in my bathing suit too. Luckily, I had thrown my cover-up over my green bikini. But the halter top on my suit and the tank top of the dress were both relatively low cut and, with holding Sophia, I was in danger of exposing my chest. Even though I had been in Florida for eight years now, I still had trouble with people going everywhere in their bathing suits. Now I was one of them.

I was sitting in a very uncomfortable chair and was telling Sophia a princess story to keep her calm. I whispered into her hair, gently rocking her back and forth when the ortho doc finally walked in.

"Well, little Miss Miller, what seems to be the problem?"

My head snapped up at the familiar voice. "Oh my God. Dr. Feel-good!" Did I really just do that for the second time? I wanted the floor to open up and swallow me.

He laughed. "You know, my name is actually Dr. Feeley, which, I know, is an ironic name for a doctor. Go ahead, make another joke. And don't think I haven't heard them all before. Better yet, why don't you just call me Holden."

"Holden? Holden Feel-Good. That's awesome. There are so many things running through my head right now. It's taking a lot of effort to hold 'em in. Get it?" I laughed.

I don't know what it was about this guy, but he always appeared at just the right moment to ease my tension.

"Haha. I've told you, I've heard them all."

"Your parents must have a great sense of humor."

"Well, considering it's actually Feeley, it's not as bad as you might think. My mom is a big Salinger fan."

I finally pulled myself together. "In case you don't remember, I'm Maggie Miller, and this is Sophia. She had a downward fall while I was holding her extended, pronated wrist, and I believe she has a radial head dislocation, but I was hoping to have an x-ray to rule out a buckle fracture before I reduced it."

Holden laughed. "Dr. Doogie out there said you had a Wikipedia diagnosis and had planned on treating it yourself." I turned Sophia to face him, and he set about gently examining her arm. She was being so brave. My poor little girl.

"Okay, so it's not just me that he looks just like him, right?"

"Nope. I'm not saying I'm getting old but when did these interns get so young? Tell me what exactly were you planning on doing."

"Ninety-degrees elbow flexion, quick supination until you hear the click, then ice."

"Good." And then he did exactly that. He winked at Sophia. "What are you?" He straightened up and ruffled her hair.

"Really upset that my child is hurt."

"No, what is your profession?" He rolled his eyes.

"I'm a PT."

"Oh, so you really could do this."

"Don't sound so surprised."

"So none of my smooth medical speak has impressed you then?"

"No, not really." It was my turn to smile.

I smiled a lot around Dr. Feel-good.

"She'll be fine in about thirty minutes or so. Watch her and make sure she has full range of motion. If she doesn't, that's when we'll do an x-ray. No need to expose her to radiation if she doesn't need it. Ibuprofen if she seems uncomfortable."

"High risk for recurrent dislocation over the next two to four weeks, right?"

"Right, so be careful about pulling on that arm. If you can, avoid holding that hand when walking. Follow up with her pediatrician in a few days."

"Dr., I mean Holden, thanks."

"Maggie Miller, it was my pleasure. You have a beautiful daughter. May I ask you something um, not related to this visit?"

"Um, okay?"

"Since Michele wanted to send you my picture, am I correct in assuming that you are not involved with anyone right now?"

"My typical response would normally be to say that when you assume, you make an ass out of you and me. But, alas, in this situation, you are not incorrect. On the other hand, while I am not involved, neither am I available."

He smiled. He handed me his business card. He wrote a number on the back. "That's my cell. I'd really like to take you out sometime. Give me a call when you're ready."

I eyed him skeptically. "How often do you hit on your patient's mothers?"

"Oh, all the time, but considering the average age of my patient is about fifty, those mothers are a whole different ball game. The nursing homes all have curfews, and I'm getting sick of eating strained peas. They're starting to get to be a drag."

I laughed, despite myself.

He continued, "No, seriously, my marriage ended about eighteen months ago. And despite the urging of everyone and the shameless flirting of many of the nurses, I haven't wanted to put myself out there yet."

"So, if I shoot you down, then it will totally crush your fragile self-esteem and scare you off of dating forever."

"I'm already crying on the inside, just thinking about your rejection."

"Oh, I think Nurse Ratchet out there will help dry them." I picked up Sophia, and she put her head down on my shoulder. "Thanks again."

I walked out, and I could have sworn that the nurses behind the desk were giving me the stink-eye.

CHAPTER TWENTY-FOUR

A week later, Sophia and I flew up to Columbus without event, which is always a good sign. I had to be careful not to hold her left hand when walking through the airport. It meant I ended up carrying her a fair amount, which was starting to get difficult as she got bigger. Lucky for me, she was still a peanut. I popped some ibuprofen with my coffee on our layover and was in okay shape by the time we arrived in Columbus. The boys were waiting for us in baggage claim. Jake ran up to us, and I scooped him right up, all sixty pounds of him. He looked older. And tanner. And in desperate need of a haircut. I looked over and Ryan was holding Sophia. I wanted to attribute the swirling in my stomach to caffeine and ibuprofen, but I know Ryan stirred that pot. He certainly did love my kids.

And I had to tell him how I felt. My decision.

We had a good week together, a 180 from last summer. We went to the Columbus Zoo and Aquarium. We went to Buckeye Lake. We went to King's Island amusement park. There was a lot of laughing, and the atmosphere was definitely lighter than it had been in the past. Ryan and I talked, but the conversations were nothing like those we had had when we first met. It seemed that we had lost our ability to have the words flow between us. But my kids were happy here.

Here, they had a family.

I still felt confident about my decision regarding Ryan, though I was torn about the idea of moving up to Ohio. I knew he wanted me to, but my life was in Florida. I had my family to consider, not to mention my business and my friends. Even Holden ran through my head as a reason to stay in Florida. Not actually Holden per se, but the possibilities he represented.

It was time for me to put myself first. I could no longer sacrifice my happiness in the name of my kids or doing what I *thought* others would want me to do. And to do that, I had to tell Ryan, once and for all.

I waited until our last night there, after the kids were in bed, so as not to spoil the week for everyone else. Old habits about self-sacrifice die hard. Ryan and I sat out on the deck side-by-side, beers in hand. We could speak without having to make eye contact. It was easier that way. The darkness that enveloped us on the humid evening also cloaked us from each other. Lightning bugs danced through the darkness.

Like we always did, we talked but not about anything of importance. Safe topics. Benign topics. Things that didn't matter. The weather.

"That's one thing I miss about the north. In the north in the summer, it gets dark and the temperature drops and there is some relief from the temperature. In Florida, it just gets dark, and the temperature stays the same." I was just prattling on, waiting for him to speak of something serious.

"Summers have got to be hotter though, right?"

"Not really. Maybe higher temps for more days in a row, but I remember it being that hot in New York in the summer as a kid. And, we didn't have air conditioning."

"We didn't either. Now I can't imagine buying a house without it."

"Yeah, everything in Florida's air-conditioned. Plus, we go out on the water, and that makes it nice."

"I'll bet it does."

"Nice, of course, until one of you ends up in the hospital."

"Now, what exactly happened?"

I recounted the events of Sophia's fall. "I knew she was okay but took her to the ER because I wanted an x-ray to make sure there wasn't a fracture. Call me neurotic."

"I think it's probably normal, but what the hell do I know about women?" he laughed.

"From my experience, not a whole heck of a lot." I glanced sideways at him to see how he reacted.

"Nice," he laughed.

It was time to steer the conversation to something that mattered.

"The best part was, in the middle of it, I got asked out on a date."

"You did? By whom?"

"The doctor who treated Sophia."

"Her *doctor* hit on you?" he said incredulously. He finally turned and looked at me. But it was a brief look, and then he turned away.

"To be fair to him, we'd met a few times before, and my friend Michele has been trying to set us up for months. Oh, that, and I'm pretty sure my breasts were hanging out of my bathing suit top." I tried to make a joke to lighten the situation.

Ryan was quiet for a moment. I just waited. Finally, he said, in a low voice, "What did you say?"

"To the doctor?"

"Yeah. Are you going out with him?"

I took a deep breath. Here goes nothing. "I don't think it should matter to you if I do or don't. Ryan, look at me."

I waited for him to meet my gaze. "Ryan, you know we can't keep doing this. We're not right for each other. We never have been."

He looked down. "I know." Then there was silence. He wasn't going to say anything else.

I stood up to go inside. Ryan stood up too and stood before me. He pulled me into his arms, and I rested my head on his chest.

"I wish we could be though," I whispered. I did. It would be so much easier.

"We could make it work." He murmured into my hair.

"Work, yes. But I don't want to just make it work. I want to be deliriously happy. I want to know what my partner is thinking and feeling. I want to express my thoughts and feelings. I want to laugh. I want to be taken care of for once. I want to be swept off my feet. Can you honestly stand here and tell me that you can give me that?"

He paused for a long time before he finally said, "But I want to."

"Can I make you feel like that? Can you get past everything that has happened and feel that way towards me?"

He pulled back a little, and we looked into each other's eyes. He didn't need to say anything because we both knew.

I stepped back again. "Ryan, I want to be happy, and I want you to be happy too. We'll always be a part of each other's lives because of the kids. And I'd like to have you as a friend. But you need to find the woman out there who is waiting for you to sweep her off her feet. And it's not me." I turned and went into the house and made it all the way to my room before I started to cry.

CHAPTER TWENTY-FIVE
November 2009

The holidays would be here before I knew it. Mrs. Milan was flying down to spend Thanksgiving with us (and I did not think she would stand us up, as Ryan had done). Ryan was coming down for a few days around Christmas. The kids being in school all the time freed me up to work a little more and to feel less guilty about the time I spent away. It also gave me something fulfilling to do. I felt like my life was where it was meant to be.

I was at the local rehab hospital, evaluating a sixteen-year-old girl who had been in a car accident and was paralyzed from the mid-chest down. She was, like all teenagers, moody and defiant. And like a lot of people who sustain spinal cord injuries, she was depressed. Her wheelchair evaluation was not going well. She was uncooperative, almost to the point of being unresponsive. We had been going round and round for over an hour and, frankly, it was getting towards lunchtime, and I was getting hungry.

Since my patience was wearing thin, I asked the therapist and her parents if I could speak to the patient alone.

The adults obliged and left us. Finally, the patient Sherri said, "I don't want a wheelchair."

"Okay. I'm kind of getting that. Why not?"

"Because I don't want to be in one. Going in a wheelchair will cause my IQ to drop about thirty points. People will look at me differently. I don't want to be some damn cripple."

"Who does?"

"What?" she looked at me warily.

"Sherri, no one wants to be in a wheelchair. Trust me, I know."

"Oh, yeah. Like hell you do." She looked at my legs.

"No, actually, I do. I was in a car accident when I was seven. I broke my back, pelvis, and both of my thigh bones. I spent almost a year in a wheelchair. They weren't sure if I would ever be able to walk again."

"No shit?" She seemed like she was warming up.

"Really. Worst year ever."

"But you are walking now," she said bitterly.

"Yeah, but it's taken a lot of hard work. And pain. It hurts every day, still twenty-five years later. And there's a good chance that I will end up back in a wheelchair as I get older. It's a real possibility for me."

"But I'm never gonna walk again."

"You don't know that. Medicine is advancing every day. But, on the other hand, there is a good possibility that you won't. So what?"

"My life will be over! It already is!" she wailed. Typical teenager. Of course, she had a lot to be grieving about.

"Are you breathing? Are you aware of your surroundings? Are you going back to school? Then your life isn't over. It's different, but not over. My mom and brother were in the car accident with me too. They were killed. My brother's life ended at nine. He never made it to middle school or high school. He never played ball again. He never got to be a dad. His life is over. Your life is just on a different path."

"Oh, I'm sorry. I didn't, I mean, that sucks."

"Yeah, it does suck. And you know what? What happened to you sucks too. But there's still a lot out there for you. You aren't brain-damaged. You don't have cancer that's eating you from the inside out. You don't have a degenerative disease where you know you will die before you hit thirty. You get to finish high school and go to college. You get to have a career. You can get married and have kids. You can do whatever you want. You just have to do it from a sitting position."

"Who's gonna want to marry me?"

"I bet a lot of guys will. If a guy is scared off because of a wheelchair, then he's not worth much anyway. There are a lot of guys not worth a whole lot out there. Trust me, I've dated a whole lot of them. If the chair helps you weed them out quicker, it's better for you."

She wiped a tear from her cheek. "So you really think I can have a normal life?"

"Yes, I do. But it will be a different normal than you're used to. And it will take some adjusting."

She leaned her head forward a little. "About having kids. You mean adopting, right?"

"Not necessarily, although that certainly is an option. My daughter is adopted, and it was the best decision I ever made." I looked at her. "But that's not what you are talking about, is it?"

She looked down, flushing with embarrassment, and shook her head.

It was hard not to smile. I knew where she was going. "Okay, so a thousand years ago when I was in college, we had to take a class called 'Psychosocial Aspects of Physical Disability' where they had lots of people with disabilities come in and talk to us. And they had this couple come in, both spinal cord injured. He was an L1 and she was a C6 or C7 because I remember she didn't have full use of her hands. I remember her showing us how she put on her makeup. They both worked and owned their own home. And they had a kid together, the regular way. They went way too in depth about their sex life, but now, thinking about it, it took a lot of courage to get up and talk about it like that. They were describing positions and stuff that was just way, way too TMI. So, yes, you can have sex. And you can even find it pleasurable. But, you're sixteen, so walking or not, you need to wait another twenty years or so."

Sherri smiled. "Now you sound like my mom."

I returned her smile. "So, I know that this really does suck, but you need to talk to the therapist about this. I'm just a loudmouth who isn't afraid to share my opinion. So just let all the people here help you. They know what they are doing and are pretty good at it."

"You seem pretty good at this too."

"Thanks. I became a PT because my PT when I was a kid was so great. I couldn't really do the job well, with all the lifting and stuff, because of my injuries, so that's why I went into the equipment end. It's all about making it work."

Sherri paused, "But I still don't want to have a wheelchair."

"I know, but it's the way it is right now. So let's get you going so you can blow this popsicle stand and get back to living. You just get to live it with better parking."

I walked out in the hall to get her parents, the Gordons, and the rest of the therapy team. I was startled to see Holden, who was standing with the Gordons. "Oh, what are you doing here?" I couldn't stop the words from flying out of my mouth. A big smile spread involuntarily across my face.

He returned the grin. "Well, if it isn't The Amazing Maggie Miller. Sherri is my daughter's friend, and I stopped in to see how things were going. I had had the impression that Sherri was being a little obstinate, but you seemed to get her straightened right out."

"Well, you know, it's what they pay me the little bucks for. I have to make the money I spent on a psych minor pay off somehow."

The adults in the hall filed back into the treatment room, and it left Holden and me standing there, staring at each other.

Finally, he spoke. "I couldn't help overhearing, well, because I was eavesdropping. That was amazing what you did in there with Sherri. I am truly impressed."

Heat filled my cheeks as I looked down. "I, um, I didn't eat breakfast, and I want to get to lunch sometime this century, so I had to do something to move the appointment along."

"No, that's not it at all."

I looked at him. "Yes, it is. I'm *really* hungry. I never joke about food."

Holden laughed. "Then, in that case, I'm taking you to lunch. Don't even think about turning me down."

I agreed and returned to finish the appointment. By the time it was over, the dancing butterflies replaced the hunger pangs in my stomach. It had been a long time since I had been out on a date, even a lunch date. But this wasn't really a date. Or was it? Holden had expressed interest in me, but that was when I was half-naked and a few months ago.

Oh, God, what was I getting myself into?

We were sitting in a café a few blocks from the hospital. It was a frequent stop for anyone who worked at the hospital, so we both knew what we'd be ordering without really considering the menu. There was an awkward silence between us. Finally, I spoke up. Sort of. "So ..."

"Yes?"

Okay, not going so well. Maybe in the years I spent pining away for Ryan, I had lost all ability to communicate with a member of the opposite sex. Yet, to anyone else, I could be candid and blunt and was always able to speak my mind. Oh, well, what the hell did I have to lose? I had been single for so long, screwing this date up would not make too much of a difference.

"Holden, I'm gonna put it all out there. I'm a single mother of two. My kids absolutely come first. I have very little relationship experience and what I do have, I manage to royally screw up."

"Maggie, I have a sixteen-year-old daughter who is driving, and it terrifies me. My ex-wife left me over a year ago, and I'm still not sure what happened, other than she," he held up his fingers for air quotes, "outgrew our marriage."

"Okay, so we're both totally screwed. And screwed up."

He laughed. And that was it. From then on, we were able to talk. And talk. And talk. I didn't watch what I said. I spoke what was on my mind.

I was me.

And it was so refreshing.

Holden, likewise, was upfront and frank. Blunt. Cocky. Yet endearing at the same time. And we laughed. So much laughing. I didn't even stop to think or overanalyze. I just was.

Holden called when his schedule permitted and texted me at other various times. His texts were usually humorous and often off-color. We were both very candid. We shared stories of our days and swapped parenting stories, as well as work stories.

It was easy to talk to him.

I never watched what I said or censored myself. With Holden, the words just flowed. After a few weeks of chatting, I grew to look forward to Holden's calls. We'd grabbed lunch a few more times but never found time for a real date. I was comfortable with that. It was nice to have some companionship, but I wasn't sure I was ready for more. Like anything that required shaving and fancy underwear and everything.

Though I have to admit, I was starting to wonder what Holden looked like outside of—and underneath—his scrubs and white coat.

As promised, Mrs. Milan came down for Thanksgiving. It was nice to work side by side with the kind woman in preparing the family meal. She even noted how relaxed and happy I seemed. I know she'd hoped for Ryan and me to end up together.

Some things just weren't meant to be.

"How's he doing?" I asked finally.

"He's happy ..." she paused. It looked like there was something else she wanted to say. She didn't have to tell me. It was apparent.

"He's seeing someone, right?"

"Yes, a lovely girl who works with Jenn. They just seemed to hit it off."

"That's good."

"Is it okay with you?"

I replied with my standard response, "It's not up to me. He doesn't need my approval. But it's fine." But as I said it, I realized that it really was fine. It didn't hurt.

Not anymore.

"I hope you find someone too. You deserve to be happy too."

At that moment, my phone rang. I smiled when I recognized the number. I excused myself and stepped outside to take the call and answered, "Happy Bird-day!"

Holden laughed. "Did I catch you in the middle of dinner?"

"No, still prepping it. What's up? I thought you were on call?"

"I am, but it's a slow day. So far. The turkey-related injuries haven't started pouring in yet. We can always look forward to food poisoning and some good burns from deep-frying gone awry." He paused, for a moment, and then continued, "So, how much do you like me?"

A lot.

The immediate answer in my brain surprised me. Yet I knew it was the truth. Still, I didn't want to show my hand just yet. "This sounds like a loaded question. Why?"

"Um, I kind of did something that I shouldn't have done and now I need you to bail me out."

"Um, okay, maybe. Is it illegal? I don't have a strong back to shovel a hole for a body. But it is Florida. I'm sure we can find some alligators or something."

He laughed. "Not illegal, just stupid and desperate. One of my partner's daughters is getting married. My ex is going to the wedding too since she is BFFs with my partner's wife. They play tennis together."

"Okay."

If it had to do with his ex-wife, feeding a body to an alligator might be preferable.

"So, I kind of freaked out about being at an event with her and her new boy toy, so I RSVP'd for me plus one."

"Okay."

"I need you to be my plus one."

"Um, okay. That's not too bad. I can do that." My stomach flipped. We'd finally get to go on a real date. I can't believe he was so nervous. He had to know I'd say yes. "When is the wedding? I need to get it on the calendar."

"Um, yeah. Saturday."

"What?!? Like this Saturday?"

"Maggie, I need you to help me out. I kind of led my ex to believe that I have a girlfriend. I know it was stupid, but she's parading around with a twenty-five-year-old. It made me feel stupid that I couldn't even get a date."

"Why didn't you ask me before?"

"Because until a few weeks ago, I couldn't get you to call me. I sent the RSVP in and told myself that I was going to work up the nerve to call you. But I didn't."

"But we talk all the time!"

"I think I repressed it. And then my partner said something about it to me today, and I had that 'oh shit' moment."

"So let me get this straight. Your ex-wife is how old?"

"Forty-one."

"And she has a twenty-five-year-old stud."

"Not shitting you, he was our pool boy."

"Nice."

"I should have realized what she was up to when she kept going back to the plastic surgeon."

"She's blond isn't she?"

"Not naturally, but yes."

Irene was blonde. "I hate blonds. They are my arch-nemeses."

"So, does that mean you'll be my date and kind of act like you like me?"

"Like you or totally in love, all hot and heavy, can't wait to rip your clothes off?" A mental image flashed through my head. Ripping his clothes off could be fun.

"Ooh, that would be even better."

"You are gonna owe me."

"Really? You'll do it?"

I laugh. "I guess I like you enough to pretend that I like you even more while you ply me with drinks and good food. It is going to be good food, right?"

"I would think so. It's at the Suntree Country Club, and it's black tie."

"Definitely good food then. I just need, oh crap." It wasn't like I had tons of formal wear

"What? Please tell me you aren't going to back out on me?" he pleaded.

"Well, I have a dress, but ..."

"But what?"

"You've already seen it. I wore it to the gala last January."

"Honestly, I don't remember it. So it doesn't stand out as being a big dud or a total bomb. Go ahead and wear it again. I won't think less of you."

"Glad to know that your first impression of me was that I was not a total dud."

"You know what I mean."

I laughed. "I do, but it's fun keeping you swinging in the wind here."

"So it's a go then?"

"Against my better judgment, it's a go." Excitement rushed through me. Suddenly I couldn't wait for Saturday.

"Maggie, you are the best. I'll show you a good time, I promise. I owe you."

"Good. You can mow my lawn and weed my flower beds."

"It's a deal. My wife gets the pool boy, you get a lawn boy."

CHAPTER TWENTY-SIX

The day of the gala arrived. After driving Mrs. Milan to the airport early in the morning, I deposited the kids with my dad for an overnight stay and went to have the works done at the spa. By the time I left there, I had been buffed and scrubbed, poked, and peeled. I also had perfect hair and make-up, something I never would have been able to pull off.

A total Cinderella transformation.

It took all day, but it was worth it. My hair was swept up in an elegant style and the make-up set off my green eyes and cheekbones. At home, I carefully slipped into my gown. It was an emerald green silk with a halter neck and a low back and a daring leg slit. Also, while the back was sexy and low, it was high enough that it still hid my scars. I had silver stilettos that would kill my back and legs but completed the look. With my sparkly jewelry and white rabbit fur wrap, I looked as good as I could get.

Holden arrived, ringing my doorbell. As I opened the door, I took a breath at how very handsome he looked in his tuxedo, his dark blue eyes twinkling with mischief. He put his hand over his heart. "How did I not remember that?"

I did a little turn for him. A slow one.

"You look stunning." Then he smiled. A wicked smile.

"Wipe that grin off your face. I can tell exactly what you're thinking."

"Good. It'll make for an interesting evening." He lifted his eyebrows.

As we headed down the walk to his car, Holden slipped his arm through mine, sending sparks dancing through me. Our first real contact. He could not stop smiling. Neither could I.

In the car, he got serious. He turned off the radio and said, "So, I know we've talked a little about things, but I need to be straight up, and tell you what happened in my marriage, just so you know the back story. Sarah and I got together in college. We met my senior year, and she was a freshman. We continued dating while I was in med school and she was finishing her degree, and got married right after I graduated. We had Cahren the next year. Sarah was a stay-at-home mom. It was a long struggle through interning and residency. Sarah was basically a single parent for a few years. Not because I didn't want to be involved but because I was trying to make my career so I could build a practice to provide for us. And I did. And Sarah built her life too. When I finally thought that I could step back and enjoy what we had worked so hard for, Sarah had decided that she was past being the doctor's wife and wanted to be on her own. With me paying the way, of course. She has told me that she *wasted* all her best years waiting for me, and she wasn't waiting anymore. She told me that she ruined her career by getting married and having Cahren. It devastated me. I mean, here I am, forty-four, with my teenage daughter who is going to be leaving for college in two years. I worked so hard to make a good life, and now that I have the means, I have no life to come home to."

I gave him an encouraging smile and waited for him to continue.

"And I know it's kind of a lousy stunt, me bringing you like this. But when I got the invitation, I kind of panicked. I thought I was doing better, you know, moving on and all. But the thought of seeing my ex-wife with another guy, well, I'm just not ready for that."

"So, what you're saying is that you're totally using me right now." I tried to make light of a deep conversation.

After he parked the car, Holden turned and looked at me. "Maggie, I haven't gone on a real date in twenty-two years. I don't know how to do this. So, I'm just gonna be me and lay it all out there. I would love to make Sarah eat humble pie, which, with you looking like that, it's gonna be a snap. But, aside from that, I like you. I like you a lot. A whole lot. You're smart and funny and caring and compassionate. Not to mention absolutely beautiful. You are interesting and the kind of person that I want to have in my life. So, if your feelings are even quasi-mutual, here I am."

Oh my.

This. This is what I've needed to hear. He put it all out there. No guessing, no games. No supposing what someone else is thinking. No doing what others think you should do.

Holden continues, "I know this is way too forward, and I'll be lucky if you don't run screaming from the car. But, judging by the look of your shoes—which, by the way, how can you even have the nerve to wear around a guy who specializes in feet—you won't be able to run fast, and I will be able to catch you."

There were so many words coming so fast out of his mouth that it was hard to keep up. But he made me smile.

"You're right, even if I wanted to run, I couldn't in these shoes. But don't ever criticize my shoes again. I know they're bad for me. Trust me, my back will let me know. But I love shoes. They are my one vice. So back off the shoes."

"Does that mean you want to pursue something with me?"

I knew there was something there between us. Oh yes, I'd felt that spark when he touched me. And my stomach definitely fluttered a little when he smiled that shit-eating grin. "I'm not used to anyone in my life being this direct with me. It's been a real problem."

"I find it refreshing, although I'm not sure how others take it. I wish I had spoken up in my marriage. I don't know if it would have changed things, though."

"Honestly, sometimes you come off arrogant and cocky."

"See, that was easy."

I smiled at him. "Yes, it was."

"Try something else. Be blunt. Just let it all hang out."

"Um, okay. I'm horrible at relationships. I have no spine. I just do what is expected of me, no matter what it costs me. I lose me to be what I think the other person wants."

I wanted to say more, but it was time to go in. Holden came to my side of the car to help me out. He took my hand this time and held it gently.

Yes, the tingles were definitely there.

As we were walking inside, he whispered into my ear, "We are going to continue this conversation. I need to find out what makes you tick so I can convince you to make our act tonight real." Anticipation coursed through my entire body, all the way down to my toes.

The outdoor ceremony was over quickly. I was acutely aware of Holden sitting next to me, our shoulders almost touching. It was as if I could *feel* what was building between us grow with each passing minute. He kept catching my gaze and smiling. We moved over to another terrace for the cocktail hour. There were space heaters out, and the night was chilly by Florida standards. Holden kept a tight hold on my hand.

I didn't want him to let go.

We started to head towards a crowd of people when Holden pulled me aside. "Before the night gets beyond us, and before people are around, I need to hear your story. I told you my failure, I need to know yours."

"Not right now Holden. People are looking for you."

"They can wait. I want to know how you're available."

"No, I don't think so."

"Aww, come on."

"No, it's bad."

"How bad can it be? You're not in jail."

Okay, here was the moment of truth. "Because you may not like me when you hear it. Besides, it's kind of long and complicated."

"Then give me the Cliff's Notes version. Three minutes or less."

"I don't really know."

"Why not? C'mon Maggie. Why are you being so wishy-washy? That's not you. I've heard you speak your mind. Are you afraid of what I will think of you? What can you possibly say that could change things? What has happened has happened. You cannot change it, you can only move on. So move on."

"Okay." Where to begin? "My great failure is my son's father, Ryan. I met him after college. I thought I loved him. I loved the idea of him. No matter how much we talked, we never actually communicated though. I fell hard and fast. He went back to Ohio and blew me off. In his defense, he had a lot of family stuff going on, but still. I found out I was pregnant and freaked out. Ryan still wouldn't respond. I moved down here, where no one could find me. I had my son, started my company, and got my doctorate. A few years later, I adopted my daughter."

The beginning of the story was easy to tell. This next part was what I was ashamed of. I took a deep breath. "I always held a torch for the Ryan I imagined, and that someday we would find each other, and we'd still be in love and we'd all live happily ever after, the end. Anyway, a mutual friend of ours found me, and as a result, Ryan found me. And he discovered he had an almost seven-year-old son. He freaked out. I freaked out, again. But I kept hoping he'd realize he was still in love with me like I was with him. He was angry, and I spent a year trying to get back the man that I thought I lost. I tried to become the person that I thought he wanted. I was no longer me."

I look down at my shoes. This is so hard to say. I still can't believe I lost myself for so long. "We never talked about what we wanted and ended up resenting each other. We've finally come to an understanding. And I've come to realize that he is not able to give me what I need. I loved who I thought he should be, not who he was. So all in all, eight years down the drain and a total fail."

"Okay, what's so bad about that?"

"Did you not hear me? Got pregnant by a guy I barely knew. Then kept his kid from him for almost seven years. Then acted like a spineless Stepford wife trying to win back this fiction man that I had pined away for. And it took me all that time to realize that we had absolutely no business being together."

"I'm still not seeing the bad part."

"You can't be serious."

"As a heart attack. What I heard is that you fell for a guy, and he was too stupid to know what a catch you were. You started fresh, are a single mother of two, managed to squeeze in more education, and build a successful business. All that, and you look freakin' amazing to boot."

"Seriously, you need to stop. You're making me blush."

He put his hand on my jaw, his finger delicately caressing. "You can keep trying to freak me out and drive me away, but it's not gonna work."

I smiled devilishly. "Don't worry, I have all night. I'll find a way to totally turn you off."

"You'll have to try very hard. I think you're beautiful inside and out. And trust me, the way you look, is anything but a turn-off."

And with that, we went to join the cocktails, already in session.

We circulated among Holden's colleagues, schmoozing and making small talk. Occasionally, he put his arm around me and gave me a little squeeze. Every so often, I'd whisper in his ear something to trying freak him out.

This was a fun game.

"I work long, crazy hours. Between the kids, and school and wheelchair clinics, and then the business. I don't have a lot of free time."

He laughed and murmured back. "You're using long hours as a defense with me? I'm not even going to dignify that with a response."

Later, after being greeted by the newlyweds, I whispered, "I drive a minivan."

He leaned down, his breath hot on my neck. "What's your point? So do a lot of people. Do the seats fold down?"

"Yep, Stow and Go, baby."

"Good, more room to fool around in the back then. Much easier than in a sedan. You should have driven tonight."

And then he winked at me. Oh boy. Was it getting hot in here?

We moved on to the reception. I had managed to restrict myself to one glass of champagne during the cocktail hour. I couldn't afford to get plastered. I already knew I was going to have difficulty keeping my hands off of Holden. The whole whispering thing was a turn-on.

I needed to behave myself.

On the other hand, he was right. The more I tried to play cat and mouse and to scare him away, the more I found myself wanting him to pursue me. And the more I found myself wanting him.

He did look rather delicious in his tux.

Broad shoulders. Big hands. Twinkling, devilish eyes. But I needed to behave. There were a lot of people from the medical community here, so there was a lot of networking going on. I needed to keep sharp.

Not to mention, we had still yet to run into Sarah, the ex-wife.

We were standing by the dance floor when I felt Holden stiffen. He didn't have to say a word. I took his hand and pulled him gently onto the dance floor. We swayed gently to Michael Bublé. I pulled him close, my hand on the back of his neck, and whispered into his ear, "I wake up with two kids in my bed every morning."

He didn't say anything for a minute, his eyes still darting around the room.

I pulled back. "See, I knew I could freak you out. I can see you're looking for your nearest escape route." I laughed.

Holden met my gaze and said, "I'm sure that's a wonderful way to wake up. I missed doing that with Cahren a lot. But I do remember that kids give the best hugs. It would be nice to have a second chance. Your daughter is adorable, and I can't wait to meet your son. I always wanted more kids, but ..." he trailed off.

312

"Sarah didn't want them?"

"No, and she's coming this way. Can we step off the floor?"

He took my hand, and we made it off the floor before she ambushed us. From the change in Holden's demeanor and posture, I knew Sarah'd done a number on him. Well, she'd better buckle in. Hurricane Maggie was about to make landfall.

"Holden," she said, as she stepped in front of us, blocking us from going anywhere. I held on tight to his hand and gave it a gentle squeeze.

"Sarah," he replied curtly.

"Well, I didn't know you were bringing your" she not-so-subtly looked me up and down, "friend tonight. No one told me."

"I didn't think it was any of your business."

I held my hand out. "Magdalene Miller. I've heard *so* much about you." I gushed.

Sarah looked at my hand, paused for a minute, and then shook it limply.

"I have not heard a thing about you. Are you a nurse?"

"No," I answered, "why would I be?"

"I can't imagine where else Holden would have time to meet anyone. He certainly never had time for a home life."

"Maggie owns a business that supplies wheelchairs and medical equipment for primarily children. She's a doctor and has quite the career. She manages to balance that with being a mother. Can you imagine that? You can talk to the Gordons about how wonderful she is. Where's Chad?"

"He's at the bar getting me a drink. He's so attentive to my needs."

I glanced towards the bar where all I saw was this smarmy-looking, spray-tanned guy, complete thick gold chains and a receding hairline. And he appeared to be hitting on another guest who was also getting a drink. While Sarah and Holden chatted about Cahren for a minute, I took the opportunity to look at her. While she was not unattractive, she was too, well, everything.

Too unnaturally blond. Too tanned (maybe she and Chad got a group discount at the spray tan place). Too much cleavage. Well, too much boobs (obviously augmented) for that matter. Too much collagen in her lips. And it was very obvious that she was trying too hard to look too young. Her dress was a sheer black top with essentially pasties covering her boobs and it was so low in the back that I was afraid we were going to see crack soon. It was not the dress that a forty-something mother should be wearing. It made her look desperate.

What was it with the guys I was interested in and these total bitches that they committed themselves to?

"So," Sarah began. "How long has this been going on?"

Holden began to speak and I jumped in. "Let me, honey. We met last January at a gala. A mutual friend had been trying desperately to introduce us. She knew we were perfect for each other." I had one hand around Holden's waist and slid the other up the buttons of his shirt.

I still couldn't help but laugh about Michele's miss-sent text and picture. Neither could Holden.

Sarah was miffed that she didn't understand what was so funny. And that we had an inside joke. "Really? I had no idea you were even interested in dating Holden, let alone actually *involved* with someone. I thought you were just making this up."

I looked at Holden and gave him a sly smile.

"I wasn't interested in dating until I met Maggie, and then I was very interested."

"And I was ending things with my son's father, and I didn't think I was interested, but Holden kept popping up and sweeping me off my feet."

He really did. I thought about him carrying my luggage off the plane and then staying to make sure I didn't need help with more bags.

"Your son's father? So you weren't married then? Interesting," she said, passing judgment, much like the church lady.

"No, I've never been married. And here's this for juicy. Ready? I have a daughter too, and she doesn't have the same father as my son. What do you think about that?" I leaned in while telling her this like we were old friends gossiping. I glanced at Holden. He had lost the worried look around his eyes and now looked amused. I gave him a wink. This was fun.

"Oh, I see," said Sarah. "I'll bet you make a killing in child support. And you're all set here." She glanced at Holden with raised eyebrows.

"No, I don't. I don't get child support."

"Oh, are they bums? Deadbeats? Trying to do a little better this time? You know, Holden can't afford to support you and me, so don't get your hopes up with this one," she said, trying to match my tone of girlfriends sharing gossip.

"Well, actually, I adopted my daughter to save her from a horrible life, and yes, her biological father is a deadbeat loser, but I'm not entitled to any child support, since he has no parental rights. And my son's father is the Assistant Solicitor General for the state of Ohio. So, I actually did okay with that one. I have a successful career and a thriving business that is also fulfilling. So, even though I'm a single mother, I don't accept his support, although he'd gladly pay it. I can support myself, very well, I might add. I mean, I chose to have the children, I can certainly support them. It's kind of sad in this day and age that a woman would still look to a man to support her. Don't ya think?"

Sarah was fuming. Anger did not look attractive on her. "I'd better go see what's keeping Chad with my drink."

"You go do that. It was a pleasure." She turned to walk away. "Oh, Sarah?" She whipped back around. This I couldn't help. This one was for Holden. I gestured to my chest, "These are real." She stormed off.

Holden grabbed me, spun me around, and planted an earth-shattering kiss on me. It seriously was one of those movie moments where we stood still while the room buzzed around us. I could feel it all the way down to my toes. Finally, a movie moment! When we finally broke apart, all I could say was, "Wow."

"Wow?"

"Yeah, wow."

"Good. I was wondering if I had lost my touch."

"Um, no. Not at all." A waiter walked by with a tray of champagne. I grabbed a glass, as did Holden. He held his up for a toast.

"To us. A real us."

"You're persuading me more and more with each minute, but I still don't know."

"I'm gonna win you over Maggie."

"I'm a train wreck."

We had drained our glasses and set them down. He whirled me out to the dance floor. As we danced, he kept trying to convince me.

"I have lived so long in a state of inaction. I'm not sure that I know what to do anymore."

"Then let me help you. I don't have a good track record either, remember. We'll figure it out together. We can do this."

I could feel myself melting into him. Oh my God, was *this* what it was like to fall for someone? It had been so long, I barely recognized the feelings anymore.

"Holden, I lost who I was for a long time. I didn't mean to. I had the best intentions in the world, but I was so scared to do the wrong thing. But that's what I kept doing, over and over. One thing would run through my head and another would come out my mouth. I can't lose me again."

"I wouldn't want you to. I like who you are. The person you are right now is the person I want to be with."

"But it's not just about me."

"We'll figure the kids thing out. Obviously, I know what I'm getting into. Kids are part of the deal. I mean, I am forty-four years old. I don't want to be with some pretty young teeny-bopper."

"But I'm only thirty-three. Well, for at least a few more weeks. You're an old man compared to me. You are robbing the cradle. Aren't I a pretty young thing?" I spin around.

He pulls me back into him, pressing closely. His body feels good against mine. *Very good.*

"Stop being difficult. You know what I mean. I told you, I'm at the place in my life where I can have time for the family. I want to have that life. I want to be settled. And I want to try for that with you. And your kids. And my daughter. Just think, it'll be like having a built-in babysitter."

We danced for a song or two more. Being with him was pure fun. Finally, Holden looked at me. "You wanna get out of here?"

I nodded, nervous about what was going to come next. What was I going to do? After saying our goodbyes, we barely made it outside before our lips met and our arms entwined around each other. I couldn't feel my feet, the kiss was that good.

Holden wanted me for me. He knew the package and was willing to take it as it was.

I pulled away slightly. "My dad lives three doors down from me. You'll have to deal with him around."

"Does he fish?"

"Of course. We live on the intercostal."

"Then we're fine."

"You really have an answer for everything, don't you?"

"I'm telling you, I'm going to do whatever it takes to make you see that you and I can do this. I fully intend to win you over. I'm going to sweep you off your feet if it's the last thing I do."

There was more kissing. Hot kissing. Sexy kissing. We reached his car too soon. "I don't want this to end."

"It doesn't have to, Maggie. You just have to be willing to be you and to let this happen. Let go and join me."

"I've been fighting for so long. Since I was seven. Fighting to survive, to walk again. Then to achieve and to realize everyone else's dreams. To make my mother proud. Fighting to get Ryan's attention, then to keep it. Fighting for my son, my daughter, my company. I don't know if I can let go and stop fighting."

"I like that you're a fighter. I am too. And I'm not going to stop fighting for you. I'll wear you down eventually."

I knew he would. I also knew it wouldn't be that far in the future. Holden was what I had been seeking all along.

Someone to hold me and tell me it was okay. Someone not to fight against, but to join me in the fight. Someone to fight for me. Someone to want me, just as I was. Someone to sweep me off my feet.

"Okay, I have one last argument."

"Try me."

"I cannot believe that I'm going to say this out loud. It's really scary."

"Go for it."

I took a deep breath. "I have not had sex in nine years."

"That's what's supposed to send me running?"

"I told you, I've been out of commission for a while. Nine years."

"That is a long time. We're going to have to rectify that."

And by golly, we did.

THE END

ACKNOWLEDGMENTS

Going at it alone in self-publishing, I was never truly alone. Thank you to fellow mortal, CCHS alum, and author Dennis Mahoney for all your advice, encouragement, and guidance.

I had the ideas, but I also had a whole lot of mistakes. They would still be here if not for the diligent editing efforts of Mary Rose Kopach, Sue Rys, Michele Vagianelis, with a special thanks to Karen Pirozzi for her expert copy-editing skills.

After being on the market for a few months, the book got a makeover. I am greatly indebted to Becky Monson for her tireless work on the cover. For her ability to see my vision even though we are a country apart and her offer to take CreateSpace on for not cooperating with me, a big huge THANKS!

A lot of friends and family may notice their names make an appearance in the book. Contrary to what you may want to think, the characters are not based upon you, but I wanted to let you know you've played an important role in my life.

ABOUT THE AUTHOR

Telling stories of resilient women, *USA* Today Bestselling Author Kathryn R. Biel hails from Upstate New York where her most important role is being mom and wife to an incredibly understanding family who don't mind fetching coffee and living in a dusty house. In addition to being Chief Home Officer and Director of Child Development of the Biel household, she works as a school-based physical therapist. She attended Boston University and received her Doctorate in Physical Therapy from The Sage Colleges. After years of writing countless letters of medical necessity for wheelchairs, finding increasingly creative ways to encourage insurance companies to fund her client's needs, and writing entertaining annual Christmas letters, she decided to take a shot at writing the kind of novel that she likes to read. Kathryn is the author of twelve women's fiction, romantic comedy, contemporary romance, and chick lit works, including the award-winning books, *Live for This* and *Made for Me*. Please follow Kathryn on her website, www.kathrynrbiel.com.

Scan now to receive FREE bonus content:

Stand Alone Books:
Good Intentions
Hold Her Down
I'm Still Here
Jump, Jive, and Wail
Killing Me Softly
Live for This
Once in a Lifetime
Paradise by the Dashboard Light
XOXO

A New Beginnings Series:
Completions and Connections: A New Beginnings Novella
Made for Me
New Attitude
Queen of Hearts

The UnBRCAble Women Series:
Ready for Whatever
Seize the Day
Underneath It All

Center Stage Love Stories:
Act One: *Take a Chance on Me*
Act Two: *Vision of Love*
Act Three: *Whatever It Takes*

If you've enjoyed this book, please help the author out by leaving a review on your favorite retailer and <u>Goodreads</u>. A few minutes of your time makes a huge difference to an indie author!

Made in the USA
Middletown, DE
26 February 2023

25396252R00191